THE FIRST HORSEMAN

Clem Chambers

First published in 2012 by No Exit Press,
an imprint of Oldcastle Books Ltd, PO Box 394,
Harpenden, Herts, AL5 1XJ
www.noexit.co.uk

ISBN
978-1-84243-654-7 (print)
978-1-84243-656-1 (ebook)
978-1-84243- 655-4 (kindle)
978-1-84243-657-8 (pdf)

2 4 6 8 10 9 7 5 3 1
Typeset in 11pt Minion by Avocet Typeset, Chilton, Aylesbury, Bucks
Printed in Great Britain by Clays Ltd, St Ives plc

For more about Crime Fiction go to www.crimetime.co.uk / @crimetimeuk

'A thriller that moves faster than a Derby winner'
— Sally Nicoll author

'Another hypnotic yarn from Clem Chambers'
— Robbie Burns author

'I stopped reading Tolstoy to get my hands on Chambers'
latest and it was worth it!'
— Charles Orton-Jones, Editor *London Loves Business*

'Jim Evans is back, in a narrative that races to a
nail-biting denouement'
— Leigh Russell, author

Praise for *Kusanagi*

'the ingredients are all in place for a colourful blockbuster
thriller... truly kinetic entertainment'
— Brian Ritterspak, *Crime Time*

'Clem Chambers' writing is as slick and thrilling as it is
authentic. *Kusanagi* is superb'
— Matt Hilton author

'Compelling. Be prepared to sit up in bed all night with this one'
— Zoe Strimpel, *CityAM*

Praise for *The Twain Maxin*

'Another blockbusting financial thriller from Clem Chambers'
— Geoff Cutmore, *CNBC*

'if Jason Bourne had to invest in shares, this is what would happen'
— Paul Mason, Economics Editor *Newsnight*

'Every Stock Exchange CEO's worst nightmare!'
— Xavier Rolet, CEO of the London Stock Exchange

Praise for *The Armageddon Trade*

'Fresh as today's headlines'
— Geoffrey Wansell, *Daily Mail*

'Part science-fiction, part Grisham thriller, *The Armageddon*
ing

Also by Clem Chambers

The Armageddon Trade
The Twain Maxim
Kusanagi

To Zoia

1

Professor Cardini was a giant, not only of science but physically. At six feet five inches he loomed over most people, and raised at the lectern he took on superhuman proportions. His hair was jet black and gleamed in the spotlights. He didn't seem to blink when he spoke. He held out a long right arm and pressed a device in his huge hand. 'Gerontology: Frontiers,' said the heading on the projection behind him. 'Summary.'

The maximum natural lifespan of a modern human is 131 years.
An improvement of five years in one generation.

The screen changed.

Nutritional deprivation may extend this to 153 years.
Impractical.

'I'm afraid few will voluntarily starve themselves for a lifetime, however beneficial the effects,' Cardini boomed, with a wry smile.

'The way ahead,' said a new slide. 'Gene therapy.'

'Naturally this is a crucial avenue of research, but recent results suggest that age is not a simple encoding that can be repaired. Age is built into the very fabric of life so it cannot be directly modified.'

The next bullet point was 'Metabolic manipulation'.

'We can slow the animal down,' Cardini went on, 'and extend its span. However, no one wants to be a tortoise, so this also does not appear to be practicable.' He clicked the device again and the word 'Virtualisation' filled the screen.

'As unlikely as it might seem, this solution is the most likely in the near future.' He scanned the audience. 'A brain/machine interface will allow for the development of mental migration into a computing platform. It is inevitable that such an interface will be created and from it such developments as needed will cascade. This, when developed into a powerful enough platform, will lead to mental immortality and enhancement.

'Meanwhile it appears that the body we are born with is designed to age and die. It is inherently a machine built to self-destruct. Ageing is a critical system built in from life's early development. It will not be thwarted. It can only be, with great difficulty, retarded.

'We are "disposable soma". Our purpose is no more than to carry the genetic code that permeates every living cell in our body created by three billion years of evolution. This is why we do not live for ever. It is for our DNA to live for ever, not us. We fight this idea because we cannot accept that our fine-tuned intelligence is enslaved to the mindless code we carry, but that code is far cleverer than we are. It made us from nothing and sends us back to nothing. What could we ever do to compare with that feat?'

He looked around the hall. Many of the scientists who had been on the edge of their seats during his presentation were now slumped in their chairs, bored.

'It seems that while we look to outwit nature, we are setting ourselves up for an uneven battle. We are a puny intelligence set against the awesome might of life-creating DNA. So, my conclusion is that we should simply avoid the conflict and instead go beyond carbon-based life into the new frontier of silicon, where our personalities might live for ever and travel freely. Imagine a mind without limit, a body without weakness, existence in a synthetic Utopia.' He smiled wryly again. 'A life,' he held out his arms, 'in the cloud.'

He bowed. 'Thank you very much.'

The crowd started clapping.

Cardini stepped down from the dais and headed towards the door along the main aisle. He acknowledged a stooped old professor with a nod. He recalled his face from many such conferences over the decades. Once he would have known many of the people in the room, but now most of his contemporaries were either retired or dead. He seldom left his labs these days, then only forcing himself out to bait the research community so they might come and tell him of their yet unpublished work. He needed to know whether they were on the trail yet.

Happily, it seemed they had not picked up the scent. They were far behind him and his knowledge was accelerating away from theirs. Compared to his breakthroughs, their crude understanding was like undergraduate coursework.

He went to the speakers' lounge to fetch his coat. There was a tray of Danish pastries by the coffee-machine. He felt a pang of hunger, the sort of physical desire the serum made almost unbearable during the first days after he had taken it. He poured himself some coffee and helped himself to a sticky type of bread, then went to sit by a large picture window overlooking Westminster.

The door opened and a woman entered. Cardini cast his eye over her. She was forty but looked thirty. Her hair was dyed dark blonde, her breasts were tastefully enlarged, her facelift of a high standard and about eighteen months old. He looked out of the window and took a bite.

'Professor Cardini,' said a voice.

He looked away from the window as the woman sat down in the chair facing him. She was an attractive specimen.

'May I have a few words with you?'

He swallowed his mouthful. 'Forgive me,' he said. 'Who am I addressing?'

'Sorry,' she said, with a smile. 'Lou Saxby. May I ask you a few questions?'

'You're not a journalist, are you?'

'No,' she said. 'I'm in politics, and I'm just interested in the subject of the conference.'

'You are interested in ageing or longevity?'

'Both. Who wants to get old?'

'Quite,' said Cardini. He noted how she had flashed her inner wrist at him and the side of her neck. She was displaying instinctual sexual submission. 'What would you like to know?' he said.

'Well, this is going to sound very silly,' she replied, brushing her hair over her shoulder, 'but I have to ask.'

'Go on.' Cardini was under the spell of the serum and could not help but admire her low-cut neckline and trim figure.

'This is going to sound like a soap advert, but how do you stay so young?'

Cardini sipped his coffee.

Lou continued, 'All the lecturers here are talking about their research into long life or staying young but they all look their age. You look twenty years younger than you are. You must know what you're talking about.'

'You flatter me,' said Cardini.

She touched his knee. 'No, really, you look amazing. You look in your fifties.'

'I hardly think so,' he replied.

He felt her touch and his primitive lower mind reacted to it. His body was at its post-treatment peak, his organs perhaps as fit as any forty-year-old's. His resurgent hormones had flooded his system, leaving his mature mind struggling against the impulses of rampant youth. 'It's a long and complicated story.'

'I'm staying at Claridges. Let me take you to lunch.' She batted her eyelashes at him. 'Will you come?'

'I will,' he said, smiling.

Cardini woke and sat up in the bed. It was six forty-five in the evening. He looked across at Lou, who was lying flat on her back, her mouth open, her hair awry. She was snoring. Her body bore the marks of at least a dozen procedures, and he wondered what she had looked like before she'd had them. Had she been a fat, ugly woman with mousy hair or a pretty girl who wanted to be prettier?

He had made a mistake in having sex with her.

His accelerated state had let his primitive mind overtake his intellect. He had taken a risk for no good purpose. He had given in to pleasure for no sensible reason and he was irritated with himself.

Yet the serum was overwhelming, the energy it engendered sweeping away his self-control. He pulled the sheets back and knelt up on the bed. He took her legs and parted them.

'Oh,' she said, coming alive, 'more?' She drew him down to her. 'You must tell me the secret.'

He smiled and kissed her neck hard.

It was nearly ten p.m.

'Why don't you stay the night?' she said, as he came out of the bathroom.

'I must get back.'

She watched him dress with the agility of someone her husband's age. Her eyes narrowed. Cardini had the answer, he must have. There was no way an elderly man could have performed like that without chemical help. It just wasn't possible to be so fit and strong at his age. She had found what she was looking for: someone who could keep her young and beautiful.

2

Cardini scanned the emails from Lou, then deleted them. He hadn't given her his email address, but she had got it anyway and was bombarding him with what amounted to love letters. The situation was fast becoming awkward.

There was a knock at his office door. Bob Renton, his chief lab assistant, entered. He seemed agitated.

'There's a woman outside who wants to see you.' He was bobbing up and down on the balls of his feet.

'Really?' said Cardini. 'I don't have any appointments, do I?'

'No,' said Renton.

'Well, then, who is she?'

'A Mrs Saxby.'

Cardini coughed. 'Show her in.'

Renton disappeared, and returned minutes later.

'Why Lou,' said Cardini, as the door closed behind his assistant, 'what brings you here?'

'You, of course,' she said, looking hurt.

'Me?' he said. 'How can I help?'

'Help?' She seemed very sad. 'I was just missing you.'

'Ah,' he said. 'Well, I'm sorry about that. My work is all-consuming.'

'I understand,' she said, 'but can we still share some time together? At least occasionally.'

'Surely that would be as impractical for you as it would be for me.'

'We can be discreet,' she said, smiling mischievously. 'Discretion is the first rule of politics.' Her eyes darted around his office.

'Just how do you propose to keep our little secret?' he asked.

'I have my ways.'

She stepped forwards and gazed up at him. He knew he was meant to kiss her. Two days had passed and the passion that had boiled through his veins on that evening had not yet subsided. She rested her right hand on his groin and smiled. 'Will you tell me your secret?' she said, caressing him through the material of his trousers.

'Of course,' he said gently, 'if that is what you want.'

'Yes,' she said, moving to pull down his fly.

Suddenly his hands were around her throat. She struggled but his grip was vice-like. Cardini looked down at her red flushed face, her eyes bugging out, her tongue protruding from her mouth. In seconds she would lose consciousness and sag.

Her knees buckled and keeping hold of her he let her fall to the floor. He held her there for three more minutes, then let go. He checked her pulse. Nothing.

He hoisted her up and placed her in the chair by his desk. He picked up the phone. 'Bob, will you come to my office?'

Within moments, Renton appeared. He looked at the woman, her feet slightly splayed as she sat. He looked at Cardini, then turned and locked the door with a key from a bundle in his pocket. 'Is she dead?' he said, bending down and staring at her.

'Quite.'

'Well, that's a turn-up,' he said, his eyes sparkling as he studied the horrified expression on Lou Saxby's face.

'Is it as much of a surprise as my overlooking your own homicidal practices?'

Renton straightened and smiled at him. 'Not quite. I'll dispose of the body in my usual way,' he said. 'I think I can deal with her car too,' he said, 'but I'll need a few days off for that.'

'Of course.'

'And I'll want ten treatments.'

'No,' boomed Cardini. 'I will give you only one.'

'Professor?' he moaned. 'Five.'

'You are well aware that that is impossibly expensive.' He paused. 'However, I will allow you two, so long as you can wait three months for the second dose.'

Renton scowled, but he dared not upset Cardini. 'Please give me three treatments. I'll accept one treatment now, the second in three months and the third three months after that. I deserve it.' He bounced up and down, nodding with determination.

Cardini stared at him.

'Three precious treatments in exchange for one vital service,' said Renton. 'That's fair, Professor.'

Cardini studied him. Renton showed no signs of backing down. 'Very well,' he said.

'Thank you,' said Renton, clearly overjoyed. 'I'll get this sorted right away. She'll be the next forty-two.'

3

Kate stood at the end of the semi-circle of students gathered around the examination table. She wanted to experience Cardini's famous course before she decided whether or not to do her doctorate with him. The atmosphere was electric.

She watched Renton pull back the white cover to reveal the cadaver. There seemed to be an element of relish in his demeanour. She shivered: death was a terrible sight.

Professor Cardini was sitting in a chair a little away from them. He looked up from a tablet he was reading, put it down and stood up. He was an imposing figure, black hair framing his handsome gaunt features.

The tag on the cadaver's toe read '42'. The woman had no head. Kate wondered what had happened to it.

'Today,' said Cardini, 'we have the benefit of a less battered subject than usual, and we will be looking at how the nerves in the arm are laid out. In this we will attempt to expose and understand many fascinating issues. For example, how does a thought, the most intangible of all things, the mere whiff of a chemical reaction in the brain, become force, the most tangible of elements?' He picked up a scalpel, his face half hidden in shadow, 'so let us begin.'

4

This was her world and Jim knew it.

Jane passed him a gun with a quiet smile, as if she was handing him a sacred item of some religious rite. It was a gift of life or death, a Glock 35.

He took it.

'You know what to do next?' she said gently.

'Not really … Jane.' He forced out her name.

'Go ahead,' she said, a little louder than she had spoken before.

He put his ear protectors in place and aimed. She'd asked him to let off fifteen rounds in five bursts of three. He aimed and fired the rounds. He reset his posture to stand passively, then repeated the exercise. She was grinning in a kind of happy, knowing, angry way he recognised. The familiar light was glowing in her eyes, with an exciting, dangerous sparkle.

He fired another three shots, barely focusing on the aim, then three more, and a final three almost as an afterthought.

He sniffed at the fumes, the hot, primitive smell of fire, a perfume that set surging the adrenalin to which he had become addicted.

Circumstances had forced Jim to embrace a maelstrom of chaos and violence. Yet he was desperate to get back to escape it and get away from the danger and ruin that seemed to follow him everywhere.

The target rushed towards him, an attacking white ghost. He peered at it as it flew towards him but could see no bullet holes.

'Outstanding,' said Jane, as he pulled off the ear protectors. 'Outstanding,' she said again studying the centre of the target which was neatly shot away. She ripped the target from its clips and handed it to him. 'You're hired.'

'You can't afford me.'

'Yeah, right,' she said, and reached forward.

If only he didn't love her, he thought, he might be able to live a reasonably normal life. But she amazed, dazzled and fascinated him. She was worth dying for, if there was ever such a woman.

5

A great pink claw reached in for the mouse. She backed as far into the corner of the cage as she could, her eyes widening in terror. The claw grabbed her and swept her out of the door and up into the air.

'This is a trembler mouse.' Professor Cardini smiled. 'We've reared it so its myelin dissolves and its nerve current drains away before reaching its destination. The neuropathy causes tremens. This is an interesting model for experimentation.'

The female mouse sniffed urgently at his hand, and Professor Cardini felt the hot surge of urine into his palm. It annoyed him a little. He struck the mouse's head against the workbench, ending its brief life with a sharp crack. He noticed one of the students flinch. She was a thin, dark-haired specimen, pale and, he judged, weak. He laid the mouse flat on the board and pulled its forelegs apart. He smiled faintly, seeing, as he pinned the paws down, the tiny marks of a mouse crucified, blood seeping from the punctures.

He sliced open its belly from throat to tail. Even now, though he had done this thousands of times, he could have gasped with pleasure at the perfection before him. The miniature work of art lay wet and quivering, exposed and vulnerable to him.

He looked up at the students. 'See?' he said, in his slow, deep voice. 'The heart still beats.'

The girl's eyes were closed. She had picked the wrong course if the death of a mere mouse was too much for her.

'This is the machine that serves as our toolbox of discovery,' he said. 'It is a small analogue of the machine that drives our own existence.'

The students looked on, hungry for mastery.

Kate turned and eased her way back through the small crowd. She had made a mistake: even at this early stage she couldn't stomach her subject. At the door she looked back. The professor caught her eye. She held it for an instant, then turned and left.

6

The sound of a helicopter passing above him filled Jim with gloom. He recognised the sound even though it was strangely attenuated and much quieter than he had expected. He had had enough of two things in his life: volcanoes and helicopters. Every time he got into serious trouble they were somewhere in the mix. The first volcano had been at Las Palmas in the Canaries: he had flown there in a chopper and ended up inside the accursed thing.

Then there had been Nyiragongo in the Democratic Republic of Congo, a volcano so active that it had recently erupted and cut Goma, a major city, in half. A helicopter had been his only means of getting out.

Finally there was Fuji, a beautiful snow-capped mountain, the backdrop to a nasty scrap in Tokyo. Thankfully, no helicopters had been involved.

Yet helicopters, unlike volcanoes, were hard to avoid. As far as Jim was concerned, a lunatic had invented the helicopter and lunatics flew in them.

As Jim got up from his desk, Max Davas, the grand master of hedge-fund managers, shadow banker to the US Treasury, would be landing in the paddocks behind the house. There was no way the old man would contemplate arriving in a car, to come crunching up the long drive like everybody else. Davas had to arrive in the grandest possible style.

Jim went out to meet him. The helicopter was huge, marked with matt grey cloud patterns that made it look like part of the sky above. It was weirdly angular with more than a hint of menace. Jim hadn't seen a chopper like it before. It reminded him of objects the military considered classified. Where rich men had Gulfstreams, Davas owned the biggest Airbus they made. For some people a 250-foot yacht was enough; for Davas, nothing short of a frigate would do. He was astonishingly rich, with billions more than Jim, and he spent money like only countries do.

Jim waited by the paddock gates and watched Davas emerge. His mentor wasn't moving with the agility Jim remembered: he had suffered a bout of pneumonia and still looked as though he'd had a close shave with the Reaper. Weeks in bed had withered him like an uprooted plant.

Davas was wearing a black blazer, dark blue jeans and black cowboy boots. He was carrying a large case. Somehow the smart informality was at odds with his uneven pace. The last time Jim had seen him, his friend had bounded across the field like a young man, full of energy and bounce. Now there was a shaky, careful determination in his walk, which was more of a stagger than a stride. Davas acknowledged him with a weak wave, as if raising his hand too high might cause him to lose his balance and fall.

Jim opened the gate.

'How are you, my boy?' said Davas, clearly relieved to get on to firm ground.

'Great, Max.' Jim smiled and shook his hand. He wanted to give him a manly hug but held back. He didn't want to embarrass him.

'Sorry for the short notice, Jim, but you know how it is.'

'I know what you want, if that's what you mean. Let me take that.'

Davas handed him the case, seeming glad to be shot of the load. To Jim, it felt almost empty.

'Let's go inside,' said Davas. 'Is your house swept for bugs?'

'Only insects,' said Jim. 'I've got no secrets.'

Davas was disapproving: 'That could be seen as sloppy. You should keep your guard up.'

They walked through a large red-brick arched portico into a long, galleried hall.

'You've done a beautiful restoration job,' said Davas, his boots echoing on the wooden floor.

'You wouldn't believe how much it all cost,' said Jim. He stopped in his tracks. 'No, I guess you'd know pretty much exactly how much this kind of thing costs.'

'Chicken feed,' said Davas.

'I suppose,' said Jim, 'but a hell of a lot of it.' He walked on.

'One day, Jim, you'll understand the scale of things. The important and the trivial will be clear to you. There have always been kings and princes and they have always lived in castles and palaces. They always will. They may not be called emperors or maharajas. They may not be seen as living gods or Dear Leaders, but they will always have everything. It's Pareto's Law. It's the eighty-twenty.'

'I can't get used to it,' said Jim, as they walked towards the door at the far side of the hall.

'Well, Jim, it's down to statistics and physics, anything but ethics.'

'I don't get you.'

'Eighty-twenty means one per cent of the people get half of the whole pie, the one in ten thousand group gets a quarter and the lucky group that are one in a million get about an eighth of everything. The guy at the top of the pile ends up with three to four per cent of all the assets in the world.' He patted Jim on the back. 'That's three to four per cent of all the money, the land, the combined wealth of the globe, and that's as a result of the eighty-twenty rule. Think about it.'

'No, thanks,' said Jim. 'It's not worth my time. I've got way too much already, I don't want to think about more.'

'Nonsense,' said Davas.

They crossed a corridor of ancient red tiles and went into Jim's study.

Jim plonked himself in a mottled brown leather armchair by

the empty fireplace. Davas took his case. He opened it, pulled out a file and handed it to Jim.

Jim flipped through its contents and sighed. It was what he'd expected, a collection of currency and bond charts with a large blank area representing the future for him to fill in with his prediction. He dropped the papers on the floor by his feet.

'So, what do you think?' Davas wondered.

'I told you last time I wouldn't read charts for you any more. I meant it.' He looked at Davas, whose right hand was in the case, holding something. Any second he was going to break into a rant. He was going to say that Jim had a God-given talent to read the future of financial markets and that gift was to help the world, more particularly Max Davas, by manipulating the bond markets so that the US could continue to control the global economy by the dominance of the dollar. The US was bust, but in fiddling the bond market and the connected currencies, Davas kept the US all powerful and, by implication, safe.

Davas had used Jim's predictions to crush the euro to the edge of collapse so that the US could fund its overwhelming debt; the dollar had staggered on as the global currency. Davas would say Jim was turning his back on God by not using his gift, that he was inviting the barbarians to pillage the West if he didn't help Davas and the US Treasury. Only he could see the possible future, and with Jim's vision, Davas could mould a favourable outcome, crafted for the good of all.

Jim had resolved that he was not going to participate in Davas's schemes. A fat American in Ohio was counterbalanced by a starving kid in India. One man's barbarian was another man's hero. Why couldn't the United States simply live within its means?

Davas pulled a metal frame from the bag and unfolded it. It was a chair of sorts, a fold-out stool with an X-frame and a seat made of a thick piece of fawn leather. 'What do you think?' He stood up and gazed down at it.

'What is it?' said Jim, knowing it was a seat.

'A Roman camp chair.'

'Wow.' Jim got up and crouched beside it. The leather was evidently new but the iron of the frame was ancient. Jim had a warehouse full of Roman pieces he had bought indiscriminately around Europe. Over months of studying the results of his feverish collecting, he had learnt what was real and what had been turned out in some resourceful faker's studio. 'Where did it come from?'

'Germany,' said Davas. 'I thought I might pay you for your help in precious Roman artefacts.'

'Nice,' said Jim, peering at it closely, 'but no dice.'

'It belonged to Marcus Aurelius,' said Davas.

'What?' said Jim. 'The Emperor?' He smirked. 'Yeah, right, of course it did.'

Davas was holding something towards him. It was a large gold ring with a carved stone in it. 'Oh,' said Jim, taking it, 'that's nice too.'

'It was found buried with the chair,' said Davas.

'That's got to be Augustus,' said Jim, marvelling at the superb carving as he turned it in the light. 'But you're having me on about Marcus Aurelius, right?' He studied the sculpted carnelian. The artistry was stunning.

'Not imperial enough for you?' Now Davas held out a golden mask. 'Have a look at this. Do you know what it is?'

'Kind of,' said Jim.

'It was found over the ring, on the frame of the chair.'

'It's a gold battle mask.'

'Well, you know who wore one in Roman times.'

The mask was exquisitely fashioned and the face hammered out on it was the official portrait of Marcus Aurelius, the last emperor of a truly great Rome. It was surely the battle mask of the Philosopher King.

'You should donate it to a museum,' said Jim.

'You can, if you wish,' replied Davas, his eyes glinting.

Jim sat down and put the mask over his face. 'Where did you get it?'

'It was found in a field in Germany about three weeks ago. When I saw it I knew I might have something to change your mind about helping me.'

'Do you think they buried it where he died?'

'Very possibly.'

Jim slid the ring onto his little finger. 'The Romans were short-arses.' He was always surprised by how tiny their things were.

'They were harsh times,' said Davas. 'It's only in this modern era that we can grow to our full potential.'

'When they buried these, they were burying Rome,' said Jim. 'After Marcus that was it for civilisation.'

'Plague,' said Davas. 'Marcus Aurelius died of it. Perhaps half the population of the known world died of it.'

'I hope you washed this,' said Jim, almost joking.

'Smallpox doesn't survive for very long,' said Davas.

'Smallpox has been eradicated, right?'

'Yes,' said Davas. 'I would say it decimated the Roman Empire, but "decimate" means only one in ten died. Instead whole regions of Europe were emptied of people. Grass grew on their roads. The barbarians simply filled the vacuum. With smallpox the empire crumbled into dust.'

Jim held up the mask and looked into the face of Marcus. The emperor had worn it at his last battle against the northern tribes and then the plague that had killed his partner in government had struck him. When the Philosopher King had been cut down by smallpox, his world had been set on a course of irreversible decay.

'Why don't you take a look at those charts?' said Davas, as Jim marvelled at the battle mask.

Jim laid the golden trophy on the low walnut table in front of him and picked up the papers.

Davas was holding out a pen to him.

'These are three-year charts?'

'I'm not expecting to get my hands on another trove like this,' said Davas. 'I need all you can give me.'

Jim knew he'd be back soon enough. 'That's a fake,' he said, waving his pen at the mask, well aware that it wasn't.

Davas didn't react.

'What's wrong with your computers?' said Jim. 'Have they gone blind?'

'In a way.' Davas looked unhappily at him. 'That's why I need you.'

Jim turned to the first chart. It was the dollar yen. He squinted at it. 'I don't look at this stuff any more,' he muttered. 'I trade a few stocks for a bit of fun, but I keep away from the big stuff.' He shook his head, as if his neck was stiff. 'Most of the time, anyway.' He stared hard at the chart. 'I see what you mean,' he said. 'This is kind of indeterminate.'

Davas was looking past his shoulder as if he didn't want to put Jim off but, equally, was desperate to watch him study the charts. 'Go on,' he said.

'Well, I'm not sure I can draw on this – it's like a bit of a fork in the road.' Jim circled a blank about two months into the future. Davas had left a large quantity of space, which represented the future for Jim to fill in with his pen. This was the skill that had made Jim unbelievably rich: his talent at inking a line that predicted the future of money markets.

'Look at the others,' said Davas.

Jim leafed through them. 'I'm losing my touch,' he said. 'This is just bullshit to me.' He went to the gold chart. 'OK, this is what I see.' Starting where the gold chart ended, the price at yesterday's close, he drew a line that zigzagged up over the next three years. But then he drew another that zigzagged down and levelled out. 'That's pretty crazy, but that's what I see. In a few months' time things could go either way.'

Davas riffled in his case and pulled out a roll of transparencies. He flicked through them until he came to the one he wanted. 'Gold,' he said, grabbing Jim's chart. He put an overlay over Jim's drawing. Davas's projection stopped where Jim's line forked: Jim had predicted a potential split in the fortunes of gold.

'We kind of agree, then,' said Jim.

'Not really.'

'But gold at nine hundred dollars an ounce, that's not the end of the world.'

'It would be very inconvenient,' said Davas, 'to put it mildly.'

'Sorry, Max, but that's all I've got.' He looked at the ring on his little finger. 'Do I get to keep these?'

'Yes,' said Davas, 'but I might have to use your God-given talent again to be certain you've earned them.'

Jim wasn't sure whether he was getting a good deal or not. 'OK,' he said, 'but only once, and not, like, a ten-year chart next time or every instrument on the whole bloody market either.'

'I understand,' said Davas. He folded up Jim's projection. 'Can you draw on the others for me?'

Jim paged through the charts. 'It's the same story. It's like there's a cliff and either the chart goes off it or it doesn't. It's like a fifty-fifty moment in history is coming up. Either something bad happens or it doesn't.'

Davas grunted in agreement. 'Well, that's what I'm getting from my computers too, and it's not good.'

'It's nothing to worry about,' said Jim.

'I don't know so much,' said Davas.

'It'll work itself out. It always does.'

Davas sat down on the camp seat. He looked drained. 'Not necessarily Jim. There isn't always a happy ending.'

7

Dear Professor,

Thank you for asking why I no longer wish to be on the course. As you know I'm a chemist. Genetics has always fascinated me, so I thought, after my master's, that biochemistry was the next step. However, I cannot work with/on animals.

She was staring at the screen, her brow furrowed like a piece of corrugated cardboard. She was angry with the situation, herself, the professor, the course, the university. She was angry with the world. She continued typing:

I really do not think I could look at myself in the mirror if I experimented on animals. Animals are no more machines than I am, and what is done to them in the name of science is horrible.

'Horrible' sounded lame. She found a better word with the online thesaurus. She scanned the new line: 'What we do to them in the name of science is vile.' Reading the sentence back, she felt a rush of release.

Animals might treat each other badly in nature, but I do not see that as an excuse to act viciously towards them too. Unlike creatures in the wild, I do not have to tear my fellow beings to pieces in order to survive. I can try to wrap all sorts of clever arguments around why I am dropping out but the real reason is that I believe treating animals as you treated that mouse is an awful kind of bullying, predicated on a level of callousness that verges on inhumanity.

She read the lines back. Was she suggesting that the professor was a vile, callous and inhumane person? She closed her eyes and thought. She was too upset to write to him just now, she told herself. She should delete the message and answer the email tomorrow. By then she'd be able to write in a less emotional and more balanced way.

She didn't want to make an enemy of the professor, especially as she needed another subject for her doctorate. She sighed. She had made two catastrophic choices: to do the course and to leave it. Her next idea had better be a good one or she'd mess up her whole life.

She opened her eyes and clicked. 'Oh, God,' she moaned, realising she'd clicked 'send'. She opened her 'sent' folder and groaned again. 'You idiot,' she cried. She opened the message and read it again. Perhaps the prof wouldn't take it the wrong way. Fat chance, she thought. It was easily the rudest message she had ever sent.

She prayed Cardini was as bloodless as his reputation suggested. Robots didn't take umbrage. She wondered if she had an email-recall function, and tugged at her long chestnut hair with her left hand as she searched for it. Eventually she gave up. To hell with it, she thought, getting up. I meant every word. She headed for the kitchenette. A mint tea would calm her down.

8

Jim got up off the grass. Pierre, in his perfect cricket whites, was running towards him. The boy was growing into a giant. Only two years before he had been a couple of inches shorter than Jim, but now he was a couple of inches taller than his benefactor. 'Hey, Jim,' called Pierre. 'I'm so glad you came to see me play. I'll show you a trick or two.'

Jim smiled at Pierre with pride. They had cheated death together in the DRC under Nyiragongo. They had been thrown together in the mountain jungle, Jim the hapless mining investor and Pierre the child soldier and defiant victim. They were both tenacious survivors, now bonded like brothers. Jim had adopted the boy and brought him to Britain, after making sure his family was provided for in the Congolese chaos.

Kings and dictators sent their pampered princelings to this school yet despite his deprived and violent childhood Pierre had managed to get along. Still, there was something outlandish about his size and athleticism that made him seem older and much bigger than his peers.

Now Jim hugged him. 'We're straight to the airport after the match.'

'You going to come home with me?'

'Not this time,' said Jim. 'I've got to see some people about a few things. We can go together at the end of term and take a look at the mine.'

'Deal,' said Pierre, grabbing Jim's hand and shaking it. 'Got to go now and play.'

'Good luck.'

Pierre laughed. 'Way!' he said looking back to Jim. 'They're going to need the luck.' He loped off, his stride long and fluid.

Jim had caught a whiff of a new English inflection in Pierre's heavy French Congolese accent. He sat down, smiling to himself. It was good to see him so obviously flourishing. As Jim sat on the neatly cut grass, memories of squatting on jungle litter, pestered by insects, his body exhausted and soaked in sweat returned to him, a legacy of that adventure, like a whistle in the ears after a noisy concert. The more he wanted them to stop, the more he noticed them.

He heard his late nan saying, 'It's a funny old world.'

He often dreamt of the jungle and woke from the nightmares with a start.

In a few short years, his talent for predicting the market had turned his life completely inside out. His ability to know if markets were going to rise or fall had set off a chain of events that had transformed him from a poor Docklands kid into a lightning rod struck by bolts of money and trouble. Often his life was like some strange hallucination and he would pull a hair on the back of his arm: pain proved he was in the real world. Sometimes it was the only proof.

His ability to trade the global financial markets and never lose seemed harmless but it had terrifying consequences. When others tried to make money in the markets, they found it hard to be right 51 per cent of the time; when he traded he was 99 per cent correct.

The outcome of this was his immense wealth. He lived in a world without the normal financial gravity that pinned everyone else to the ground. Enormous wealth changed everything, and for Jim it made the world a very dangerous place. However surreal his situation felt, it was as solid as a punch on the nose. While dreams couldn't hurt, the real world seemed intent on wreaking his comeuppance.

Millions of people try to make a living from speculation, but only a few are successful, and even the fortunate few probably win through luck. The law of the efficient market levelled all players, from huge banks to the smallest retail investors. Efficient markets made them into little more than desperate gamblers doomed by the laws of probability to fail in the end. Sometimes the gambles paid off, sometimes they didn't, but in the long run even the mightiest ran out of luck and money. Banks blew fortunes as surely as the smallest private investor blew their savings.

Jim suffered no such levelling. He traded and he won. He read financial charts like a navigator could plot a route on a map. It was a blessing and a curse. Perhaps Fortune was trying to get even, he thought. Perhaps it needed to wreak a counterbalancing loss to even out his bloated success. And that loss would have to be catastrophic. Which was how things seemed to develop for him: one potential disaster followed another. Sometimes he felt like a bug in a piece of software, a glitch that needed deleting. There had been too much craziness in his life.

Pierre was opening the bowling. That's a bloody long run-up, thought Jim. Pierre set off. He was running very fast when he let fly. Jim whistled as the ball pitched up short and the young batsman flinched back as it hissed past his head. A youth by the boundary just managed to stop it and save four byes.

'How fast was that?' muttered Jim. Too fast by half, he thought. Good job the kids were wearing helmets. They were going to need them.

The ball came back to Pierre, who studied it as he returned to his mark. He scratched the spot with his boot, so he could find it again and charge from the same place. The batsman was banging the crease as if there was some kind of defensive magic in digging a small divot in front of the middle stump.

Pierre set off with a little kick. The batsman started to bob up and down. Pierre let fly.

Jim winced as the ball flew past the batsman at shoulder height. The wicket-keeper, ten yards back, tried to catch it but it was too fast, rocketing over the boundary for four byes.

The umpire said something to Pierre, who nodded.

Jim had no idea about cricket and wondered if dialogue with the umpire was good or bad. It looked like a cautionary word and that seemed sensible. If he was the umpire he'd tell Pierre to slow down – but wasn't bowling like that the point of the game?

Pierre looked over at Jim, gestured at his eye and then at him, smiling happily. Pierre meant him to watch closely. Jim nodded. Pierre turned away, rubbing the ball hard on his whites as he returned to his mark. He stood still for a moment, steeling himself for the sprint. He set off and by the time he reached the wicket he was running flat out.

Jim didn't see the ball fly, just heard a thud at the batsman's end and saw a stump fly backwards out of the ground.

Pierre took off vertically, spinning around with his arms in the air. There was a chorus of shouts from his team mates.

This was going to be a short game, thought Jim.

Pierre swung into the passenger seat. 'Nice car, Jim,' he said. 'All my friends are well jealous of me.'

Jim smiled and started the Bugatti Veyron. 'It was Stafford's idea,' he said. 'He says I should have this kind of car. It's suitable for a man of my standing, so he reckons.'

Pierre laughed.

Jim reversed out between the two parental Range Rovers. 'You played bloody well,' he said, checking to make sure he wasn't going to hit anything as he pulled away.

'Thanks,' said Pierre. 'I love cricket – it's like friendly fighting.'

'I'm not sure the other team would agree about the friendly bit,' he said, nursing the car forwards.

'Only bruises,' said Pierre, 'no blood.' He waved out of the window at a friend.

Jim glanced at the historic school building, then at the uniformed children watching him pass. He scratched his head, ruffling his short black hair. It was a world he had no understanding of. He slowed to a crawl as he took a tight turn.

'How's Jane?' asked Pierre, swivelling in his bucket seat and lowering the window. He waved again, then poked his head out and shouted to another boy, laughing.

Jim didn't reply.

Pierre pulled his head in. 'What did you say?'

'Nothing,' said Jim. 'I didn't say nothing.'

'Oh,' said Pierre. 'That's not good.' He closed the window and screwed himself into the seat. 'Does this car go fast?'

'Like shit off a shiny shovel.'

'You going to show me?'

'Probably not,' said Jim. 'I've not really got the hang of it yet.' He grinned. 'But if we can get a stretch of clear, straight road, I might give it a go.'

'Wicked!'

Jim was finally out of the obstacle course of the school precinct, pleased to be on a proper road. He pushed the accelerator a little and the car surged away. He eased off and settled at the speed limit. 'Nought to a driving ban in three and a half seconds,' he said, laughing.

'OK!' said Pierre. 'Go ahead!'

'Maybe later,' said Jim. 'There's plenty of time.'

'So how about you come back to the DRC with me today?'

'No can do,' said Jim. 'Got to see a man about some mosquitoes.'

'Mosquitoes?' said Pierre. 'You can see plenty back home.'

'That's right,' said Jim. 'But this is different. There's a professor in Cambridge who's trying to find a way of stopping mosquitoes spreading malaria. I'm thinking of funding him.'

'You giving your money away again, Uncle?'

'Uncle?'

'Kind Uncle, gives his money away to all the girls.' Pierre was laughing again.

'It was your idea, remember?' said Jim.

'No,' said Pierre.

'You told me mosquitoes were to blame for so many deaths.'

'I might have.'

'It set me thinking and you're right. The fucking mozzies are, like, the worst thing on earth. Little flying bastards spreading death.'

'But all this money you keep giving away, you'll run out of it.'

'I don't think so,' said Jim. 'Anyway, if I do, I'll make some more.'

'Good plan. How's the professor going to kill the mosquitoes?'

'I don't know,' said Jim. 'I'll find out tomorrow.'

Pierre put his hand on Jim's shoulder. 'Can't you go faster?'

'No,' said Jim, 'not yet.'

Pierre groaned. 'Jim, you're so boring.' He laughed. 'But that's OK.'

'Thanks,' said Jim.

'I'll probably be boring too when I'm old and twenty-five like you.'

An image of Pierre at fifteen, in his worn green irregular army uniform, a battered Kalashnikov slung over his shoulder, flipped into Jim's mind. Now the boy, once named Man Bites Dog, was just a teenager watching the world go by. Jim grinned. 'Let's hope so.'

'So what's happened to Jane? Please nothing bad.'

'Nothing bad,' said Jim.

'Go on.'

'Nothing bad.'

'You can tell me, Jim.'

Jim stamped on the accelerator and the Veyron shot forwards.

'Whoah!' said Pierre. 'This is great!'

Jim looked into his rear-view mirror. Was that the flash of a speed camera?

9

A broad smile slowly spread over Professor Cardini's face. He slapped the side of his right leg with his giant gnarled hand. 'Ha.' He laughed, in a single deep rumble. 'Plucky,' he said, raising a bushy eyebrow.

Dear Kate,
I appreciate your honesty in the matter. Over the years I, too, have had my reservations.
If you can come to my office at eleven thirty tomorrow I have something I would like to share with you.
I hope that will be a convenient time as my schedule is very tight.
Sincerely,
Cardini

Kate sat in front of her Notebook, holding a cup of tomato soup, which she put down – she was worried that when she read Cardini's email she might drop it.

'Oh,' she said. She sagged in her chair with relief. Thank goodness he's cool, she thought. Perhaps he wasn't such a horrible man, after all. She remembered the look he had given her as she'd left the laboratory and shivered, then picked up the soup and sipped.

Dear Professor,
See you at eleven thirty tomorrow.
Kate

10

Jim threw the presentation down in disgust on the distressed gilded-leather-covered desk top. He looked up at Stafford, his butler, who sat on a delicate eighteenth-century chair opposite him. 'How can this be so hard?' he said, his voice tinged with despair. 'If I dig a well, people might get poisoned by arsenic in the ground water, or some local guy'll start charging for access. If I hand over money to someone else to give away, they drive around in an SUV lording it over starving people. If I pay five hundred dollars to ten thousand families, the money leaks away, and before you know it, they're depending on me to keep paying. What am I supposed to do? How can you give money away without polluting everything?'

'As you say, it's not easy,' said Stafford, quietly.

'Most of these projects,' said Jim, springing up, 'are just filling in for evil governments who go around stealing all their people's stuff.' He threw his hands into the air. 'Rather than funding boatloads of food, I'd be better off sponsoring an invasion to kick bastards like that out.'

'It's been attempted,' observed Stafford.

'Well, I'm trying to give my money to charity, not start another United Nations.'

'Quite.'

'So what's the answer?' wailed Jim.

'Determination?' suggested Stafford, with a hint of irony.

'Well, this thing tomorrow better not be another British middle-class lifestyle sponsorship plan playing at being a charity.'

Stafford stiffened a little. 'It's a research group and it looks very interesting.'

'Mosquitoes,' growled Jim. 'I hate them.' Then he smiled. 'If the professor drives a Merc, I'm not putting in a single penny.'

'Professors are allowed nice cars, you know. You're funding a scientist not a saint, are you not?'

Jim wrinkled his nose, as if there were a very smelly piece of cheese under it.

Stafford rose. 'Would you like some lunch?'

'It's OK,' said Jim. 'I'm going out – I'm dying for a Big Mac.'

Stafford tried not to look aghast, but failed.

11

The real-tennis court echoed to the grunts of Jim's physical exertion and the thumping of staccato steps on the floor mats. His fists made slapping, squeaking sounds on the receiving gloves of his coach. He was sweating profusely.

'Stop,' said the coach.

Jim straightened.

'Very good, you showed a lot of speed there.'

Jim grimaced. 'Trouble is, Pat, I don't feel I'm making any progress.'

'You're doing fine. You learn fast.'

'But it's not real, it's just play-fighting.'

Pat pursed his lips. 'It's close enough.'

'I need to do it without this head guard on, under real conditions.'

Pat drew a breath. 'But you'll get hurt.'

'Pat, I'm not doing this to look cool. I'm doing it for my own protection.'

'I know. You said.'

'I'd have you punch the lights out of me but I can't take it to the side. I'm all screwed up there.'

'I remember you telling me so.'

'But I have to be able to react in a real situation, against real blows, under real pain. I need to be able to respond properly if I get into trouble. I need to practise on something that's as real as possible.'

Pat was blanking him. 'You'll be fine,' he said, smiling gently.

'Look!' said Jim, pulling up his shirt in frustration. 'I can't afford to get any more messed up.'

He watched his coach recoil. His right side might have been chewed up by some large and ferocious animal. He dropped his shirt, bowed and parted his hair, showing a long scar across his scalp. 'I've been in a fair amount of trouble,' he said, 'and next time I don't want to rely on luck to keep me alive.'

Next time? Pat had looked Jim up on the Internet: he was some kind of retired super-rich, boy-genius banker – but something had messed him up good and proper.

'You don't have to kill me,' said Jim. 'You can pull your punches a little.'

Pat started to take off his focus pads. 'OK,' he said, 'but don't ever say you didn't ask me nicely to beat you senseless.'

'Brilliant,' said Jim.

Pat looked doubtful. 'I'll be putting my head guard on and you'll be keeping your gloves.'

'Sure,' said Jim.

Pat returned with his head guard in place and a pair of practice boxing gloves on. 'I'm not messing up my knuckles on your face,' he said, waving his right hand at Jim.

Jim smiled. 'OK,' he said, and put in a mouth guard.

'Are you ready?' said Pat, sounding reluctant.

Jim nodded, crouched, and began to weave.

Pat kicked his legs out from under him, then towered over him ready to land a punch.

Jim rolled away and up. In that moment he had felt what it was like to stand up against a world-class fighter. Pat's speed was breathtaking. And Jim was paying to be trained by the best. 'You should have hit me,' he said. 'Punish my mistakes ... Well, punish them a bit, OK?'

Pat moved towards him. Jim could see he was going for a grapple, so he fended off the grab with his left hand and tried to land a punch with his right. Pat's head seemed to fall out of the way of his blow and Jim hopped off.

Jim's concentration was intense, adrenalin coursing through his body. In a split second he saw Pat consider several moves. He was going to fire a shot at Jim's temple so Jim shot a blow to his stomach. He felt it was the wrong move as it went off, so he twisted to avoid Pat's jab, which seemed to come in slow. Jim's punch was heavy, given extra energy by his turn. It was a contact that scored hard. With better poise he could have fired off another shot, but he needed to hop back into balance first.

Suddenly he felt a sharp blow to his left eye and a cuff to the other side of his skull. He was instantly confused and falling.

Pat was looking down at him.

'Nice one,' said Jim, weakly, shaking his head.

'Not so bad yourself,' said Pat, and pulled Jim to his feet.

'That was great,' said Jim, trying to blink his left eye.

'I hope that's enough.'

'For now,' said Jim, pasting on a smile. 'I learnt more in that minute than in all the other lessons.' His eye was swelling. He took his gloves off and his mouth guard out. 'Ow,' he said, touching his eye. 'That was awesome. I didn't see your punches at all. Incredible – amazing.'

Pat wondered why his pupil was looking so happy, if somewhat dazed. 'I think you might quite possibly be mad,' he said.

'Thanks,' said Jim, dizzily. 'I appreciate that.'

Stafford put the tray on Jim's desk. 'Best fillet steak,' he said. 'The best thing for it.' He regarded Jim's black and red eye. 'Can you see properly?'

'Yes,' said Jim, 'no problem. It wants to close a bit, but I can keep it open.' He took the steak, which was cold and wet, and clapped it on his eye, which enjoyed the cold but was irritated by the pressure. 'Are you sure this'll help?'

'No, but it comes recommended by folklore.'

12

The Veyron was ludicrously fast. It was almost impossible to drive without sailing instantly above any speed limit. Consequently his foot lay lightly on the accelerator at an uncomfortable angle and he kept having to take it off altogether to slow down. The novelty of the car was quickly wearing off. He'd get Stafford to find him something slower. He took his foot off the accelerator again and braked – he was doing 115 m.p.h. after daydreaming for just a few moments. At this rate he'd arrive at the professor's lab horribly early, with a handful of speeding tickets.

Stafford had selected a number of cars for him, assuring Jim that they were right for a man of his station in life. They sat in his garage collecting dust. They were pretty enough but he hated the way everyone stared at him as he drove past. He'd get less attention if he walked down the road naked, he told Stafford.

Stafford ignored his protests and bought the latest concept from any supercar company that came along. He put into storage the vehicles he considered out of fashion. He would drag Jim to see his latest acquisition and practically force him to take them for a drive, like some old owl trying to fledge one of its brood.

In return, Jim tried to make Stafford take them for a drive: he knew that Stafford was in love with his shiny car collection. Yet Stafford demurred, 'I shouldn't be able to get back out of it,' he would say, flapping a hand dismissively at the low driver's door. 'I doubt a man of my weight would even fit inside.'

Jim would shrug and smile. There was no harm in him assembling a few flash cars to polish in the stable block.

13

Bob Renton had a funny, springy walk and a black-bearded grin permanently on his face. There was a kind of happy determination about him, enhanced by the implied authority of his white lab coat. His gait seemed to suggest he was doing several jobs in parallel, all of them exciting, important and running according to plan.

That scenario was perfectly likely because Renton was Professor Cardini's chief assistant and the linchpin of the professor's many research projects. His faintly eccentric but jovial demeanour ensured he was an object of mirth among the students. He seemed to pop up everywhere around the lab, as if he could appear at will wherever he chose. He was the go-to guy for all necessities and help in the lab. He always seemed to be there.

He showed Kate into a little study. It acted as a waiting room for those wishing to see the great Professor Cardini.

Renton seemed to look at her oddly. It was as if he was enjoying something different about her from what she guessed other men were thinking when they eyed her in a particular way. Like a bad memory, Bob Renton made her want to shudder.

'Would you like a cuppa?' he asked, in a friendly way, standing a little taller on the balls of his feet.

'No thanks, Bob,' she said politely.

'He shouldn't be too long,' said Renton, smiling, his chin pushed forwards.

'Thanks.' She sat down in a worn green armchair, crossed her legs and looked out of the window. The door closed.

It was a lovely summer day and a breeze was fluttering the

leaves of the horse-chestnuts outside. She was not going to wonder what the professor would say to her: she had thought it over a thousand times. She would soon know, she told herself, as a small blue sports car drove noisily into a parking space outside.

Renton closed the door of his room and locked it. He opened the video monitoring software and pulled up the feed from Cardini's anteroom. There Kate sat. He clicked up the remote control centre, the master controller of many of the lab's experiments, and sent an instruction to the container in the far-right corner of the room – it looked like a mouse trap. A little door opened in its side and a fan inside began to turn, blowing a silent gust of air though the flat white plastic housing. The mosquito rose on its legs and instinctively flapped its wings as if resisting. The airflow dislodged it and it was blown out into the wider world.

It flew up to the ceiling and landed, hanging upside down. As moments passed it began to smell Kate below. With only one millionth of the neurons of a human, it located her, calculated her position and prepared to fly to a place on her body where it could pierce her skin and feed. It flexed its legs, dropped from its hold, turned and flew.

Kate was watching a young guy get out of the sports car. She wondered what make it was. It looked like one of the Mazdas she had always fancied having one day, whenever she could afford a luxury like a sports car. He was wearing a suit that didn't quite go with the car. He'd have been better off in jeans and a leather jacket. He wasn't bad-looking in a funny way … In fact – she craned her neck – he was pretty handsome, perhaps even dangerously so.

Renton watched the screen. It was kind of pointless. He couldn't see the mosquito because it was too small. Neither was the girl likely to jump up and scream when it bit her. He would just have to hope it did its job, which, as a hungry mosquito, it most surely would.

The buzzer sounded in Reception. Who could it be? He switched feeds. A young guy was standing at the desk. Was he the professor's meeting? If so, he was early. He switched off the monitor and got up.

'It's down the hall on the corner,' said the receptionist.

'Thanks,' said Jim, and turned to go. The place reminded him of his comprehensive school, which he hadn't thought about since he'd left it at sixteen. He had gone to work for an investment bank as a gofer on the trading floor and never looked back.

How different this place was from a bank. There were tiles rather than marble, and wood, painted many times in an off-blue colour, rather than the steel and ebony of London's financial heart. Here he detected a whiff of cleaning fluid, not coffee, in the air.

Jim wandered down the long gloomy hall. He opened the door at the end. A girl inside started. 'Oh,' he said. 'Sorry. Is this the right room for Professor Cardini?'

'Yes,' she said.

'Good,' said Jim. 'I'll join you, if you don't mind. I've got an appointment with him but I'm really early.'

'Me too,' she said, 'but he's late.' She smiled.

'Don't move,' said Jim. He was staring at her arm. 'Just don't move.'

She looked at him questioningly and froze.

'You've got a mosquito on you and it's about to tuck in. Shall I get it?'

'Yes,' she said. 'Where is it?'

He lunged and slapped her arm gently. 'Got it!' He picked something off her just above the elbow. He held it up. 'You were nearly lunch,' he said, admiring his handiwork.

'Thanks,' she said, smiling nervously.

He became aware that someone was standing behind him. He turned, mosquito in hand, to see a bearded guy in a lab coat.

'Hello,' Jim said. 'Just saving this lady from a blood-sucking insect.'

'Are you Jim Evans?' the man said, peering at the tiny corpse between Jim's fingers.

'Yes,' he said, 'I'm very early.' Jim rolled the insect between his fingers, dispersing it like dust.

'I hope that thing didn't bite you, Kate,' said the man in the lab coat. 'The locals aren't as nasty as our subjects, but even so.'

She shrugged.

The man in the lab coat stepped forward. 'Kate, do you think you can come back at one? The professor's running a bit late. I don't think he can see you before his meeting with Mr Evans here.'

'Sure,' said Kate, surprised. 'OK.'

'Mr Evans is a philanthropist and his time is incredibly valuable.'

'No, no,' said Jim. 'I'm way early. I don't mind waiting, that's OK.'

'It's all right,' said Kate, with a resigned smile. 'I'm dying for some lunch.' She stood up and grabbed her jacket. 'See you at one, Bob.' She grinned at Jim. 'Nice black eye.'

'Thanks,' he said sheepishly. 'It's my new look.'

The man in the lab coat opened the door for her. 'Thanks very much, Kate.' He followed her out.

What a crap way to treat people, thought Jim, sitting down. He would happily have swapped the crusty old professor's company for hers. Even a five-minute chat would be better than an hour of waffle from a fat cat angling for a handout.

14

The door opened and a tall man, perhaps over six foot six, in his late fifties, entered. Jim knew immediately it was Cardini. He stood up.

'Welcome,' said the professor, in a very deep voice, holding out a huge hand at the end of an immensely long arm.

'Hi,' said Jim.

'That's a bad contusion you have there, young man. It looks untreated.'

'It's OK,' said Jim.

Cardini was now up close to him, studying the bruise. 'I don't approve,' he said finally. 'That needs to be looked at. Come this way.' He led Jim into his office. 'Please sit down,' he said, then went to his desk and brought out a bag. 'I used to be an eye surgeon, you know.' He put his giant hand gently on Jim's head. Jim noticed him raise an eyebrow as he noted the long scar across his scalp. 'I'm going to look into your eye to check your retina is intact. Try not to blink if you can.'

Jim was dazzled by a bright light.

'Very good,' said Cardini. 'No damage.' He stood up and took a little pot from his bag. 'This,' he said, holding it between thumb and forefinger, 'is something I've been working on for thirty years. It will help your injury – may I put some on you?'

'Sure,' said Jim.

Cardini took a pair of white rubber gloves from his bag, removed the top from the pot and dipped a cotton bud into the contents. There was a faint smell of pears. 'You may feel strong heat where I apply the balm. Do not touch your eye for ten minutes while your skin absorbs it. It is a cellular stimulant, and

47

if you have it on your fingers you may spread it elsewhere, producing unintended consequences.' He dabbed it on Jim's eye.

'Wow,' said Jim. 'I can feel the heat.' Warmth spreading around his eye, then down his cheek, as if blood was flooding from a gash.

'I wasn't expecting to treat someone today,' said Cardini, standing back, 'but it's always a pleasure.'

The intense heat on Jim's face was almost painful, but not unpleasant. It was like the taste of a hot curry on his tongue, except the tingle was on his face. 'What is that stuff?' he asked, reeling a little.

'Telomere eukaryotic retranscriptase.' Cardini smiled.

'Right,' said Jim, puffing. 'Whatever it is, it's hot stuff.'

'Let me show you around.'

Jim stood up, flustered, distracted by the pulsing heat in his face.

Cardini was watching his expression with a degree of amusement. 'We have a lot of programmes on the go at present, thanks to very generous donations from America.'

They left the office, went down the hall and climbed a flight of stairs.

'Our speciality is in finding genetic solutions to medical and general health issues, but we also focus on biomechanics,' said Cardini, launching into what seemed to be an informal presentation. 'We have some of the most advanced programmes on genetics, biomechanics and meta-organic synthesis on earth.' He stopped at the top of the staircase and looked at Jim. 'Where is your degree from?'

Jim normally said, 'Tesco,' to that kind of query, but his face was taking most of his attention. Someone seemed to be pressing a hot bread roll to his eye. It was, surprisingly, a rather nice sensation but it made it hard to concentrate. 'I didn't go to university,' he said. 'I went straight into banking.'

'And well it did you, too,' said Cardini. They walked along a corridor on the first floor. The professor swiped his pass over a pad and opened a swing door. 'This is our mosquito lab. We're trying to build the perfect mosquito, a specimen that can replace the current insect in nature.' The walls were lined with glass tanks that housed pink rats.

'Hairless rats?' enquired Jim.

'Food for our subjects,' said Cardini.

Jim looked closer. There were mosquitoes in the tanks: some were squatting on the rats and feeding off them. He felt a bit queasy and turned away.

'We're trying to make a mosquito with adapted salivary glands that won't carry malaria but, of course, we need it to out-compete the normal species and enable it to replace it by out-breeding it in the wild. This, of course, is the difficult part. Out-designing evolution is, without doubt, the greatest of challenges.'

'Out-designing evolution or God?' asked Jim, almost by accident. His internal censor had gone off duty, defeated by the fierce heat in his face.

'Ha ha! It would be a great disappointment if the people's God was responsible for such a killer, would it not?' He leant forward and gave Jim an amused, quizzical look. 'Of course, if we succeed, we can forestall the journey of many to test the supernatural axiom.'

'You mean by saving lives.'

Cardini continued: 'We are making solid progress with the mosquito. If we can solve the final problems we can change the world for ever. And that is what you are trying to do, is it not?'

'Well,' said Jim, 'not really. I'm just trying to help people. Does that mean changing the world?'

'I think so,' said Cardini. 'Great advances always change the world. Take penicillin,' he boomed. 'When it was discovered there were but two billion people in the world. Now, thanks to this panacea, there are seven billion. Dr Fleming is the grandfather of five billion people.' He looked deep into Jim's eyes. 'Of course there is danger in progress, but it takes a man of vision to face these consequences with courage.' He lowered his head. 'Are you a man of vision, Mr Evans?'

Jim didn't answer. His face was beginning to itch and he was trying not to scratch it for fear of getting the balm on his fingers. His left ear was whistling. He caught sight of a cowering rat covered with feeding mosquitoes. 'I'm not sure I'm too keen on genetic engineering,' he said. 'What happens if you screw up? It's like programming, right? Well, you know what happens with software – it's always crashing.'

'There is no second place in nature,' said Cardini. 'A flawed design will be gobbled up by the voracious environment that is life.'

'What about a mistake that works – like those frogs in Australia?'

Cardini nodded. 'Toads,' he corrected. 'A good example. Cane toads are not genetically engineered, quite the opposite. They are very "of nature". Meanwhile, in all the years of genetic experimentation there has never been a single accident. It is clear that nature is far more dangerous than science. All you need do is ask yourself if you would prefer to sleep in a laboratory like this or in a jungle.' He laughed at his own joke.

'Jungles are OK,' said Jim. 'I've slept just fine in jungles.' His eyes were drawn back to the glass case.

'However, if you are uncomfortable with genetics, we have our biomechanics lab.'

'What do you do there?'

'We're attempting to build replacement organs: kidneys, livers, hearts. There is a desperate shortage. Thousands die on waiting lists, hoping that some unfortunate will pass theirs on to them. One must die so others live. Clearly that is no real solution.' Cardini held his giant hands out in supplication. 'So we're trying to create artificial ones. Would you like to see?'

'Yes,' said Jim, happy at the prospect of departing from the ghoulish mosquito lab.

They went up to the second floor, where a distant pulsating hum filled the atmosphere with an unsettling reverb straight out of a Chill Bill ambient track like *This time Orpheus does not look back*. Cardini gave him a lab coat and asked him to put on a pair of plastic clogs that looked rather like Crocs. They slipped masks over their noses and mouths, then went through a series of airlocks.

Cardini took him into a small room, with glass cases lining the four walls. 'This is a pig's kidney,' he said. 'We're washing it so that all the cells come away. This will leave the structure behind. In this room we wash all the organs and next door we try to grow human kidney cells on them. Let me show you.'

They walked out into the corridor and into the next room.

'This kidney is very advanced,' said Cardini. 'We have fitted it with artificial human veins, which we have grown and populated with cultured human cells. It's very close to being complete.'

Jim marvelled at the apparatus holding the kidney, with its tubes of blood and fluid pumping through and over it. 'Will this be used for a transplant?' he asked.

'Sadly not,' said Cardini. 'We must build and test innumerable versions before we can even start thinking about applying for medical approval. Even if this were a perfect kidney, we'd be years away from *in vivo* application. Not many of us will see this work reach a point when it saves lives. The timescale crosses generations.'

'Pity,' said Jim.

The door opened and Jim recognised Cardini's assistant. 'Excuse me, Professor, but you have an urgent call from America.'

'A bit early even for them,' barked Cardini, clearly irritated. He turned to Jim. 'Forgive me, but Bob Renton here will show you around while I'm away. I shall return in a few minutes.' He looked at Renton. 'Would you be so kind?'

'My pleasure,' said Renton.

'Please excuse me,' said Cardini, and left.

Renton smiled at Jim, his beard sticking up on his chin. 'What do you think so far, Mr Evans?'

'Call me Jim,' he said. 'You're Bob, right?'

'Yes,' he said, rising up on his toes.

'Well, Bob, this growing kidneys thing is amazing.'

'Yes. Deliciously Promethean.'

'Yes,' said Jim, getting the gist – in as much as 'Promethean' sounded positive. 'And you're growing livers and hearts too.'

'Yes – let's go and see them.' Renton opened the door. 'Of course, the real goal is nerve and spine. Once you can build a nervous system, it's only the brain that's irreplaceable.'

'You're never going to grow a brain in a jar!'

'No,' said Renton, 'but we're making good progress on nerve and spine.'

'Really?' said Jim, as they entered another room where a liver was being bathed in a misty fluid. 'So you'll be looking to make people with broken backs walk again?'

'We're close, Jim, very close.'

Jim stopped and stared at him. 'Amazing. I thought that was science fiction.'

'Would you like to see?'

'You bet,' said Jim. 'One liver looks just like another to me.'

'Come this way. It's upstairs.'

15

Cardini sat stiffly in his desk chair, an old phone pressed to his ear. 'Howard, you must calm yourself. I'll attend next week as planned. I know the process is distressing but we've been through it before and it's occurring as expected. No good will come of exciting yourself over it.'

He listened to the reply.

A window popped up on his computer: Renton had entered the myelin lab. He scowled. 'I must go now, Howard. I have an urgent matter to attend to.' He hung up, cutting off the agitated reply, then got to his feet and strode towards the door.

Through the window in the security door Jim could see the lab was dark and up-lit, unlike the others. As they went in, a faintly musty odour was partially masked by the smell of disinfectant.

A lab assistant at the far end of the room looked at them for a second, then returned to his work.

Renton led Jim to a case containing what at first glance looked like a small industrial robot. There was a red fluffy thing on its wrist, some kind of joke hand. He logged on to a computer, operated a joystick and the robot moved. The hand opened and closed and the fingers flexed like those of a theme-park automaton. 'Extraordinary, isn't it?' His eyes were lit up with pleasure.

Jim was about to say something else but … 'Is that a real hand?'

'Of course.'

'Like off a monkey?'

'Macaque.'

Jim watched the hand as it articulated. 'How does it stay alive?'

'We feed it like the animal did, with blood and nutrients.'

Jim's eyes were riveted to the hand in horrified fascination. 'With monkey blood?'

'Yes, but that's nothing,' said Renton, typing. At the side of the robot a metal curtain pulled back and something stirred. 'We'll let the monkey work the robot.'

Jim jumped back, appalled.

The one-armed monkey peered through the window and the arm began to move.

'The nerves in its shoulder are wired into a tiny receiver-transmitter,' said Renton, who had fallen apparently into a state of ecstasy.

The hand turned to the monkey and pulled on a cord hanging above the robot. A piece of apple fell into the cage beside the animal, which picked it up and bit into it.

'Of course, it takes a smart monkey to recognise its own arm and use it.'

Jim gaped. That's awful, he wanted to say, but the words didn't come out. He was mesmerised by the one-armed monkey, chewing its apple.

'You can imagine the applications. Some of these nerves are connected at the spine, and if we can take the feed directly from the spine or brain then it doesn't matter whose body—'

'I'm sorry,' said Cardini's deep voice behind them. Jim started. 'I'm afraid I must take you out of here. This project is funded by the military, and Bob shouldn't have brought you in.' Cardini was glaring at Renton. 'As you can imagine, if we succeed in this project then many thousands with damaged spines can be given their lives back. The military, the US military in particular, is investing heavily in research to help their veterans, many of whom have lost limbs.'

'That poor monkey,' blurted Jim.

'Indeed,' said Cardini. 'A small sacrifice in the fight against such great misery.'

As he followed Cardini out of the lab, Jim glimpsed at least another dozen such cabinets. He was relieved when the lab door closed behind them. He felt nauseous.

Cardini noted his expression as he closed the door. 'I hope that didn't upset you.'

'I didn't like it,' said Jim. 'I didn't mind watching you grow a mixed grill downstairs, but I'm gutted for the monkey. I can't help thinking of me like that, in a cage, in his position.'

'The monkey would live a shorter more brutal life in the wild,' said Cardini.

'But it would be a lot happier.'

'Hm,' grunted Cardini. 'I don't believe a monkey experiences happiness or unhappiness, Jim ... Unlike the people we are trying to help,' he added gravely.

'Well, I hope you find the answer quickly, for everyone's sake.'

'So do I,' said Cardini.

Jim's eye was itching again, as if little needles were working under his skin. He put his fingers to the bruise and touched it gently. The skin was soft and smooth. He rubbed it carefully – surely ten minutes had passed.

'I think,' said Cardini, as they walked down the stairs, 'you should consider our mosquito project. Here, at least, we kill only vermin for the sake of human life.'

When Cardini looked at him, a flicker of what Jim interpreted as contempt showed in his eyes. 'Are you having a pop at me?' he wondered.

'Yes,' said Cardini. 'I probably am.'

'What's probability got to do with it?'

'Very little,' he said, sighing.

'I know you mean well,' said Jim, following him down the bare concrete stairs, 'but I've got to be honest. Chopping a poor monkey's arm off so you can get him to move it by Wi-Fi makes me feel kind of sick.'

'I know,' said Cardini. 'But you have a purity that only youth can afford. If you were lying paralysed in bed covered with bedsores, how many monkeys would you want to die for you?'

Jim stopped. 'Loads,' he said, 'but that wouldn't make it right.'

Cardini continued on his way down the stairs. At the bottom, he said, 'Well, Jim, it's been a pleasure to meet you. It's not often I meet someone so young and full of life and righteousness. My normal donor shakes in his boots at the thought of his moment of judgement or his approaching oblivion.'

Jim had no idea what he meant. 'OK,' he said. 'Well, thanks for having me.'

'I hope you'll consider what we're doing here in a broad context and forgive some of the harshness you've seen.'

'I understand what you're trying to do, Professor, but I still feel sorry for the rats and that monkey.' He grimaced. 'And for all the other poor bloody monkeys I didn't see.'

Cardini didn't respond but Jim felt his disdain.

'Well,' said Cardini, eventually, 'I wish you good day, and if you should want to help us, I'm sure history will be very grateful.' He held out his hand, took Jim's, dwarfing it, and shook.

There was movement high above and Jim glanced up to see Renton looking down from the landing. Jim's eyes narrowed. Cardini and Renton were a creepy pair.

He went out into the daylight, got into the Veyron, opened his iPad and logged on to the markets. He felt like a retired sportsman checking on the next generation of players battling away in a never-ending round of tournaments. He couldn't let the markets go: he was a junkie for the game he'd been forced to give up.

When he looked up, Kate was walking towards the car and the lab beyond. He lowered the window and stuck his head out. 'Hi,' he called.

She veered towards him. 'Hello,' she said.

'I'd offer to take you to lunch but you just ate.'

'I didn't actually,' she said, resignedly. 'I was just making excuses.'

'Do you fancy lunch, then?'

She hesitated.

'OK, I can hang about waiting for you now as a punishment.' He grinned.

She tossed her head. 'OK, then, but if you get fed up, just go.'

'Deal.'

16

Jim was flipping through the financial charts on his iPhone. The Dow was going to open up and stay strong all day. The dollar would keep slipping, and by the end of the week it would be down about two per cent against most of the major currencies.

To him financial charts told a story not just of the past but of the future. It was a skill that legions of traders tried to develop. The successful analysis of financial charts was meant to be the key to untold wealth, but it seemed that only Jim had mastered the art. While other traders pored over their charts hoping for a hint of what was to come, Jim could read the outcome as if it was printed in bold. His clairvoyance had made him his fortune, a sum so great that he didn't even know exactly how much he was worth. He was so rich that the interest, even at the current derisory rate, piled up faster than he could sensibly give it away. There was no end to the prosperous middle-class people who begged him to donate to their slick and shiny causes, but aid at one level was too often a curse at another. How could he help without worsening the situation he was trying to relieve? You could send clothes to Africa, like the Americans, and end up destroying a country's industry so that in the end it couldn't even make its own. You could send shiploads of food and by accident bankrupt a nation's farmers. Giving money away was like putting fertiliser on land: it so easily became poison in the rivers.

Trading was much easier than philanthropy. The market was either going up or down. You made that call and you were either right or wrong. You made money or lost it. There was no one to tell you that you had lost when you had won, or that you had bought when you had sold. You took your positions and you came off richer or poorer. It was a black or white world where the rules of engagement were simple. If you were right enough, you made a fortune; if you were wrong you went broke. Unlike the real world, the markets were simple and fair.

Yet here again things got complicated.

As he could read the markets like no other, he was rich beyond his wildest dreams but he had been caught in a position where he could no longer participate in the activity that had made him. Not only had he more money than he wanted or needed, his reputation and the scale of the trading he needed to do to make it worthwhile were so huge that any dealing he did pushed the market out of equilibrium. Like a teenager trying to ride his old toddler tricycle, he risked breaking his cherished toy. Yet he kept up with the charts and read the financial news, as an inverterate gambler avidly scans the racing pages.

There was a tap at the window and Jim looked up. 'Get in,' he said, waving to Kate and putting the phone on the floor by the base of his seat.

Kate opened the door and slipped into the little capsule. 'This is very cosy,' she said.

'Where to?'

She gazed at the sleek chrome and leather of the cockpit. It was bling, but kind of exciting too. The philanthropist with the black eye must be some kind of Flash Harry venture capitalist. He'd be full of himself and pretty obnoxious, she was sure. She smiled at Jim. 'McDonald's.'

Jim almost let out a sigh of relief. 'Great idea,' he said. 'Show me the way.'

She put a book she was carrying on her lap and buckled herself in. 'It's just at the bottom of the hill.'

'The hill?'

'Go left.'

He caught sight of his face in the rear-view mirror as he

pulled out of the parking space. His eye was no longer black and swollen, the bruised area was red and ringed in yellow and green. He wondered what the hell was going on inside his face.

17

There was only so long Jim could make a Big Mac last. Time flew, and soon enough he was pulling up outside her digs to drop her off. She lived in a tall Edwardian house, which, Jim noted, had been broken up into several student flats.

'I really enjoyed lunch,' he said, smiling.

'Me too,' she said.

He reached across her – she didn't recoil – to open the glove compartment and take out a plastic box of calling cards. He prised it open. 'I'd like to see you again,' he said, handing her two cards. 'Can I get your phone number?'

'Of course,' she said. She reached into her bag, rummaged around in it and finally took out a bright green plastic pen. She wrote on the back of one of the cards and gave it to him.

He jammed it awkwardly into his trouser pocket. Their eyes caught. There was a frozen moment as if God had pressed the pause button. Kate looked amazing, he thought, with her long shiny reddish hair, her large, kind, friendly eyes and curved pink lips, which glistened invitingly. He held himself in check. If only there wasn't someone else. Kate's body, lithe and sexy, tilted towards him in her seat. He felt as if Jane was standing outside at the passenger window, watching him.

He sank back in his seat. 'I'll call you,' he said. She must have someone too, he thought. A girl like her would have any number of smart university guys chasing after her – she'd have a boyfriend for sure. She'd think him a pushy prat if he hit on to her too quickly.

Kate popped her seatbelt and opened the door. 'Please do,' she said, and batted her eyelids at him. How many supermodel girlfriends did he have? she wondered. The chances of hearing from him again were one in a million. A pity, she thought. Jim was a really cool guy. "Bye," she said, and closed the door.

Jim watched her walk away, then turned his attention to driving and pulled out. When he called her he'd get her voicemail, and in a way he would be relieved and happy. He still hoped his phone would ring and that the caller would be Jane. He still wished his email would play a fanfare and it would be some terse cryptic message that meant she was back in his life. He'd almost given up hope. Soon he was going to have to admit it was over between them. He was either going to have to write Jane off for good and move on, or find out where the hell she'd got to so he could try crawling back to her. Both paths seemed like an awful punishment, but moving on seemed worse.

They had split on good terms, almost like professionals going their own way at the end of a project. Neither owed the other on aggregate after the danger they had endured. They had saved one another's skins. She'd seemed to think that splitting up was the sensible thing to do and he'd understood the logic. They knew they were oddballs and it had seemed clear that neither of them could fit into the other's world.

Yet without her there was still a giant emptiness in his heart, an injury to his brain that could not repair itself. He hungered for her.

There was a flash and he glanced at the speedometer: he was doing seventy in a thirty m.p.h. zone. He groaned. Pretty soon Stafford was going to have to replace the shot-up Maybach limo with one that didn't look like it had been the subject of a car-bomb attack, because at this rate Jim would end up as a passenger with a driving ban hanging around his neck. Then Stafford, or a newly hired chauffeur, would have to drive him around.

18

Kate had been about to send Jim a flirtatious SMS but thought better of it. Instead she Googled him. 'Billionaire Jim Evans, Britain's Most Eligible Bachelor Under Thirty,' said the headline. She clicked on the images and there he was, in a blurred long-distance shot. She couldn't make out his face but she could tell it was him. 'Oh dear,' she said aloud, putting the phone down. Texting no longer seemed such a good idea. She saw him in her mind's eye. Was he cute or was it just the money? No, he was extremely cute, even with a flaming red eye – which somehow enhanced his appeal with a touch of dash. How had he really got it? 'Training'? Training for what, exactly? She picked up the phone and reread the message she'd been about to send him: 'Nice to meet you. I enjoyed lunch.'

Silly. She deleted it, turned the phone upside-down and put it on the table.

She read two other articles about Jim. He was starting to seem a bit sinister. 'No one knows exactly where his fortune comes from,' said an article. That was a good reason not to contact him ... but the slightly dangerous angle was enticing. She closed the browser. If he liked her, he would call. They all did. Then she would decide whether or not to respond. She turned the phone over and looked at the screen. No, he wouldn't. Who was she kidding?

It gave him a satisfying thrill to draw up outside his Jacobean mansion in the Veyron. The ancient house oozed mystery, its ornate façade stern yet welcoming. This house and his place in London's Docklands were his anchors. How many dramas had gone on during those buildings' long histories? How many adventures and tragedies had washed past as the tide of history had ebbed and flowed? Was his story any more outlandish than the lost histories of the rich men who had owned this mansion over the four centuries before he had bought it?

He got out, hearing the crows calling from the trees beyond the rose gardens as the wind blew light clouds across a blue sky. He surveyed the scene. This was all his. He had to start enjoying his luck a bit more, he thought. He had to start wanting the things he had but, compared to the abstraction of the markets, physical things left him cold.

Stafford was standing in the doorway. Jim wished he wouldn't do that.

'Welcome back, Jim.'

'Hi, Stafford,' he said, bounding up the steps.

'Would you like tea, sir?'

'No, thanks,' said Jim, heading for the cloakroom and a toilet break. He pushed open the door, glimpsing himself in the large mirror over the basin. He stopped in his tracks. 'Bloody hell!' He leant close to the mirror. His eye was completely healed. Gone was the bloody red circle that had replaced the swollen black bruise and the skin didn't even show the jaundiced tint of earlier. It was as if he had never had a black eye. He touched the skin, which was smooth – smoother than it was on the undamaged side. He bent closer. There wasn't a mark where there had been a swollen mess just hours before.

'Amazing,' he muttered. He must call the professor and find out more. But first things first.

19

Cardini looked disappointed. 'So, Bob, do you think the mosquito bit the subject or not?'

'It's hard to tell. Maybe it did, maybe not.' Renton grimaced, bobbing up and down on the balls of his feet. 'It landed, but that doesn't mean it fed.'

'In your opinion?'

'It's hard to have one.'

'If you did, what would it be?'

Renton screwed up his face, his black beard jutting out.

The phone rang.

Cardini stared at it disapprovingly.

'Shall I get it?' suggested Renton.

Cardini thought for a moment. 'No.' He picked up the receiver. 'Cardini,' he said sharply, as if he was engaged in something vital.

'It's Jim Evans,' said a young voice.

'Jim,' boomed Cardini, as if he was welcoming a long-lost friend, 'good of you to call.'

'That stuff you put on my face is amazing.'

'Yes.'

'I mean really amazing.'

'Yes.'

'My black eye's completely better.'

'Yes.'

'That's impossible, right?'

'Apparently not.'

'Can you tell me more about it?'

'I could,' said Cardini, smiling to himself.

'Can it do more than just heal bruises?'

'Yes, very much more.'

'Like what?'

'Jim, I'm not particularly happy to discuss my research over the phone.'

'Right,' said Jim. 'I was wondering maybe if I could fund this line of research. I mean, it's not like the other stuff you're doing.'

'You mean the animals?'

'Yes.'

'No,' said Cardini. 'I am my own guinea pig.'

'Right,' said Jim, sounding surprised.

'I hope that's sufficiently humane for you.'

'You can't say fairer than that,' said Jim, who was pulling Cardini up on Wikipedia. 'Can I—' He coughed violently. He had caught sight of Cardini's birthdate. The man was nearly eighty, not fifty. 'Can I—' More coughing.

'Are you all right?'

Jim took a deep breath. 'Can I come up and talk it over with you, then?'

'Tomorrow morning,' said Cardini. 'I have to go to America, so my time is very short.'

'No problem. Nine o'clock?'

'Yes indeed.'

'See you then.'

'Good day.' Cardini hung up and looked at Renton. 'We must speed up our work,' he said. 'Bring the girl in and test her for the infection. If she isn't infected, infect her. Examine the development, then terminate the test. Do it once I have left for America and make sure there is no trace by my return.'

'Yes, Professor.'

'Do your utmost, Bob. The first horseman's entrance must soon be upon us.'

20

Kate stared at the message she had typed on her phone. She was filled with paralysing indecision: her mind was unable to command her hand to press the button. 'Enjoyed lunch,' seemed almost sendable but she had typed several versions and they'd all looked awful. What was wrong with her?

Her phone buzzed. She flipped to the message and almost dropped the phone. It was from Jim. 'I'm back up in Cambridge tomorrow. Fancy another burger?'

'Pizza?'

'Sure. I'll call when out of meeting.'

'gr8.' She regretted that one the moment she pressed send.

Jim looked at the message: 'gr8'. She liked him. He smiled.

He opened his trading screen. The dollar was going up and the euro was going down. He jumped on the dollar and joined the ride.

'Happy days,' he said, as Stafford came in with a mug of tea.

'Very good, sir.'

21

Jim shook Cardini's hand and sat down in front of the professor's desk. It was worn at the front where so many people had sat before, leaning themselves or their papers on its edge. The varnish had worn off to show the light-coloured wood below.

Cardini pushed a document towards him. 'You will need to sign this, Jim,' he said.

Jim picked it up. 'Confidentiality Agreement,' said the cover page. The date was written on it in flowing script. 'OK,' he said. 'Let me give it a read.' He turned back to the first page. It was typical legal bullshit, he thought, but if he talked in his sleep about what the professor was doing he'd be sued. He flicked through the pages to make sure there was nothing wildly odd in any of the paragraphs, then turned to the signature page. 'Got something to write with?'

'Of course.' Cardini produced a black fountain pen with a large red crystal set in the top. He unscrewed it and pushed the cap on to the rear of the barrel, then offered it to Jim, who took it.

'Don't think I've ever used one of these before,' said Jim. 'Writing with a biro is crazy enough.' He scratched his signature, which looked horribly childish. He liked the way the shiny wet ink dried into the paper. 'There you go,' he said, handing it back.

Cardini took the document. 'I will send you a copy.'

'So, what the hell is that stuff you put on my eye?'

Cardini was smiling. 'Telomere eukaryotic retranscriptase.'

Jim nodded. 'You said that before and I tried looking it up but

I couldn't find anything.'

'You won't find anything. I tend to call it TRT for short.'

'I saw some stuff about telomeres, but it didn't help me understand what made my face heal so quickly.'

'As you may have picked up,' Cardini began, 'telomeres are areas of the chromosome that terminate them. Telomeres are a part of our DNA that protects our genetic fingerprint from corruption.' He nodded, his expression suggesting he was reconsidering the subject and finding it very much to his satisfaction.

'When your DNA replicates it comes unzipped, if you will.' He made a motion with his hand as though something was being torn apart. 'It then re-forms, pulling the other half of the genetic puzzle back together from the surrounding chemicals afloat in the cell. The telomeres enable this zipping and unzipping to take place without destroying the viable DNA at both ends. Without the telomere the DNA division process would cause catastrophic corruption in the chromosome. Without telomeres, as we understand them, the outcome of a cell dividing would be unsustainable.'

Jim was listening intently.

'Without telomeres, cancerous mutations would soon destroy an organism. Your cells simply would not survive the many divisions required for your body to grow and survive. Without telomeres, life would remain primitive. Telomeres are crucial for complex organisms. Sadly, this protecting DNA terminating code wears away with each cycle, shortening with every round of regeneration. The telomeres are an inert buffer, which is eroded by each tick of our genetic clock.' Cardini arched an eyebrow and looked grave.

'This,' he boomed, 'limits the cell to a finite number of divisions before it must die. Once the telomere is consumed … the cell is destroyed. The telomere is like the spring of a watch that is slowly unwound, except there is no key to wind it up again. The untold billions of telomeres in your body are the inbuilt timer of your life. When their cycles have run their course, just like the cell, you come to an inglorious end. As the telomeres shorten, so do we age. Telomeres in aggregate dictate your allotted span. They programme your mortality.' He examined Jim's face, which was mainly blank. 'Do you see?'

'Yes,' said Jim. 'Well, I sort of get your drift.'

'Good,' rumbled Cardini. 'Telomere eukaryotic retranscriptase lengthens telomeres. Retranscript means "to write again". You see? It is an enzyme that extends the telomeres in the chromosomes and in effect makes the cells young again.'

'So how did that make the bruise on my face go so quickly?'

'TRT, as I prefer to call it, creates a chronomatic reaction.'

'And what's that?'

'It speeds up the biological processes in damaged tissues. Healing or growth can take place up to a hundred times faster. You are young and the dose was low so certain effects of TRT will not be so dramatic in your case.'

'It seemed pretty dramatic to me.'

'It is not possible, for example, to take forty years off your cells,' he chuckled, 'but in older people, well, TRT winds back the clock. It temporarily reverses the ageing process by amplifying the organism's natural ability to repair and rejuvenate old cells.'

'This is like a revolutionary medicine, right?' said Jim, now perched on the very edge of his seat.

'Yes.'

'So why isn't it all over the newspapers? Why haven't you got a Nobel Prize? Why isn't the whole world parked outside your door?'

Cardini stiffened. 'Because no one knows about my discoveries.'

'But why not?'

Cardini looked at him so fiercely that he almost shrank back in his seat. 'There are problems.'

'What problems?'

Cardini sighed, a low grumble that resonated in his chest. 'There are seven billion people in this world, Jim, but before the discovery of penicillin there were just two billion. I believe that without that one compound there would still be just two billion people on this planet.' He paused. 'It is said that the average Indian peasant spends a quarter of their income on antibiotics and this expenditure on that medicine is responsible not just for their health but for their and their children's very existence. Yet this miracle compound is terribly underestimated. People imagine that such drugs are simple things, like chocolates, and that, once discovered, they can be produced cheaply at will.'

Cardini stared at Jim, his eyes unblinking. 'But when it was discovered, penicillin, for example, could only be produced in tiny amounts.' He leant forwards. 'The drug's first subject was a policeman dying from a terrible infection behind his eye.' Cardini interlaced his fingers. 'The penicillin had been extracted from mould grown in racks of bedpans and when it was given to the dying man he began to recover. Yet even though the team at Oxford extracted as much as they could, even redistilling it from the patient's own urine to eke it out, they did not have enough to save his life."

Cardini sat back. 'Soon he lapsed once more into a coma and died. It was fourteen years from the discovery of penicillin before there was enough to treat even ten people. It was yet another ten years before use was truly widespread. Even with such miraculous properties it took a generation for the compound to reach mankind en masse.'

'Sorry, Chris, I don't understand the problem.'

'I can only make the tiniest amounts.' He stared at Jim as if it was his fault. 'It must seem perverse, particularly to your generation, but little has changed in chemistry in the last two or three decades. In computing, progress has been exponential, but in chemistry and medicine, it has been linear. A computer chip in the nineteen seventies may have had just a thousand transistors but now it has two billion. Meanwhile chemistry cannot make a molecule of ten thousand atoms, let alone a million.'

Cardini's eyes bulged, apparently with fury.

'When compared to the progress in electronics, chemists are working in the dark ages. We cannot even imagine creating proteins of any real complexity, let alone anything as complex as a simple cell. The best we can do is to modify existing life and have it do the biochemistry for us. The basic chemicals we call drugs are the simplest of compounds, perhaps a dozen or two elements glued together. Anything complex must be extracted from life itself, be it plant or animal. There is no real capacity to make anything but the simplest pharmaceuticals from scratch. We are little better than the primitives that stewed plants and drank the decoction thereof.'

'How do you make it?'

'We take human blood and distil it.'

'How much blood does it take to make the treatment you gave me?'

'About thirty tons.'

'Thirty tons of human blood?' said Jim, nearly falling off the edge of his chair. 'How the hell do you get it all?'

'We take what we can from blood banks across the country as its age passes its mandated storage limit. We have access to about a thousand tons a year. Happily we do the medical profession a service in disposing of it for them but the supply is nowhere near enough for my work. Extraction from human blood is not the answer. To advance we must synthesise the drug, and we have not yet done that. Or, rather, I have not yet implemented it on anything but a minute scale.'

'A thousand tons of human blood,' said Jim. 'How do you process it all? That's twenty tons a week.'

'There is a facility outside the city dedicated to it.'

'Can I see it?'

'Jim,' said Cardini, sternly, 'I must bring you back to my earlier point. We need to synthesise the compound. Extracting it from life is simply not a feasible long-term solution.'

'What about blood from abattoirs? Cows and chickens, that kind of thing.'

'Five million dollars would be the price for such a medicine. Five million for a single dose.'

Jim put a finger to his cheek. 'It cost five million dollars to fix my eye?'

'That was not a full dose,' said Cardini, 'but that is not the point. There is not enough biomass to produce the compound at scale in this manner. It is a drug beyond the reach of all but kings.'

'I shouldn't think kings get many black eyes,' muttered Jim, who was now deep in thought.

'Were you listening, Jim?' said Cardini, somewhat plaintively.

'Yes,' said Jim, eyes glazed. 'You need to find a way to synthesise it.' He shook himself. 'Have I missed something?' He looked into Cardini's face and saw the Wikipedia picture: a dark-haired middle-aged man with scary black eyes. 'You're eighty-one, aren't you?'

'Yes.'

'And you look fiftyish.'

'So I'm told.'

'And that's because you take your drug?'

Cardini lifted his head a little and peered down his nose at Jim. 'Yes.'

'And you're emptying our blood banks to make enough for yourself.'

'In effect,' Cardini held up the finger of his right hand, 'but not quite.'

'Not quite?'

'Jim,' said Cardini, 'the cost of this project is truly great and I have a patron who funds it. I help him in return. I have small amounts of serum surplus to requirements. It accrues, but is scant. I need further funding to take the next step.'

'You could get that anywhere, surely.'

'The world is run by old despots and maniacs. For their lives and the lives of their loved ones they would kill millions without hesitation. If I told the world of my discoveries, labs like mine would appear across the globe and humanity would be fed to them. Humanity would become Ouroboros.' Cardini noted Jim's blank look. 'The snake that consumes its own tail.'

Images of Second World War death camps flashed through Jim's mind. 'You don't believe that, do you?'

'No doubt you read the papers.'

'Yes.'

'You see the monstrosities, the evil, the sickening violence? What is it all for? It is for material gain or glory.' Cardini scowled. 'Imagine the price some would be prepared to exact to be years younger again, to be, well, to be strong. Those people would stop at nothing.' He leant forward on his desk, his hypnotic eyes riveting Jim to the spot. 'I ask you to fund my project because you are young. You do not need the serum to be fit and healthy. You do not need the drug to be young. Not now and not for years.'

'Right,' said Jim. 'I see.'

'Of course I will supply you once there is a purpose, if we have not made the breakthrough needed by then to produce the serum as cheaply as the common aspirin. Twenty-eight is possibly a potential physical peak, but I have thought perhaps the early thirties is another period worth preserving.'

'When I'm twenty-eight you can keep me at that age?'

'The serum will do that.'

'Keep me physically twenty-eight years old, no matter how many years go by?'

'Indeed.'

Jim's eyes bugged out. 'For how long?'

'You can be twenty-eight almost indefinitely.'

'How long is "almost indefinitely"? Ten, twenty, thirty years?'

Cardini didn't reply immediately – he seemed to be checking a mental calculation. 'Three to four hundred years,' he said slowly.

'You're bullshitting me, right?'

'You see, Jim, this is why I keep my secret. The implications of my research are too great at this stage.' He smiled. 'Not a week goes by that an old professorial friend of mine does not die and pass for ever into the void. With their death, a treasury of knowledge is lost for good. It is as if a unique library is burnt alongside the cadaver.

'Each of their threads must be relearnt and picked up by a new mind. Our progress is set back by most of the span of a life with every catastrophic death. Death makes our human progress just a slow crawl forward on hands and knees. I am the first scientist who can pursue his work beyond a few decades. I will continue to discover and build on my discoveries, with the weight and momentum of my knowledge as huge assets magnifying my abilities. With my faculties undiminished and growing, I may serve humanity for many generations more. The possibilities are revolutionary.'

He held out his giant hands as if he was cupping a large invisible ball.

'I have extended a human boundary and I can use it to transcend the cruel evil of mortality. A lifetime of five hundred years is enough to overcome this tragic impediment. Our life span is the same limit that drives greed and war and hunger. With a life of five hundred years, human potential expands beyond imagining. The petty needs of a short life, which drive so much chaos and misery, disappear.'

'It's hard to take in,' said Jim, rubbing the skin around his eye, which yesterday had been swollen and black. He thought of Stafford, his butler, best friend and ally. For a few million he could make the old man young again. He'd write that cheque on the spot. 'What happens when you take the drug?' he said. 'I mean, it's got to have nasty side effects, right?'

'As long as you keep taking it, there are none, but the effects wear off so you have to remain medicated or the process is reversed. As the serum is metabolised, the ageing process begins again and accelerates. A balance needs to be maintained between rejuvenation and degeneracy. Sadly, the later the treatment starts, the less life can be extended. Perhaps I will live two hundred years more, but if you begin treatment at thirty you may live five hundred or perhaps a thousand more years. I hope to be able to widen the use of the technology so that, within fifty years, the serum will be one of a number of treatments. If I can discover these new solutions, I may go on for yet further centuries myself.'

Jim's mind boggled. This was either the biggest lie he'd ever heard or the most amazing truth. Maybe the professor's story was one big pile of bullshit – but he had the evidence of his own eye to prove that it wasn't. And Cardini certainly didn't look his actual age.

Jim jumped to his feet. 'Can you take me to your factory?'

Cardini took a sharp breath. He looked at his watch, then back at Jim. 'Yes, why not?' He stood up, unfurling himself to his great height. 'Then, I hope, you will believe me and become my benefactor.' He looked down at Jim. 'With your help we will be able to find a way of producing this panacea for all. Together we will make history. Together we can save the world.' Cardini smiled, but not in a friendly way. The smile seemed to come from an internal pleasure that was hardly connected with Jim's presence.

He walked up to Jim and patted him on the back. 'Come on, let us go, you and I. Out to where the sky lies etherised as a patient upon a table.'

Jim wondered what he meant.

22

For all its speed and technical wizardry, the Veyron was a small car and the professor was crammed into the passenger seat. He struggled to buckle his seatbelt in the confined space. 'Very good,' he said, as it finally clicked into place.

Jim fired up the engine.

'Turn left at the entrance,' commanded Cardini, 'then right at the main junction. After several miles I will point out the next turn.'

'No problem,' said Jim.

It wasn't an elaborate route, and a little more than ten minutes later Cardini was indicating that Jim should pull into a road that entered some woodland. At a gate among the trees, Jim spoke into an intercom and it opened. Down a private track out of sight of the road lay a modern warehouse-style building, with a small office area embedded in the left side.

'I will ask you to say little to the staff you meet,' said Cardini. 'They are technical employees and not apprised of the compound being extracted. They believe it to be a vital component of a highly poisonous nerve agent. The result of their work is completed by me in my lab so what is made here is an inert waxy fat, which I alone activate into the final compound. I hope you understand the need for total secrecy.'

'OK. I'll try not to put my foot in it.'

Cardini heaved himself out of the car and stretched his long arms upwards. 'That's better,' he said. 'I suspect in a few weeks' time I'll be in need of further treatment. My joints do not feel as young as they did last week. Such is the battle waged. Come,' he said, dropping his arms, 'let me show you.'

A small man in a white coat came out of the office. 'Ah, Professor,' he said, in heavily accented tones. 'Such a nice surprise to see you, we weren't expecting you.'

'Good morning, Dr Ramos. This is an associate come to see our work.'

Ramos shook Jim's hand. 'Very good to meet you, sir,' he said.

Jim wondered where Ramos was from. The Philippines? 'Good to meet you too,' he said.

'Follow me,' said Cardini, striding to the door. 'Time is not my friend today – or, for that matter, on any other day.'

Jim and Dr Ramos marched after Cardini.

The reception desk was empty and looked as if no one ever manned it. Cardini's thumbprint opened the door beyond. They followed him through and he unlocked another door.

Dr Ramos grabbed a white coat off a peg and handed it to Jim. 'Please,' he said. 'It's not necessary but it looks correct.'

Jim put it on. It felt kind of good to be a man in a white coat, like he'd been granted some added level of intelligence.

They went into the lab. Two white-coated people were at a desk, monitoring screens, and through the window in front of him Jim could see huge steel vessels and piping, filling the space beyond. The white coats rose and stood to attention. They looked as if they might be Filipinos, like the doctor. They were smiling deferentially and inclining slightly forwards.

'Very good. Please carry on,' boomed Cardini.

'Thank you, thank you,' they chimed back.

'Let us continue,' said Cardini. The door ahead of them clicked open for him as he applied his thumb.

'This,' said Cardini, impressively, 'is where we process the blood. We smash the cells into tiny fragments in these three large tanks. Smash them chemically. During each stage of the process, the chemical units that make up the feedstock are decomposed into small component pieces.' He seemed invigorated by the idea. 'By molecular standards the chemical pieces are still gigantic, but in comparison to the cells they come from they are tiny. The infinitesimal compounds we seek are among the vast soup of biochemistry, like flecks of gold in a mountain of gravel. Over here, we effectively distil the result,' he waved his hand to suggest the metaphor was not very accurate, 'in the same way that you might separate a fraction of oil in a refinery or a paper mill.'

He looked at Jim as if he had judged him and found him wanting. 'Did you know vanilla is extracted from the paper-making process?'

'No, I didn't.'

'Well, when you distil a tree it breaks down in much the same way as a barrel of oil. One fraction may go to make a newspaper while another will become the flavouring in your coffee. If only the extract we seek was so prevalent.' He fell silent, then took a sharp breath and continued. 'That is the kind of process we are using here to find our extract.' Cardini gestured at a series of pipes. 'The resultant output is separated into three distillation fractions plus an output of waste. The waste we dry by reverse osmosis and the solids are then burnt or donated for research to others. The remaining pure water is ejected as effluent. The three fractions are then reacted together. The output of this is a complex soup of molecules, none of which we can hope to construct by themselves, mixed together to create a complex of compounds. Come.' He opened another door.

Jim smelt pears as he went into the room, which contained a large machine, rather like a giant printer.

'Here,' said Cardini, 'the resultant combinations of molecules are laid down on absorbent paper and as it dries the different molecules spread out.' There was a buzzing from the machine and something inside the huge contraption moved its length, buzzing and grinding along a hidden assembly. A brief silence followed. Then he went on, 'This is a unique machine built for our project. I admit to being particularly proud of it.'

Jim recognised a kind of giant paper feed coming from a large cylinder above the rear of the machine. It resembled a twenty-foot-wide toilet roll. There was another grinding, buzzing noise as more paper went in.

'As the molecular printout dries, the machine feeds the result along this bed and downstairs, where the paper is cut to separate the vital fraction. This fraction is removed from the paper and through here the molecule is separated by machine. Follow me.'

'Atomic force microscopes,' said Dr Ramos.

'Microscopes?' said Jim.

'Come, come,' said Cardini. They followed him into a dimly lit room filled with silent white-enamelled machines. Only the breath of air-conditioning gave any indication of activity.

Jim scanned his surroundings. Twenty-five machines were laid on the floor, cables and fine piping snaking away from them. Faint light glowed from their controls.

Cardini waited for Jim to turn to him. 'There are three floors like this,' he said proudly. 'The resultant mix of compounds that comes from the initial distillation process contains a very little of the molecule we require and we have no chemical way of extracting it. What is worse, it has an isomer, that is to say a photographic twin, which is a mirror image of the molecule we want but has no efficacy. The only way to extract our target is by microscopy. A computer-imaging system coupled with these microscopes identifies the compound and the system extracts it with the same tiny element used to see it. The chemical is picked out of the fraction, one molecule at a time. Fortunately, as the size and distances involved are so small, the system itself can work very fast.'

'Millions of operations an hour,' said Ramos.

'Quite so, quite so,' agreed Cardini. 'So, with our array, we can make a milligram or two a day.'

'How much does one of these microscopes cost?' asked Jim.

'Many millions,' said Cardini. 'Well, they were many millions when we started, now they are a million or two. I'm not sure whether that's because we have bought so many or simply the march of technology, but they have become cheaper. In any event they are still a very expensive component of the process. They are also somewhat fiddly.' He threw a look at Ramos. 'But the doctor here keeps the machines at work as much as is possible. Our efficiency is a remarkable achievement.'

'It's nothing,' said the doctor. 'A machine is a machine. It does all it can within its man-given parameters.'

'So there you have it,' said Cardini. 'Our little refinery in all its finery.' He smiled, but not at Jim.

Jim looked at the doctor and then at Cardini. He was bubbling over with questions but knew he couldn't ask any of them until he had Cardini alone. 'Amazing,' he said finally. 'Let's get going.'

23

As Jim swung the car round, the tyres squealed and spun a little. He took his foot off the accelerator. 'Well,' he said, as he drove gingerly down the long, thin lane, 'I'm gobsmacked.'

'And?' asked Cardini.

'Remind me why you need me.'

'Because, Jim, I need to invest a great deal to make this process commercially viable – or, rather, viable for the masses. I cannot open a Pandora's box by going public. I am caught in a trap. I need a huge investment to make the necessary breakthroughs and the time to do it without setting off a chain reaction of disaster.' Cardini shifted uncomfortably in his cramped seat. 'I cannot simply make more serum in the way I am making it now. I must find a donor young enough to give me the ten years I need to discover the answers required. To bring the compound to mass production, I require more resources. I can spend your donations on research rather than production. If you can fund me I have solved my final challenge.'

'How much do you need?'

'One hundred million a year?'

'Ouch,' said Jim. 'A hundred million pounds a year?'

'Dollars, Jim, happily not pounds.'

'A billion dollars over ten years?'

'Yes, until the process is perfected. Then the market will fund all that is needed and more, of course. Can you afford that, Jim?'

As he pulled out on to the public road, Jim threw Cardini a glance. 'I can afford about a century's worth at that rate.'

'That's impressive,' said Cardini. 'Almost as impressive as my compound.'

'No,' said Jim. 'My money is not impressive. It's just bits of paper with ink on them. What you're doing is so big I can't get my head around it. My mind's boggled.'

'I'm going to see my patron this afternoon to treat him,' said Cardini. 'If you come with me, you will see him, the treatment process and the transformation. Then you will understand. Will you accompany me?'

'Yeah.'

'I am flying from Cambridge airport to the east coast of America by private jet,' said Cardini. 'Can you be ready for around three?'

'Hold on,' said Jim. He pressed a button on the dash. 'Stafford,' he said.

'Good day, sir,' came Stafford's voice over the speaker.

'Stafford, can you run my passport up to Cambridge airport? I've got to go Stateside for a couple of days. Need it by three.'

'Certainly, sir. Is everything in order?'

That was Stafford's way of asking if he was in trouble. 'Peachy.'

'Very good, sir. Please call nearer the time and I shall meet you.'

'I'll be at the private jet terminal, I guess,' said Jim.

Cardini nodded.

'I'll call when I'm ten minutes out.'

24

Jim parked under the shade of a tree outside Cardini's lab. In the direct summer sun, the blue Veyron would heat up like a greenhouse. He got out and scrabbled for his phone. He'd better tell Kate that lunch was off.

Kate's phone bleeped. She glanced away from her screen to it. In a little speech bubble it said 'Jim: Cant.' Her heart sank. She opened the message. 'Cant make it today, got to dash to the states. Lets do pizza when I get back.'

Where's the sorry? she thought. 'Sorry, Kate,' she muttered, 'got to go and see one of my millions of gold-digging girlfriends.'

She wasn't going to reply, she decided. Then she typed, 'OK,' and sent it to Jim.

As they entered the building the phone vibrated in Jim's pocket. He glanced at the reply. 'I've got to do some social re-engineering,' he said. 'This trip means I've got some grovelling to do.'

'By all means go ahead.'

'Sorry,' Jim typed awkwardly, as he walked after Cardini, 'I'll make it up to you. How about extra toppings on that pizza?'

Kate looked at the message. Why didn't he just call? It was obvious: SMS meant he wasn't serious. A call would suggest there was a chance he wasn't messing her around and they might actually meet again.

'Extra toppings it is,' she replied. She was deflated. For a few short hours, she'd felt she'd met someone special and that something special might come of it. In fact, she knew she'd met someone special: he had a funny look in his eye that made her want to sneeze – always an early warning that a boy was about to get under her skin, then break her heart.

She sighed. He wouldn't get worked up about her, a simple student. She was no glamour-puss stalking the beaches of Monaco or wherever guys like him hung out. Why would anyone fall for her, let alone a mega-successful guy with the world at his feet? She had been doomed from the get-go, she told herself. And it was probably a lucky escape, she thought, paging back through the messages. At best he'd toy with her.

Jim looked up from Kate's message. He'd blown it. 'I'm in trouble,' he said to Cardini.

'Nothing serious, I hope.'

'A girl.'

'Never mind,' said Cardini. 'Can't be helped.'

Jim heard dismissive contempt in Cardini's voice, which rankled. It can be, he thought, looking at his mobile's screen. 'Got to make a call,' he said, hanging back as Cardini went into his office. He dialled.

'Hey,' he said, as she answered. 'How are you?'

'Fine.'

'Sorry about blowing our lunch out, but something's come up and I've got to fly out at three.'

'That's OK,' she said. 'Sounds exciting.'

'Yes,' he said, 'very. I've also got to get some work done before I go, so that's put a spanner in the works too.'

'When do you get back?'

'Don't know,' he said. 'Thursday or Friday, I should think. I'll keep you posted.' He hesitated. 'Fancy doing something this weekend?'

Clearly she hadn't expected that. 'Yes,' she said, after a short silence. 'What?'

'Don't know,' he said. 'Whatever you like. How about a day out in London?'

'That sounds nice.'

'I'll come and pick you up.'

'I can get a coach.'

'Coach?'

'The bus station is practically by my front door.'

'I'll come and get you.'

'No, really, it's very easy for me to get the coach. Think of the time and carbon dioxide saved.'

He wanted to protest but didn't. 'OK, then,' he said. 'Look, I've got to rush, got to get back into my meeting. I'll inbox you. Sorry again about lunch.'

'Don't worry.'

''Bye,' he said.

''Bye,' she said.

''Bye,' he said again.

''Bye,' she repeated.

Jim wanted to get the last goodbye in but stopped himself. That was odd, he thought. He normally hung up on people abruptly, a bad habit picked up on the trading floor that he was trying to break. What had all those 'byes been about?

Kate felt as if something was fizzing up inside her. She could see his face in her mind's eye as she sat grinning. She looked out of the window: it was a beautiful day. She got up and made for the kitchen. It was time for a lunchtime soup.

Jim walked into Cardini's office.

'I want to show you something,' said the professor.

Jim snapped away from Kate to the present. 'What have you got?'

'See this?' said Cardini.

Jim went behind his desk and looked at the computer monitor. There was a picture of a jellyfish on the screen.

'This is *Turritopsis nutricula*,' said Cardini, 'the best example of an immortal creature we know. This animal has an infinite ability to repair itself, to such an extent that it can start again as a polyp.'

Jim automatically pulled a face as if 'polyp' didn't mean anything to him.

'It can return to being a baby jellyfish, if circumstances require it to,' Cardini explained, perhaps a touch impatiently. 'My compound is a key part of this process, an ability to refresh the cells during these processes. Yet with further understanding I will be able to begin to turn back the overall biological clock of an organism to set its age at whatever point is required. Now I can merely regenerate the cell and refresh it. If I can learn the next secret of this creature I will be able to reset the very clock of life.'

'You mean you'll be able to tell your body to be twenty-five again?'

'That is the ultimate goal and I am close to it, very close indeed.' He pulled up a plan on his screen. 'I will build a new lab and in it I will build a plant to synthesise TRT, step by step, molecule by molecule, like a child builds a castle with toy bricks. Never has such a complex compound been made from base chemistry. It will be a giant step forward in technology. It will be for medicine as the technology behind the silicon chip was for electronics. It will be the beginning of a whole new paradigm.' He flipped through blueprints, as if Jim was meant to understand them.

'How many people will you be able to treat with the output of this plant?'

'Tens of thousands,' said Cardini. 'Perhaps hundreds of thousands.' He brought up a picture of what looked like a large dusty root. 'Once upon a time progesterone was the most valuable medicine known to man. It is the hormone vital to female reproduction. It was the only infertility treatment available in the mid-years of the last century and had to be extracted from the ovaries of pigs.' He looked at Jim. 'You can appreciate the analogue with our vastly more complex problem. In any event, enterprising scientists discovered it could be extracted from wild yams and set off to South America to bring one back. They extracted from one single tuber enough hormone to sell for three million dollars. They then considered that the hormone might be more effective with a little amendment and found a compound a thousand times more powerful, so powerful, in fact, that the drug made a woman's body believe it was pregnant. Thus the world was changed by a chemist and a potato.'

He sighed. 'If only our situation was as simple, yet breakthroughs at the molecular level can be as spectacular for medicine as they are for computing. Outcomes, as with the human population, can multiply exponentially.'

25

With a smile, Kate texted Jim, 'Safe trip.'

There was a buzz at her door, which made her start. Nobody ever came to call. Someone must have pressed the button by accident. It was probably a leaflet delivery person, trying to get in to push junk into everyone's mailboxes. She hoped no one would open the front door. The world didn't need more landfill leaflets.

The buzzer sounded again. She leaned forwards and peered out of the side of her bay window. Through the net curtains she could see Bob Renton. 'Hello,' she said, into the intercom.

'It's Bob.'

'Hold on a minute.'

The front door clunked and he pushed it open. She stood up and went to her door, which she opened. Renton smiled at her as he stepped into the hallway. 'I was just passing,' he said. 'The professor was wondering if you could drop in tomorrow. He wants me to complete a formality or two.'

'Formality?' she wondered.

'Exit paperwork – they like me to get it in person to make sure there aren't any loose ends. It's funding stuff, stupid bureaucracy, but we get into trouble if we don't get it done. I can also work on a letter of reference with you, so it can be just as you want it. It's so much easier to do that kind of thing in person than via email.'

She hadn't thought about getting a reference from the professor. What would he say? 'Silly woman left the course almost immediately, but otherwise a sound person'? 'OK,' she said. 'What time?'

'Would around five be all right? That's a quiet time for me. It shouldn't take long.'

'Five is fine,' she said.

'Great,' he said, hopping onto the balls of his feet. 'I'll be on my way, then.' He nodded. 'See you tomorrow,' he said, his eyes widening in what looked like keen anticipation.

Kate blinked. 'See you.' She stepped back and closed the door. She felt she had been a bit short with him. She wandered over to her couch and looked at the TV she never watched. She felt like switching it on to distract her from the strange impression Renton's wide-eyed grimace had left.

Had she heard the main door close? She got up and looked out of the window. There was no sign of Renton walking off. He couldn't still be standing in the hallway, could he? She went to the door and listened. She couldn't hear a thing. But how could she? The door was a solid piece of wood.

She definitely hadn't heard the front door clank shut, as she always did when one of the other students went out and let it slam behind them. She peered into the peep-hole but, as usual, couldn't make out anything on the other side. What would Renton be doing standing outside her door anyway? Waiting for her to say goodbye properly? That would be ridiculous, but even so she couldn't just sit there and imagine him not gone. Yet if he hadn't gone, she certainly didn't want to open the door to find him standing there.

She was being silly and mad and compulsive – but she needed to know and know for sure. Sometimes the problem was, had she closed the door? Turned off the iron? If she'd left it on, would the ironing board catch fire? She had to make sure it was turned off. Et cetera. Once the nagging question had lodged in her head, she had to go back and check whatever it was, and then, as she walked away, go back and check it again. When that kind of doubt entered her head, she was filled with a crippling uncertainty that undermined her whole world.

Renton was surely not in the hall, but was the door open for just anyone to come in? That was all she wanted to know: it wasn't about Renton waiting there, it was about the door not being closed.

She had to look.

She opened her door a little way. There was a flash of movement, the blur of a figure passing with a clump and a bang. She squealed in shock and slammed the door. As it closed, she realised it was the guy from the floor above, bounding towards the exit in his normal galumphing manner. She snatched the door open again and peered out. He was standing by the front door, looking back. 'You all right, girl?' he said, almost laughing.

'Yes,' she said. 'You startled me.'

'Sorry,' he said sheepishly. 'Happens all the time.' He left the building, the door banging loudly behind him.

How embarrassing, she thought. She checked the hallway again and tried to force into her memory a mental note that the front door was shut and the hallway was empty. In the circumstances it wouldn't be difficult.

26

Stafford was standing in the small departures area of Cambridge airport. Unlike Heathrow, or any other major airport, Cambridge was little more than a collection of large sheds set to one side of a giant field with a strip of tarmac running down the middle. There was a Citation X outside, which Jim guessed was to take them Stateside. It needed a pretty big private jet to make the Atlantic jump and the Citation had the range. It was junior to his Gulfstream by a long way but the fight for luxury air supremacy was not of much interest to him.

Davas, his mentor, had his own Airbus, with concert hall, garage and 3D cinema, but that seemed silly to Jim. He didn't want a flying palace, just the right recipient for his philanthropy, so that giving such a lot of money away wouldn't cause chaos for all concerned.

Davas had laughed at him. 'Spend it,' he said. 'Let the market distribute it. The market is fighting twenty-four seven, three sixty-five, to allocate resources in the most efficient way possible. Don't worry about saving people. They'll save themselves.'

Yet Jim had seen so many people unable to save themselves, and he had seen bad people do bad things and flourish. In the end they'd got their just desserts, but the process seemed to take far too long. Money was raw energy and it could speed a bullet as cheaply as it could save a child from death by dehydration. Davas was right: the market worked 24/7 and 365, but there were good people and bad, and they all fought for and struggled to keep the resources that money encapsulated. The market might be nearly perfectly efficient but it was most certainly not nearly perfectly benign.

He glanced at the plane. He would happily have swapped the luxurious flight for a long chat with a pretty backpacker in a cramped seat at the rear of an old jumbo.

Stafford had brought a Louis Vuitton holdall with him. 'Here are enough essentials for three days,' he said, handing it to Jim.

It was heavy. 'What's in here?' said Jim.

'A notebook, of course, and some incidentals,' said Stafford.

'Thanks,' said Jim. 'Brilliant.'

Cardini was standing back from them, apparently lost in thought, a member of the small cabin crew carrying his bag away to clear it through security for him.

'See you in a day or two,' said Jim, taking his passport from Stafford's outstretched hand.

'Have a safe journey,' said Stafford.

Jim imagined his butler at thirty-five. He'd probably been quite a good-looking guy then, rather than the heavy, owlish old bloke who peered at him now from beneath bushy eyebrows. 'Take care,' he said, turning away. 'OK, Professor, I'm all sorted.'

A pretty stewardess in uniform asked him for his passport and they walked towards the door as she checked the paperwork on her clipboard. 'Thank you,' she said, as they stepped outside.

Jim looked back through the glass of the door. Stafford was watching them go, a blurred oval of black and grey.

He turned and followed Cardini over the concrete apron and up the steps. Cardini ducked his head as he entered and the plane seemed a little too small for his great frame.

Jim thought his Gulfstream would have been more comfortable. Yet it was nice that he didn't have to spend the fifty thousand pounds the flight would have cost, even though that was small change to him, these days. He sat down across a table from Cardini and automatically buckled himself in.

'So, Jim,' said Cardini, 'I've been meaning to ask but I've

hesitated.' He leant forwards interlacing his fingers, which seemed to Jim unnaturally long. 'I hope you don't mind me asking you a personal question.'

'Sure.'

'What is the source of your immense wealth?'

'Drugs and guns,' said Jim. Cardini didn't flinch. Jim laughed nervously. 'That's my favourite joke,' he said apologetically.

'One never knows about these things.' Cardini shrugged.

'I made my money in the markets,' said Jim.

'Made? Have you stopped?'

'Yes,' said Jim, 'mostly. How much can a bloke want?'

'More, is normally the answer to that question,' said Cardini.

The stewardess was coming towards them. 'What can I get you, gentlemen?'

Jim noted the door was already closed. 'I'll have a beer,' he said.

'Virgin Mary,' said Cardini.

The plane was moving.

'I'll bring them to you, gentlemen, as soon as we get up to altitude.'

'No vodka in your drink,' Jim commented. 'Is alcohol a no-no with TRT?'

'Indeed not,' said Cardini. 'I just resist the temptation to put toxins into my system.'

'So, no booze?'

'None,' said Cardini, in a haughty tone.

'Well,' said Jim, 'not only will you live for ever, it'll feel like eternity too.' He tried to detect a hint of amusement in Cardini's raised eyebrows but failed.

As the jet headed for the main runway, it suddenly occurred to Jim that it was going to be a long, boring trip. He got out his phone and texted Kate. 'Taking off.'

27

Kate looked away from the picture on the wall. She had forgotten to set her alarm and she needed it to remind her of her appointment with Bob Renton. She didn't want to upset anyone enjoying the calm of the lovely Fitzwilliam Museum but … Fitz meant 'bastard', she mused, as she switched on the ringer. Fitzwilliam meant 'bastard of William'. She wondered whether the William was one of the old kings and, if so, which of the four. William II had been gay, she seemed to recall, which would seem to disqualify him.

So 1700 minus thirty minutes would give her half an hour to get there on time. She tapped back thirty minutes as she looked at the painting. So, the man who had founded the museum had been the illegitimate son or grandson of a king or a duke. The guy behind this amazing place would have been an outcast if his father, or grandfather, whoever, hadn't been royalty. Instead of being a pariah he'd got to be a big cheese. What hypocrisy, she thought.

She set the alarm with a jab of her thumb and put her phone back into her handbag. She felt uncomfortable but didn't know why. It was probably that the Victorians, the biggest humbugs of them all, would probably have refused even to acknowledge that there was one morality for the rich and another, meaner one, for the poor.

She sighed. She should let the pictures chill her out. Yet the woman on the ship heading across the sea, red scarf flying in the wind, didn't fill Kate with calm: it filled her with dread, as if there was a storm ahead. She thought about studying some Turners, or maybe Constable, and headed off to find just the right picture to contemplate.

She wondered where Jim was and what he was doing. She wanted to tug at a strand of hair but stopped herself. The temptation would pass.

28

Cardini looked as if he was falling asleep, which was more than a little annoying to Jim, who was waiting for him to make his next move in their game of chess. It didn't seem right to give him a shake but after several games, in which Jim had been crushed like a bug, he at last felt he was about to deliver Cardini a nasty surprise. A draw by default seemed a frustrating result. You couldn't say you'd beaten someone at chess because they'd passed out.

Cardini's eyes batted open and he grunted. 'Ah, yes,' he said, moving his black knight back and across.

Jim studied the move. He was in trouble again: what he had thought was a strong position had been split deftly in two. 'Bugger,' he said.

'No,' said Cardini. 'Buggered, I believe, would be more accurate.' He took a little bottle from his inside pocket, unscrewed the cap and had a sip. He watched Jim watching him take his medicine. 'This will be a trying few days,' he said, 'cause for a little support, I fear.' He held out the bottle to Jim. 'Would you like to sample the effect?'

Jim looked at the little vial. 'Of course,' he said, 'but you know how it is. Just say, "No" – right?'

'It's a mild tincture,' said Cardini. 'No more than a tonic, really, in comparison to a treatment. I would recommend it.' Cardini's hand was most of the way across the table, holding the vial out to him.

Jim looked at the little bottle. It held a watery, slightly opaque liquid. His nose caught the perfume of pears. Appetising. He took the bottle.

'Only a drop on the tip of the tongue,' said Cardini.

Jim poured a little into his mouth. It tasted like pear-flavoured olive oil.

Cardini took the vial from him and replaced the cap, watching Jim's expression.

A wave of heat rolled down Jim's throat and the flavour, in a sudden rush, seemed to shoot along hidden nerve pathways to his brain. He closed his eyes tightly: he had never tasted anything inside his brain before, only on his tongue. If was as if his mind had suddenly become part of his mouth. 'This is crazy,' he gasped. 'It's like someone's baking a cake in my head.'

'That will soon pass,' said Cardini.

'Pity.' He opened his eyes as the delicious fumes started to die away. He looked down at the board. 'Ha.' He laughed. Cardini was screwed. He moved a pawn forward. 'I think that's serious "ownage" on your king's side,' he said.

Cardini grinned. 'Yes, of course,' he said. 'Now I have clarity I can see how that has been a risk for some time.' He laid his king down in defeat.

'Wait,' said Jim. 'What are you doing?'

'Checkmate in eight moves,' said Cardini.

Jim sat up straight. 'Really?'

'I'm afraid I've been too generous. Mental acceleration is a side effect of the tincture.' He handed the vial to Jim. 'You may keep this,' he said.

'Thanks.'

'I will, of course, invoice you for ten million.'

'Dollars?' asked Jim, looking at the tiny bottle.

'Pounds. You are British, are you not?' Cardini burst into thunderous laughter.

'OK,' said Jim, 'fair play.' His whole body seemed to be warmed from within, as if an internal oven was heating him to the perfect temperature.

'So, Jim,' said Cardini, 'tell me how you came by the rather charismatic scar across the crown of your head.'

Jim put his hand to it. 'This?' he said.

Cardini nodded.

'North Korean ninjas attacked me.'

'Really?' said Cardini, jovially. 'And where was that?'

'On the Strand,' said Jim, grinning widely. He laughed a little.

'The Strand in London?'

'Yes.'

'And what were they doing there?' asked Cardini, beaming.

'Trying to steal the Japanese Crown Jewels.'

'Really?' said Cardini, like an indulgent grandfather to a little kid. 'And what had you to do with the Japanese Crown Jewels?'

'I'd bought them by accident,' said Jim, chuckling. He was finding his own story quite funny.

Cardini sat back. He'd never experienced hallucinations or delusions when taking the serum, and neither had McCloud. The effect on Evans was intriguing. Perhaps it was his age; perhaps it was a normal reaction that the few subjects of the treatment hadn't experienced.

Jim held his right side. There was an intense heat there. 'This is getting into all the right places,' he said.

'You have an injury there?' enquired Cardini.

'Just a few,' said Jim. 'Fragmentation grenade. I nearly died. Got a pretty nasty hospital infection too, but that cleared up in the jungle in Congo. Now there's just a stupid metal box holding my ribs together.' He was nursing his side and rocking back and forth. 'I'm pretty much fucked up, really,' he said, his head dropping, a broad gormless smile on his face as he luxuriated in the fingers of heat that seemed to be massaging him. 'But, hey,' he said, 'you can't expect to save the world and get out in one piece.'

Cardini let the heavenly heat of the serum take over his own thoughts. Once the effect had run its half-hour he would consider Evans's reaction, but until then he would let the sensation of healing take him on a wonderful ride.

Jim put the bottle into his pocket. He picked up his glass of beer and drank the last few drops. It was the most amazing beer he had ever tasted. He looked at Cardini. He could see the professor's face in exquisite detail. Every pore and line was delineated in crisp form and colour. It was how he had seen things when he was little. He had forgotten how everything had been so vivid and startling; now he was remembering. It was as if the TRT had peeled a thick layer of invisible padding from his senses. He remembered looking up with awe at the big blue sky capping the grey tower blocks of east London, the wonder of pulling at tufts of vibrant green grass pushing up by the fences of an empty building site. It was an intense world and it was now back in his mind.

'This is scary stuff,' he said, lying back in his seat.

'There is nothing to be afraid of,' said Cardini. 'The initial effects are not long-lasting. However, any ailments you had before your dose will be addressed, not that I imagine you had many. I'm hoping to see signs of optimisation.'

'Optimisation?' said Jim, sitting up a little.

'Don't worry,' said Cardini, his deep voice rumbling. 'It's just a hypothesis of mine.'

Suddenly Jim felt sleepy, as if someone was putting a warm woollen blanket over him. 'I think I'm going to ...'

Cardini regarded the young man, as his own body healed at an accelerated rate. He recalled how it had felt the first time. That had been a momentous day.

His own minor dose would rob him of a few minutes of his total life expectancy, but he needed to be at his best for McCloud. As Cardini's patron inexorably approached the point at which he might die before a new treatment could be administered, he was becoming less and less predictable. While he might avoid the final plunge into death for perhaps thirty years, his transit around the tipping point became longer and more unpleasant.

The old man had come late to the fountain and stared death

in the face for weeks at a time only to be yanked a few yards from the edge for a month or two by the serum. The stress of his closeness to death seemed to be warping his mind. For McCloud, Cardini's miracle was no longer enough: as his health became more and more precarious, he demanded more serum, a longer, deeper return to youth. It was a demand that Cardini could not satisfy – yet.

Yet Cardini was sure he would find the answer. The secret lay in the humble jellyfish and he would unravel it, if not in time to save McCloud. He would resolve the mystery of how a humble jellyfish could throw off its old tissue and grow again anew.

Yet that was not the answer. Return to the infantile state would reset the minds of his subjects, blanking all they had learnt. Cardini had to find a physical reset that did not clear the mind of its memories and learning. The goal was an old head on a young body. If he could not achieve this, he would look to transplanting the head. That might take a century of research but it would be a solution and there was time enough for him to find it.

29

Kate's alarm was buzzing. She came out of her reverie, shoved her hand into her bag and switched it off. She was a little confused: the time had shot by. She must have been asleep in front of the painting. Thank heavens for her alarm. She might have daydreamed for hours in front of the golden hazy Turner, its dirty white and faded blue sky drawing her into its misty world. She would have been soaring in that featureless sky for ever if electronic reality hadn't dragged her back to the bench she'd been travelling on. Now she'd better hurry to her meeting with Renton.

She couldn't abide the thought of being late. Being late told the world you either didn't give a damn or that you were not in control of yourself, perhaps both. Being on time was a kind of personal hygiene, an action that showed respect to others and likewise yourself.

She walked out into the street. It was a lovely afternoon and she had plenty of time. She looked at a bench as she passed it. If she sat down for ten minutes she would still get to Renton on time, but she walked on. She heard a siren behind her and looked around. A police car was heading up the road, blue lights flashing, then another, and another. A whole load of coppers were going somewhere in a hurry.

A guy dodged out of her path as she nearly walked into him. He pulled a face at her and she pulled an apologetic one back.

She reached her car, with the customary relief that she had found it where she'd left it. It started too, as it always did, but she thanked it each time, as if one day it might get into a huff and refuse to oblige.

She glanced occasionally at the minute hand of the clock on the dash as she trundled down the final stretch to the lab. She was going to be rather early.

The police had been going somewhere in a hurry, and the consequences of the incident stretched back to where she was now. Whatever the blockage, though, it seemed to be clearing quickly. She could see the entrance to the car park only a few metres ahead. There was bound to be no space. She turned in and there was plenty.

She trotted into the building and took out her phone. It was exactly four forty.

30

A little alarm popped up on Renton's screen: four forty. Time to finish his preparations. He minimized the window and went back to looking at the image of the woman run over by a bus. The entrails spread over the road were fascinating. He had seen the guts of thousands of animals but there was something especially riveting about a human evisceration. He wondered about adding it to the collection. No, he decided finally. It was too humdrum, just a giant version of a rabbit roadkill. For a start there was no look of horror or agony on the dead woman's face. It was all a little too normal.

He closed the picture and went to log off, but decided against it. No one ever came down to his office in the basement and he would be back in a few moments with the sample. He hated password codes, having to type them in just to get on with what you had to do. So irritating.

That was why he was going to wedge the door open. All the keypads on all the doors were an illusion of security. Anyone who wanted to get in could do so with little more than a balaclava and a short crowbar.

He opened his office door, jammed it open, and bounced off down the corridor.

31

Kate found the stairs to the basement unsettling. The environmentally correct illumination didn't seem to throw enough light to make them feel wholesome. It was gloomy and kind of crypt-like. The basement itself was just as eerie, and each time she had been down there in her short stay on the course it had given her the shivers.

I'm going to see creepy Renton down the creepy stairs in the creepy basement, she thought. She heard distant footsteps, which made her heart race a little, but they faded and were soon gone. She stepped into the main corridor, dimly lit and empty. I'd swap a bit of global warming for a little more light, she thought, looking along the shadowy alley to Renton's office door. There was something empty about the place, as if there was no living soul on any of the floors.

The office door was held open with a grey rubber wedge that was old and sorely distorted from jamming doors for untold years. She knocked lightly and went in. Renton's computer was on, and his worn corduroy jacket hung over the chair. A door at the far end of the long, thin office stood open and the light inside showed through.

'Bob,' she called, heading for the inner door.

She thought she caught the flicker of a shadow beyond.

She opened the door. 'Bob?' She went in. She gasped at the sight of a simple chair and table. She closed her eyes. What was she seeing? What was she thinking? What was she doing?

She opened her eyes. There was a chair, a long examination table and a square metal trolley.

The stainless-steel trolley had things on it: scalpels, silver duct tape, plastic zip-ties. She stepped forward. Was that a bag or a hood? She looked at the plain chair. She looked back at the examination table. She was standing in what looked like some kind of bodged-together operating theatre. The white enamel dish had a pack of what looked like sealed syringes in it. There were surgical instruments in a shiny silver pile. There were bandages, cotton wool and plasters.

What was going on? What kind of surgery could possibly be performed in a cellar? It reminded her of a set from some cheap horror movie. She recoiled. Had she stumbled into some kind of SM dungeon? Was it the scene of real torture? Could it be anything else? Her abdomen pulsed and her stomach churned.

The door slammed behind her. She jolted and swung around, trying to suppress a shriek.

No one was there. Thank God. But was she locked in now? She sprang to the door, turned the handle and pushed. It was locked. She pushed it hard and shook the door.

She stopped, stepped back and took two deep breaths. She grasped the handle again, turned and pulled. The door opened. She let out a groan of relief. She closed it again and went back to the table. Was this meant for her? Her legs turned to jelly and started to shake. It was meant for someone, so why not her?

No one would be around at five p.m., just herself and Renton. She pulled her phone out. Four forty-seven. If she hadn't been early, she would have been dragged into this room by Renton, a knife to her throat. I must be mad, she thought. That can't be right. Then she caught sight of a large wheeled canvas holdall in a corner of the room. She could imagine herself inside it, dismembered like a broken doll.

She had to get out of there right away. There was no time to look or think. She just had to run.

There was a clunk. The outer door had closed. She could hear movement. She lunged for the trolley and picked up the scalpel. Her mind was racing. What was the best thing to do? Sit tight and hope that, after she didn't arrive as expected at five, Renton would give up and go home?

If that happened she could let herself out. The room was bare. She looked back at the bag in the corner. She couldn't hide in or under it. She should just open the door and walk out, she thought. That would give her the element of surprise and she could escape. If necessary, she could back it up with the scalpel.

That was what she had to do. She had to be the aggressor, not the victim. She looked down at the door handle. She had to turn it and walk out into the next room. She had to go for it.

She tried to summon up the strength.

Call the police, she thought. Just call the police. She pulled her phone out again. One signal bar. She dialled 999, but as she did so the signal bar disappeared. She could have cried.

She looked at the door again. She had to go through it.

Renton looked up from his screen. Funny, he thought. I left the door open. He got up and went to it. He clasped the handle and turned it slowly, listening.

Kate stood by the wall where the door would swing open, covering her. It moved slowly. Whoever was on the other side, undoubtedly Renton, was opening it carefully because they expected someone to be there. She clasped the scalpel behind her back and pressed herself against the wall, trembling, her hands clammy with sweat.

A head appeared. Renton's.

If she had been in any doubt as to the purpose of that room, her glimpse of Renton's face and the wild excitement in his eye dispelled it.

The door slammed.

If only she had opened it herself and run past him, she would have had a chance.

Kate heard the key rattle in the lock. She was trapped.

Renton ran back to his desk. Well, well, he thought. The bird had flown straight into his trap. No need to hold the chloroform to her face and drag her into the room. She was waiting for him. He pulled a doctor's bag out from under his desk and took out the cloth and bottle. Chloroform was such a wonderful weapon: it allowed for a struggle but not enough of one to cause much trouble. People always underestimated his strength, one of his many little secrets.

He soaked the cloth with chloroform. In a few minutes she would be his, and his alone, for ever.

She stood in the middle of the room dialling 999.

No signal. No signal.

She heard the key in the lock. She dropped her handbag to the floor and stuffed her phone into it. She held the scalpel behind her back. This is your last chance to be strong, she thought, your very last chance. This is it. This is the only moment that counts. This is the one time in your life where you need to be big and bad and tough and nasty, like all those horrible people who get whatever they want by being vile and wicked. She was hopping from one foot to the other. You have to win. You can't let him get you. The door was opening.

Renton flung it wide. 'You're early,' he said, 'but that's OK.' He stepped in.

She saw the folded cloth in his hand and caught a whiff of something chemical, like ether.

Renton really was there to do something terrible to her. He was going to do what she had been scared even to imagine.

'Don't worry,' he said. 'I'm not going to hurt you.' He closed the door behind him. 'Don't be frightened, take my hand.' He extended it as if to shake hers.

Why should I? So you can pull me towards you and cover my face with that cloth? Do you think I'm stupid?

'Come on, let me lead you out of here.'

You're left-handed, she thought, just like me.

He looked so very friendly now, almost kindly. He inched his right hand forward. 'Don't be afraid. I know you know that you aren't meant to be in here. Let's go outside.'

A shadow flickered over his face as he moved, his friendly face suddenly demonic. His eyes flashed.

She stood a little taller and turned a little from the door. He mirrored her.

'Come on now. Take my hand and let's get going.' He threw a glance at her hidden left hand.

She saw him cast his eye to the table, but she blocked his view. 'OK,' she said hesitantly, holding out her right hand.

He grabbed it – and she lunged at him, the scalpel disappearing into his belly. He cried out and let go of her hand. His knees buckled and he fell.

She bent down, grabbed her bag and leapt for the door. She swung it open and slammed it behind her. Then she whirled around: there was a key in the door. She turned it in the lock and took it out of the key hole as Renton groaned. There was blood on her left hand. She let out a little cry.

'You're in trouble now,' she heard Renton roar. 'Better come back in and finish me off because I'm going straight to the police. You're an animal-rights terrorist, and you've tried to kill a simple researcher for your twisted politics.' He gave a crazy giggle.

Then she heard him pick himself up and walk heavily to the table. 'Amazing what a one-inch blade can't do. There's not even much blood.' Something fell to the floor with a clatter. She started. It had sounded like a bundle of keys. He might have a key to the door. She turned and ran.

Renton peeled off his lab coat, opened his shirt and stuck a plaster on the cut. Then he took the keys from his lab coat and went to the door, unlocked it and walked out stiffly. He sat down carefully on his chair and opened his screens. There she was, running up the stairs and out of the building. She was heading to the car park. He got up and threw on his jacket.

He took out his phone and called her, watching her running away till she stopped, pulled out her phone and looked at it. She might guess it was him.

'You,' she said, before he had spoken.

'Yes,' he said, 'me. You have twenty minutes before every policeman in Cambridgeshire is looking for you. Better run, rabbit, run.'

'I'm going straight to the police.'

'And what will you tell them? There's nothing to see here but lab equipment, silly girl. Nothing but my stab wound against your crazy story.'

He watched her shoulders sag in the CCTV shot. 'Run, rabbit, run,' he shouted, into the microphone. She would flee and he would follow and, if circumstances allowed, he would strike.

She was holding something. A worm of anxiety slithered through him and he glanced back to his workspace. She had the specimens. He disconnected the call and let out a howl of rage.

She looked at the phone. He'd ended the call. He might be coming after her right now. She sprinted for her car.

32

Renton sat uncomfortably in the driving seat of Cardini's silver Mercedes. He was hot and in pain. He had forced himself, with great discomfort, to get upstairs and be in place to follow the girl. Pain was a fitting punishment for letting her get away. The place just below his ribs where the tiny blade had penetrated was burning. It was little more than a flesh wound, he calculated. She hadn't twisted the blade, just stabbed with it. It was hardly a wound at all.

He would treat it himself later, but first he had to discover where she would run to. He watched her on his android phone as she drove out of the car park, taking a route that, while out of site of the campus cameras, would bring her past the entrance to the lab. It was the fastest route to the rest of the world that she could take. Going left would have been smarter – it would have been harder for him to find and catch the little blue Ford Focus. Instead she was going to drive straight past him and he would follow her wherever she went.

The blue Focus flicked by, followed by a white van. Renton pulled out behind it and fell back a little so he could see the faintest glimpse of the girl's car.

Kate was shaking as she drove, her arms numb, her grip feeble as if her hands might fall off the steering-wheel. She was sobbing to herself in frustration.

'Call the police, call the police,' she kept saying to herself. She had stabbed Renton, that much was obvious. What would he do? Go to the police? Surely a sicko like him wouldn't do that. She started to rummage in her bag for her phone. Her fingers caught a sharp piece of card. Jim's. Her eye glimpsed something in the wing-mirror. There it was again – a flash of silver behind the white van that was following her.

Was it Renton?

She went back to rummaging in her bag. 'Phone, please,' she begged, 'please.' She shook the bag sharply and suddenly her phone was in her hand.

Call the police, said the voice in her head, for the umpteenth time.

What if he wasn't following her? Then the police would think they were dealing with a mad woman saying she was being followed by a man she had stabbed, with his stolen property in her footwell.

'Why did you take that?' she muttered. Because I thought it would have stuff in it that would prove Renton was planning to do horrible things to me. It was an evil-looking box and whatever was inside it was evil too. It was black, functional and secure: it looked like it was meant to hold something nasty. But it was light: perhaps he'd meant to put something in it, something of hers. She shuddered.

She picked Jim's card up and read the address. Jim was a rich guy: he would have lawyers, he would know people: he would help her, she knew he would – she prayed he would. 'Oh, God,' she moaned. Now she was praying for help from a stranger who wasn't even in the country.

She punched Jim's address into her beaten-up old GPS. It said she could be there in thirty-seven minutes. What harm could another thirty-seven minutes do?

Stafford was standing in front of the main door at the top of the steps as the Ford Focus came to a halt. There was a young woman in the driving seat, a local, perhaps, who had come to enquire about a fundraiser or the use of a field for some event or other.

She got out and looked up at him. He cut an imposing figure, he knew, in his grey striped trousers and black jacket. She smiled and walked up the steps to meet him. 'Good day,' he said. She looked extremely nervous. His right eyebrow rose. She's not nervous, he thought. She's terrified. 'How may I help you?' he said, smiling kindly.

'Jim,' she said. 'Jim said I could come and stay whenever I liked, so here I am.'

'I'm afraid—' began Stafford.

'That Jim's gone away to America.' She nodded vigorously. 'I know, but he asked me to come anyway.' She looked quickly over her shoulder.

Stafford followed her gaze up the drive, then turned back to her. There was a desperate determination in the girl's eyes. 'Of course,' he said. 'Let me fetch your bags.' He made to go down.

'No,' she said. 'I didn't bring any.'

Stafford stood back to attention. 'Very good. Will they be following?'

'I'm not sure,' she said. 'I have to speak to Jim, to work out what I'm doing.'

Stafford watched her face twitch involuntarily. She was in shock. 'Please come in,' he said. 'Allow me.' He tried to take the small black box in her left hand.

She smiled. 'I'm fine,' she said, and appeared to sag in relief.

He held the door open and she walked into the mansion's hall. The floor creaked as she crossed it and their footsteps echoed.

She climbed the ancient wooden staircase behind Stafford to the gallery, then followed him along a corridor. The carpet was ragged and worn and ran irregularly down the passage, whose polished boards groaned with every step. The pictures on the walls were portraits of well-painted but ugly noblemen and women set against beautifully painted but contrived country scenes. The smell of polish filled her senses. The house was as perfect as a museum.

Stafford opened two large doors and ushered her into a giant bedroom filled with ancient furniture, a huge bed set against the far wall. Four windows looked out on to the parkland beyond.

'Please feel free to wander about,' said Stafford, 'but be careful not to disturb anything in the master's study, especially near his computers.' He held out a small wooden block with a button set in the middle of its length. 'If you need anything, press this and I will be on hand.'

She took it. 'Thank you,' she said. 'Thank you.'

Stafford stood at the edge of the ha-ha, the light gently fading. In another hour it would be dark. He watched Lady Arabella riding around the cornfield towards him. Two wood pigeons swooped from above the tree to his left – he could have snapped his shotgun breech closed and despatched them. However, as he imagined they knew, he preferred not to shoot. He watched them fly off. He was a little disappointed, but meeting Lady A as she passed on her daily patrol would more than make up for it.

'Good evening, my lady,' he greeted her. Her long chestnut hair was flared out behind her; no riding helmet today.

'Good evening, Stafford,' she said, smiling down at him. She rubbed the horse's neck. 'You seem to have someone parked at the bottom of your drive looking rather shifty,' she added, her voice high and clear. 'Mercedes, about thirty metres to the right of the gatehouse. Unsavoury, if you ask me.'

'Thank you, m' lady,' said Stafford. 'I'll attend to it right away.'

She smiled at him, as she had when their paths had first crossed where Jim's grounds met her family's estate. Somehow he would make a point of being in the same places at the same times and she appeared to do likewise. Their meetings had become a pleasant unofficial appointment in the day.

There was something fascinating about the butler, something unusual, she thought. Of course, there was no such thing as a butler any more. It was a fiction, a reconstruction of a relic, an invention worthy of a Disney movie. A butler, if you ever met one, was a costumed manager, as much a servant as any vice president of marketing she might meet socially. Stafford was clearly a gentleman, and the retainer of allegedly the richest young bachelor in Europe. She fancied getting a look at his boss: Stafford was clearly gatekeeper to him and a very charming one at that.

She was happy to flirt a bit with the old man. If she looked at him through narrowed eyes, she could see him as he had been in his prime, beneath the older, heavier form. Beneath his servile exterior, she sensed the strength and character of her late father; a man guided by principles as archaic as the estate she rode around.

'I hope to see you tomorrow,' said Stafford, raising his green checked cap.

She smiled in acknowledgement as the horse walked on.

Stafford's shadow passed across the driver's window of the Mercedes and he rapped on the glass. The man inside sat up with a jolt and lowered the window. His eyes were fixed on the broken shotgun under the butler's arm.

'What are you doing there?' asked Stafford, imperiously. The car was parked so that its occupant could observe the house's gates. The terrified young girl and this vehicle were linked, he felt sure. Something was afoot, but he had no idea what it was. Without doubt Jim would be mixed up with it.

'Resting,' said the bearded man, in a friendly but unctuous way that made Stafford bristle.

'You had better move along,' he said.

The man started his engine.

Stafford took this as conclusive evidence that he was up to no good. An innocent person would have shown shock or enquired as to why he had to move off a public highway.

'Sorry,' said the man, putting his seatbelt on. 'I didn't mean to trespass.'

Stafford got a good look at his face. He had apologised for

something he was planning to do but had not yet attempted. He stood back from the car to let it pull out and away. Was that blood on the driver's shirt? He memorised the number plate. Lady Arabella had been right: the situation was fishy, very fishy indeed. How observant of her, how clever. And how negligent of himself not to have CCTV that could see on to the road at the perimeter. He huffed to himself and set off towards the gate.

There was a sudden eruption to his left and a horse crashed across the bank and down on to the road. Lady Arabella trotted over to him. 'So, what do you think?' she said, appearing slightly excited.

'Up to no good,' said Stafford. 'No doubt about it.'

'I'll make sure the estate keeps a keen eye open,' she said.

'Much appreciated,' said Stafford, sketching the faintest of bows.

'I shall probably see you tomorrow,' she said gaily, turning the horse around.

'I hope so,' said Stafford, knowing full well that he would be standing on the ha-ha apparently waiting for pigeons when she rode by.

It would be another wonderfully bitter moment. He retained the desires of a man in his prime but not the reach. Thirty years previously he would have made a play for her, but now, like a decrepit climber, he had to stand back and admire the magnificent prospect of the peak rather than risk humiliation and injury by attempting to conquer it.

He wondered why she indulged him by always riding by at the same time each day. She must be, as he was, a creature of habit, routine and discipline.

He allowed his head to drop as he walked to the gate.

33

Kate looked out of the window of the large salon. She could see Stafford trudging up the gravel drive, shotgun over his arm, looking like the master of the estate. The mansion was huge, empty and strangely friendly for an echoing and potentially scary old house. She had imagined that big houses like this would feel cold and haunted, like a vandalised mausoleum in an abandoned wood. Instead the massive building felt like a home that had been loved and filled with comfort. It would be a haven from which she was sure to be ejected as soon as Jim made contact with his butler. Then she would be adrift in the freezing seas of a dangerous world.

Was she wanted by the police?

Where could she go?

Home to her parents to face the music?

She had nowhere else to run to.

Was the maniac Renton looking for her?

She felt trapped by a series of binding problems, penned in by an infinity of awful outcomes.

She was tugging at her hair, she realised. She dropped her hands, then flicked away the strands she had broken or torn out and let out a little groan. If only she was smart enough to know what to do. If only she could fly above it all and see her whole predicament laid out in a simple diagram. If only she could just evaporate and reappear somewhere else at some other time.

34

'Really?' said Jim, as Stafford's voice cut in and out, beamed across the international network. Kate had shown up at the house and was staying there. That was unexpected. Perhaps it meant that Jane would magically reappear in his life at the most impossibly awkward moment. He smiled at how ironic that would be.

He liked the idea that Kate had sought him out. She was his kind of girl. And he was as lonely as hell. 'Of course,' he said, in reply to Stafford's enquiry as to whether she could stay.

The connection was frustratingly fractured and he was unsure whether the choppiness was creating the concern in Stafford's voice or whether it was real.

'Anything else I need to know?' he asked.

'No … stage.'

'Say again?'

'… stage.'

'Say again,' said Jim, looking out at the South Carolina forest.

'Not at this stage.'

'OK,' said Jim, 'over and out.' He hung up. He gazed across the fawn leather back seat of the Lincoln Town Car to Cardini, who sat impassively, like a marble statue in a suit. 'So tell me about your client McCloud,' he said.

'When the environment is right, I will be happy to do so, but it would not be appropriate in this car.' Cardini looked at him gravely. 'We should be at his compound in about another hour, inside what is allegedly the largest private home constructed in America in the last fifty years. It is a house of truly palatial proportions. Even the kings of France would have approved.' He went on reflectively, 'Though it must be said that modern methods render the construction of titanic buildings a modest challenge. No more are giant structures works of genius, like the European cathedrals or the monuments of the ancients.'

'How big is his place?' asked Jim, scratching his head.

'Big enough for a small army,' said Cardini. 'Perhaps even a large one.'

The countryside was impressive to a British guy. There were no fields or villages or towns. Instead there were miles and miles of forest. It had been burnt down by the early settlers, who had washed the ashes for potash, then shipped back the extract of a whole ecosystem to Britain as fertiliser. Just as they had killed the buffalo for its skin and the birds for a few feathers, they had murdered the virgin abundance of America for a fraction of the whole.

The land had been farmed until the pillaged soil could no longer support agriculture. Then, abandoned, the forest had returned and reclaimed it. In a few hundred years all that outrage and turmoil had come and gone and left no trace.

The Town Car slowed and pulled off the highway. After about half a mile they arrived at a gatehouse. A guard came to the driver's window and the driver signed a form. The guard glanced into the car and returned to his gatehouse. The barrier in front of the vehicle dropped into a hole in the road and the gate with its hinged fence swung up. The car drove forward and up a hill. Jim looked around, expecting to see a large house at any second, but as they went over the brow there was nothing except another hill, covered with trees.

'You may wish to sit back,' said Cardini. 'We have several miles to go yet. The McCloud compound is on a quarter of a million acres.'

'I don't do acres,' said Jim. 'How big is that?'

'Four hundred square miles.'

Jim sat back as instructed. 'Huge.'

Cardini nodded. 'Much of it is mountain. No use for anything except hunting.'

They passed up a steep rise.

'You'll see the house when we come over this ridge.'

Jim sat forward.

The nose of the car dropped and the car turned around a curve that looked down into a broad valley. Jim's jaw dropped. 'That's not a house. It's like a Vegas casino without the flashing signs.'

Below was a massive pink building, part modern glass holiday resort and part fantasy cartoon fortress. It was built in the shape of a triangle, like a big hotel, and at the end of each spur there was a pink Disneyesque castle. It looked like a collaboration between a futuristic architect and a three-year-old with a pack of crayons.

Jim was grinning. 'What the fuck?'

'What indeed?' said Cardini. 'Only great wealth can create such true art.' A crooked smile crept over his lips.

Jim strained to see more of the building as the car swept around the bend and the trees quickly obscured the view. 'Why is it pink?'

'Ah,' said Cardini. 'That would be because it was McCloud's late wife's favourite colour.'

'Right,' said Jim. 'Why not?' He laughed. 'I'll look it up on the net when I get back.'

'I'm afraid you won't be able to,' said Cardini. 'McCloud made his money from satellites and, oddly enough, there are no pictures of this area on any public satellite images.'

'Impressive,' said Jim. 'I wouldn't want anyone to see it if it was mine either.' He sat back again, wondering whether all his money would drive him bonkers one day too.

35

Renton sat in his office, deep in thought. He felt weak and ill. He had thought the wound below his chest was trivial, but now he could tell he had sustained more than a flesh wound. He had taken off his shirt and put on a clean white lab coat to cover himself.

He cast his eye over the glass vial on his desk top. Just two-thirds of the contents remained.

He would put a drop of the serum on his tongue, then read the work of great mathematicians. Under the influence of just a tiny drop, the meaning of obscure works unfurled in his mind. What was impenetrable to him in normal circumstances was suddenly revealed. Ideas that seemed isolated in their relevance seemed joined together in a tapestry of revelation. He saved these moments for special times and rationed the priceless elixir with which Cardini had bought his undying devotion.

Now he would resort to the serum to repair his wound. He peeled off the plaster, lips pursed against the pain of the adhesive tearing out his body hair. There was a congealed scab, a bruise around the wound and an ugly swelling that was growing steadily.

He had to get the samples back. The girl was irrelevant. The samples were everything.

He took the hypodermic and filled it with half of the vial's contents. He injected the wound with half of the measure and the rest into a vein in his forearm. He felt the warmth rush through his body immediately and a sudden exhilaration in his mind. He would allow himself an hour for healing, then set off again to the house where the girl had taken the samples.

He picked up his copy of Godel's *On Formally Undecidable Propositions of Principia Mathematica and Related Systems* and set the slideshow of his favourite pictures running on his twenty-eight-inch monitor.

The face of a man whose brains had been ejected by a large-calibre bullet through the side of his skull filled the screen. Renton smiled to himself and opened the book.

36

Kate looked at the long table, laid at the end just for her. 'Can I eat somewhere less formal?' she asked sheepishly.

'Where would you like to be?' said Stafford.

'The kitchen?'

'The kitchen,' said Stafford, not quite as a question but as if eating in there would provide him with some logistical problem. 'Of course,' he said, after the shortest of pauses. Jim often had dinner in the kitchen. He smiled. 'Come along then. It's downstairs.'

The kitchen was a large red-brick cavern furnished with the latest equipment. A giant table in light wood stood in the centre. It was clearly the focus for the preparation of giant meals, and its surfaces carried the scars of many years' service. Behind it was a huge Aga, in scale with the table. It, too, looked as if it had been specified to cook in bulk.

Stafford pulled out one of the chairs and offered it to Kate. She sat down. 'Would you care for a glass of wine?' he asked.

'Thank you.'

'Red or white?' he queried.

'White, please,' she replied.

'I have a nice Pouilly-Fuissé,' said Stafford.

'Lovely,' she said, not knowing what kind of wine it was. 'Did you speak to Jim?' she dared to ask.

'Yes,' said Stafford, stripping the lead foil from the bottle. 'He sends his regards.'

'Oh,' she said. 'Great.'

He twisted in the corkscrew. 'He didn't say when he'd be back. It might be a few days.'

'I don't mind waiting,' she said, 'if that's OK.'

The cork came out with a sharp pop. 'Of course,' said Stafford. 'I'm sure that will be fine.' He sniffed the cork, then poured the glass and brought it to her.

'Aren't you having one?' she asked.

'Perhaps when I retire,' he said, 'if there's any left.'

'I won't drink a whole bottle,' she said, laughing.

'Very good,' he said. 'Would you care for a starter?'

37

The entrance to McCloud's house was like the reception area of a large office complex. It was a white marble space accessed by two revolving doors. A party of three, two security men and a tall, thin, sandy-haired man of about thirty, was waiting for them.

'Professor,' the young man greeted him, throwing a concerned look at Jim. 'We've been waiting keenly. Who is this?' There was a hint of disapproval in his tone.

'My assistant, Dr Jim Evans.'

'We weren't anticipating another guest.'

'My apologies,' boomed Cardini, 'but you gave me insufficient notice to inform you.'

'This is not within the protocol,' the man said, his voice rising in pitch as he cast another glance at Jim.

Jim stared back at him steadily.

'I'm sorry,' said Cardini. 'You must clear it with Mr McCloud or we shall leave.'

'Mr McCloud is in no condition to clear anything,' the sandy-haired guy said sharply, bristling with annoyance.

'Then,' said Cardini, straightening to his full height, 'we shall leave.'

The man seemed to sag. He shook himself. 'No, no,' he said, as if the idea was silly. He stepped forward quickly to offer Jim his hand. 'Pleased to meet you, of course, Dr Evans. I'm Joe Marius.'

Jim shook his hand and Marius stepped back.

'Come, Professor,' he said, pouting at Cardini. 'Let's lose no more time. Mr McCloud is in sore need of your attention.'

'Lead on,' replied Cardini.

Marius spun on his heels and strode ahead in fast staccato steps, the click of his soles sharp on the marble surface.

There was a picture of water-lilies on the wall. Jim wondered whether it was a real Monet or a fake; he couldn't tell. He'd only be able to judge if there was a price tag on it. If the first number was trailed by seven zeros it would be genuine – or, at least, sold as such. Artworks, he had learnt, were the most valuable objects by weight in the world. A few pounds of Impressionist made the equivalent in gold seem pretty worthless.

Jim had thought about buying some Van Goghs after seeing the old movie with Kirk Douglas. All the experts had assured him of his great taste, but when he discovered that Van Gogh had painted a thousand pictures in ten years he was left wondering how the hell a crazy, poverty-stricken drunk could have made a fantastic picture every three days for a decade. It seemed unlikely that a sane hard-working artist could have made two masterpieces a week so he concluded that many, perhaps most, of the thousand paintings must be fake. Jim lined up dozens of them on his computer screen, courtesy of Google images, and it seemed to him that, from the styles, at least three painters had been involved. However, none of the experts who fawned over him seemed to see that so he had dropped the idea of becoming an art collector.

He was trying hard not to be a member of the stupid rich. The stupid rich were a small but powerful group. It didn't take brains or class to be rich, just skill or perhaps luck. A soccer star was as easily conned by an art dealer as any little old lady by a boiler-room stock-pumping spiv. A Russian oligarch might rearrange your anatomy if you crossed him, but was just as likely to fall for a good salesman flogging crap as any country bumpkin. Jim tried to avoid stepping into the many traps laid for 'new money' but he wasn't completely sure he'd managed it.

He caught up with Marius and Cardini.

They entered a lift, one in a bank of three. They went up to the fourth floor and exited into what looked like a hospital.

Is this all for McCloud? he wondered.

They walked down a long hallway and Jim tried to work out what was behind the doors, all numbered. Across from Room 4 there was a double door. 'Operating Theatre 1', said a silver plate on the wall next to it.

Marius opened the door at the end of the corridor. Cardini walked in past him and Jim followed. Medical equipment was neatly lined up around the room, all on racks and trolleys. Two nurses sitting by the door rose and hurried out of the room.

A bed stood by the window and in it lay a slight figure whose outline barely made its presence felt.

'Good afternoon, Howard,' said Cardini.

Jim stayed back. The old man in the bed was clearly very frail. The lifeless pallor of his skin, his motionlessness form, underlined how close to death he was.

Cardini opened his bag and prepared a hypodermic. He injected McCloud in his forearm, then put a plastic tip on the needle and replaced it in his bag. He turned to Marius. 'For now our work is done.' To Jim, he said, 'Come, we will return later this evening.'

Jim's room felt distinctly like a hotel room. It had the kind of sterility of a planned space rather than the warm haphazardness of a personal area. He showered and changed. It would be midnight back in London and he was starting to feel the hour, even though the sun was only just falling to the horizon here.

38

Renton took the Google Earth printout from the passenger seat again. Although he had memorised every inch of it under the influence of the elixir, the effects were wearing off fast and his detailed recall was fading rapidly.

The plan was simple. He would drive slowly up to the house. Ring the doorbell. Overpower the old man or whoever who came to the door, cut their throat. Find the girl, kill her and take the samples. If anyone else was there he would kill them too. He would then take all the horsemen back to the lab. Prepare the final batches and flee. The tickets to Mumbai, Lagos and Washington were booked. Nothing could stop him.

He blinked. Now that the TRT's effect was wearing off, it seemed so much more of a daunting challenge. Even minutes ago the prospect of driving to the door of the great mansion had seemed trivial, the slitting of the old man's throat no more than the termination of a lab rat. That clinical perspective was draining away and a sensation of panic was welling in his stomach.

He screwed up his face in anger. He put his hand into his pocket and pulled out the vial. It contained a few drops, leftovers that represented a weekend of heavenly bliss and flights of genius across a limitless horizon of mental clarity. There would be so much more for him once he had executed the plan, he thought. He would have such pleasure whenever he wished it and for ever.

By the faint beam of the light above his rear-view mirror, he sucked up the drops into the hypodermic, then injected them into his neck. 'Argh,' he gasped, rolling his eyes. A hot sensation flooded his brain, like a *wasabi* rush in the nose. He stretched his neck left, then right, and felt a satisfying pop where his skull met his spine. He started the engine. How could it be anything but easy to destroy these people when they did not even close their gate at night?

The car pulled across the road and on to the gravel of the drive, which crunched and crackled as he drove slowly along. He glanced down at the handle of the hunting knife that poked out from between the pages of a road map. He imagined it at the throat of the old man who had chased him off. He imagined the blade biting into the neck; he could see it slicing into skin, flesh and windpipe. He thrilled with anticipation. About two hundred yards ahead, the house stood, dark and brooding, looming up beyond the bushes and trees.

He was grinning to himself.

Stafford sat up in bed. When his iPhone vibrated like that, droning inside its rubber bumper, it always meant something bad was afoot. He grabbed it and his glasses. A car was coming up the drive.

DISARM??? flashed the screen of the iPhone, as the infrared image of the blue-grey car approached.

He couldn't see who was behind the wheel of the Polo but it seemed to be moving at quite the wrong speed.

He waited for the action to start.

There was a blinding flash and Renton slammed on the brakes. The whole house and driveway were suddenly lit up like a night-time football match. Metal bollards had appeared from the ground in front of him, their caps flashing blue, their lengths red. TURN BACK, said two signs that had appeared from nowhere.

Renton steadied himself and switched off the engine. He picked up the map, pushing the knife's handle inside the main fold to hide it, and got out of the car. He walked slowly towards the house.

*

Stafford put on his dressing-gown and saw on the screen that a man, looking rather similar to the fellow who had parked outside that afternoon, was making his way to the front door. He left his room and walked swiftly down the stairs. As he entered the main hall there was a shriek. His hand went instinctively to the right pocket of his silk dressing-gown as he spun round.

It was Kate. 'Don't answer the door,' she said, running towards him on the landing. 'Please listen to me, don't open the door.'

He looked at her searchingly. 'What is this about?'

'It's complicated,' she said, 'but please don't open the door to that man.'

'Should I call the police?' said Stafford, leaning slightly forward and fixing her with an owl-like stare.

She looked yet more panicked. Her mouth opened and she stared at him as if a fishbone was stuck in her throat. 'No,' she said finally.

'Somehow I thought you might say that,' said Stafford. 'Go to your room and lock the door. I'll deal with this.' He trotted off.

Renton looked up at the house. The lights had come on inside. He could feel a new strength in his muscles as they pumped themselves up with fresh vigour. As soon as the door was opened to him, he would tell the old man that he was lost, his GPS had broken, and ask for help with the map. Then he would push himself inside the house and strike. The excitement was invigorating.

He reached the worn red-brick steps that led up to the door. He paused, feeling the knife through the crisp paper of the map.

He placed his left foot on the first step and put on his friendliest smile.

There was a quiet rustling behind him and a tinkling sound. He turned.

The old man was standing twenty feet behind him, a Rottweiler sitting on either side. The left one was shaking its head, its nametag ringing and rattling. The old man supported himself lightly on a heavy, gnarled shillelagh, the other hand in the pocket of his burgundy silk dressing-gown. 'How may I help you at this unearthly hour?' he said. The dogs got up.

Renton noted that they weren't on a leash. He turned to the old man and took two steps forward.

The dogs stepped forward too.

Renton looked uncomfortably at them. They were a little too purposeful to be pets.

'Don't I recognise you?' said the old man, sounding slightly angry. The dogs stood stiffly to attention and stared at Renton as if they knew exactly what he had come for.

'No,' said Renton. 'I'm looking for the Porterfield Country Hotel,' he said, shuffling to one side, away from the house. 'This isn't it, is it?' he said, in a friendly but rather scared way.

'No, it isn't.'

Renton was wheeling around now, the old man and the dogs moving accordingly.

'I'm sure I've seen you somewhere before,' barked the old man.

'No, we've never met. Sorry to have bothered you,' he said, manoeuvring himself so that he had a clear route back down the drive.

The dogs were gambolling slowly after him as he walked past the old man and away. They were humiliating him, driving him like a wayward sheep. He could turn and stab them, then go for the man, who might try to hit him with the stick, but he felt incredibly strong as the TRT pumped through his mind and body. He could take them all on and win with ease.

He stopped, grabbed the hilt of the knife in his right fist and turned.

As soon as the dogs saw the blade, they charged. Renton raised it to strike, but the first Rottweiler clamped his wrist with its open jaws, while the second crashed into his chest and flattened him.

Renton was pinned to the ground, stunned.

The second dog had his throat in its jaws. He could feel the teeth pressing down on his flesh, just short of tearing into his gullet. If the dog chose it could sever his windpipe. The knife was out of reach, on the gravel, and he lay transfixed. The second dog was only a command away from ripping him to pieces, like a brought-down stag.

The dogs made no sound. They waited motionless and throbbing above him. He could feel their heat.

The old man looked down at Renton, holding a hunting knife in his right hand. 'The next time I see you will be the last,' he said, fixing Renton with a beady stare.

Eventually he turned away and walked up the drive. 'Come on, boys,' he said.

With that, the dogs released their grip and ran to his side.

The old man turned to watch Renton run down the drive. His throat was covered with foamy dog slobber but he didn't dare stop to wipe it off.

Stafford looked up at the house. Kate was standing in the window looking down at him.

He rubbed the dogs' necks. 'You can stay out tonight and play,' he said. 'Go on.' They jumped at each other, wagging their stumpy tails, and dashed off across the drive into the darkness beyond.

39

Stafford took out the front-door key and went into the hall. At the top of the stairs, Kate was looking down at him. She was dressed and she was carrying something in her right hand. She walked down the stairs.

'I think you have some explaining to do,' said Stafford.

Kate looked at him with a mix of awe and terror. Words didn't form. 'Those dogs,' she said, 'are they yours?' She blinked. 'I don't mean are they yours, I mean …' She stopped. She held out the black box. 'I took this from him.'

Stafford reached out to take the box but she held it back. 'No,' she said. 'It might be very dangerous. Let me show you.'

'Come through to the library,' said Stafford. 'Let me pour us a drink and you can tell me everything.' He turned away.

'Mr Stafford,' she said, 'what if he comes back?'

'The dogs will deal with him,' he said.

'Mr Stafford,' she said.

He stopped and turned back to her.

'Thank you,' she said. 'I'm really …' She halted mid-sentence.

'You are very welcome.'

'I meant to say I'm really scared but grateful sounds better, doesn't it?' She let out a nervous laugh.

Unconsciously Stafford patted the pistol in his dressing-gown pocket. 'I'm sure your story will be fascinating.'

She sat on a long green leather sofa, her legs curled underneath her. He occupied a brown leather chair, a low table between them. He had listened to thousands of witness statements and confessions, and the truth was always the same: it made sense. It flowed and fitted together. The improbabilities stuck out against the mundane and the teller told the story with the vividness of the moment, making no attempt to justify or embellish.

The man Renton was clearly some kind of insane monster. Stafford had come across such monsters before and he had worked with men like that too. The highly functional insane turned up in many places, especially in his old profession, and while they were rare, they could leave a huge wake of chaos behind them, especially when they finally lost their meagre grasp on normality.

He could smooth over the situation for her. He could make sure that there would be many red flags against Renton's records. If anything unusual happened within five miles of Renton in future, he would be on the 'go-see' list.

'Well, Renton will now find it hard to prosecute you for stabbing him, seeing as he has paid us a visit, fit as a flea, only a few hours after you fought him off. I have everything on video, of course.' He smiled.

Kate shifted on the sofa, her feet on the floor now. She looked as if she was going to jump up, but she slumped back. 'What about the box?'

'Well, I was going to ask you ...'

She sat forward and unclipped the top. The lid flipped back and the front fell forwards. There were four trays. Stafford leant forwards. She pulled out each tray and laid them on the table. Inside each one there was an enclosed Petri dish. In each dish, on a clear jelly, something was growing. White spindly snowflakes spread across the first, like crystals of quartz. In the second, green-white billowy mould spread like a fungus on a damp, decaying wall. In the third, patchy translucent dots were expanding into jelly-like blobs. In the fourth, red bubbles were growing in grid formations where the jelly had been contaminated with whatever was feeding and dividing in the clear incubating soup.

'What are they?' said Stafford, torn between the curiosity to look closely and the instinctive repugnance he felt towards whatever was growing in the dishes.

'I don't know,' she said, 'but whatever it is, it's important to Renton. He didn't risk everything to come after me. I think he came for this.'

'Why do you say that?' said Stafford.

'I just know.'

Stafford looked at the dishes. 'I'll have these seen to,' he said.

'By whom?'

'Acquaintances,' he said, looking askance at them. 'Do you think you might put them away now?' He watched her put them back into the box and close it. He would call Porton Down in the morning and have them collected. One way or another that would be the end of the matter.

40

The serum's primary effects were wearing off fast as Renton drove towards the M11. He was starting to panic. All the things that could go wrong were churning in his mind as it computed the infinite possibilities of disaster.

He had to go back to the lab, start with the first horseman he had and forget the rest. There was plenty of viable culture and the other strains would have to come from nature after the release. As long as the initial first horseman was successful, the rest wouldn't matter. He had to forget the girl and the other cultures, work fast and prepare. He could be on his way within three days. He would go to Lagos or Egypt first and start there. Once the first horseman was established in Africa the situation would become uncontainable in any event. The cull might take two or three years longer to become established but it would happen.

He had to keep Cardini ignorant of the mess. He dreaded to think what his reaction would be if he discovered the truth.

The girl had been intended as a simple test of the vector, to see whether they had managed to improve its ability to carry into humans. Confirmation meant the unleashing of the horseman would be optimal.

Yet this step was unnecessary, as Cardini knew. Every laboratory animal tested had been infected by the re-engineered vector. It carried the horseman and spread it, then outbred the natural vector with its improved reproductive capacity. But Cardini wanted the tests to be completed on a human subject. Cardini was a methodical perfectionist.

Suddenly Renton was grinning again; the path ahead seemed wide and certain.

He'd been a student, he recalled, when he'd asked his then professor, an earnest but visionless academic, 'Aren't you worried you might accidentally make a bacterium or virus that could kill everyone?'

His professor had smiled patronisingly. 'Actually,' he had said, 'nature is working full time on that right now. Billions of invisible life forms are trying to find a way into us to feed and reproduce. I'm more afraid they will find the answer to their challenge before we can understand a way of locking them out. Compared with the risks to humanity from nature, the risk of creating a monster ourselves is infinitely remote.'

What a fool that man was, Renton thought. Cardini's vision dwarfed such a limited and arrogant mind. Man could and would out-engineer nature. Great men would wield the microscopic world, and in doing so control humanity's numbers by cull.

His cull – or, rather, Cardini's cull – would revolutionise the world, in the same way that the Black Death had torn down feudalism to replace it, eventually, with the Enlightenment. All he needed to do was infect the lab rat with the Ebola virus, feed it live to the modified mosquitoes, fly to Lagos or Cairo and release them. Then, one bite at a time, the world would begin to change. As the mosquitoes spread and bred, the blood-borne plague would be carried with them. Mosquitoes had been the vector for malaria since the beginning of history, spreading it with their salivary glands. Cardini had re-engineered them to regurgitate their stomach contents when they fed so they would infect their prey with the blood-borne disease of their previous hosts. Now Aids, hepatitis C, Ebola, West Nile virus, SARS and others would be transmitted from human to human and animal to human via an ever-present flying syringe. Humanity would become a giant and growing incubator of all the diseases that destroyed it.

Not in the north, though, not in the civilised lands, only in the hot, fetid countries that teemed with the ever-growing billions who doomed the world to environmental decay and destruction. Humanity would kill the seas, clear the forests and pick the planet clean of all resources. The world needed the Amazon rainforest to cleanse the air; it needed unplundered seas to support the environmental cycle. It needed six billion fewer of the humans who were driving the world to catastrophe.

He was about to set the spark that would give birth to the blaze that would turn the earth again into a paradise where a thousand million people could live and he, Renton, would enjoy immortality.

41

McCloud was sitting up in bed, glaring. He looked considerably different from the collapsed husk of three hours before. 'What's this kid doing here?' he said, wagging a finger at Jim.

'Dr Evans is assisting me,' said Cardini, with the sort of authority that would have silenced most people.

'You don't need no goddamn assistance,' said McCloud. 'Who are you, son?' he asked Jim.

'I'm Jim Evans,' he replied.

'Check that out,' said McCloud to Marius.

'I already have,' said Marius.

'And what did you find?'

'Britain's most eligible bachelor under thirty,' he said, as if that was a crime. 'Banking. Net worth five billion dollars. Far East connections.'

'Far East connections?' queried Jim. 'Your data's dodgy.'

'Japanese Order of the Chrysanthemum.'

'What the hell is that? Some kind of flower-arranging medal?' growled McCloud.

Marius shook his head. 'I have no idea.' He turned to Jim. 'There sure isn't much about you for a man with your kind of money.'

'I'm a trader, not a pop star,' said Jim.

'You must be a mighty big trader, son,' said McCloud.

'I was,' said Jim, 'once.'

McCloud coughed.

'That's enough for now,' said Cardini.

McCloud continued to cough. Eventually the spluttering subsided. 'So what are you here for, son?' he said, a gasp still in his voice.

'I don't know. I think Chris wanted to introduce me to you.'

McCloud turned his glare on Cardini. 'Think I'm going to croak?' he snapped.

'Due to your recent pattern of unpredictable behaviour,' said Cardini, sternly, 'that is becoming increasingly likely.'

McCloud put the oxygen mask over his face. He drew some breaths, then removed it. 'You underestimate me,' he said, trying to sound strong.

'Perhaps,' boomed Cardini, 'you overestimate yourself, Howard.'

'I told you Cardini, long ago, that I always get my way.'

Jim wasn't sure whether he sounded pathetic or threatening.

42

The sun was going down behind the mountains and there was a fiery orange sunset. At the back of the mansion, a long veranda swung in an arch across the centre of the building.

'This whole place is like some huge deserted hotel,' said Jim. 'A holiday resort without any guests.'

A waiter came out on to the terrace and walked over to them. 'What can I get you, gentlemen?'

'A gin and tonic,' said Cardini, in a voice so deep it made Jim hanker for one too.

'Coke,' said Jim, asserting his independence to himself.

'I'll be right back,' said the waiter.

'I thought you didn't like to put poisons in your body,' said Jim.

'Under certain circumstances I make exceptions,' replied Cardini. 'And this is one of them.'

'I'm not too sure why you brought me here,' he said. 'Let's say I don't feel very welcome.'

'I wanted you to see TRT in action on a real person, one at the very edge of his natural lifespan, and understand the importance of what I've invented, the potential, the power. It's all well and good talking about it, showing slides, but nothing is more potent than seeing the effects with your own eyes.'

'OK,' said Jim, 'but I saw what it did to my eye. I believe you.'

'Today you saw what it can do in a few short hours to a whole organism. Tomorrow you will see yet more improvement. I want you to understand in your soul how TRT has the power to change everything, humanity, its future and more.' Cardini gazed over the mountain tops to the dying sun.

'I'm not about changing the world,' said Jim. 'Changing the world is strictly for the nerds of Silicon Valley.'

'Yes,' said Cardini, 'and it is hard to find the right person to help me take the final steps.' He looked seriously at Jim. 'We are all doomed, of course.'

'You mean me and you are doomed to die eventually?' said Jim.

'No,' said Cardini. 'Humanity is doomed. So is the planet.'

'Really?' said Jim. 'I don't agree.' He blinked as a memory of the nuclear showdown he had helped avert flooded his mind. 'We might have been scuppered a couple of years ago but that's all fixed. I can't see any problems as far as I can draw a stock chart and that's decades.'

Cardini was staring at him with an expression that Jim had seen directed at him before. It said, 'Who is this idiot and what is he talking about?'

The professor looked away and sighed. 'How do you think the world will continue with eight, nine, fifteen, twenty billion people living on it? What do you think will happen?'

'We'll muddle through.'

'Muddle through? Even now the planet is dying.'

'Is it?'

'Don't you read the newspapers?'

'No,' said Jim, 'not as a rule. When I read something in them I know a little about, they're always dead wrong. When you read about stuff in the papers that you know about, do they get it right?'

Cardini's silence was telling.

'Common sense should tell you that the world can't continue to support ever-increasing numbers.'

'When I look at Google Earth, Chris, I can hardly find anyone. I just see miles and miles of empty spaces.'

Cardini gave a deep cough. 'I believe the point has been reached at which human numbers are killing our planet and that soon powerful forces will destroy not only the environment we know but also the atmosphere, which will be stripped from the planet by new and devastating processes. Environment feedback loops will start to create a series of vicious circles that, once uncontrollable, will leave the earth like Mars, lifeless.'

'It can't be allowed to happen, Christopher,' came a voice behind them.

Jim turned. McCloud was walking slowly towards them supported by a Zimmer frame. He stopped. 'Forgive my slow progress,' he said, smiling wryly. 'I'm starting to feel better and thought I should get up to be with my guests.'

He resumed walking towards them. 'Don't come to meet me,' he said. 'I need to use my legs. The more I walk now, the stronger they'll get over the next few days.'

'You should have remained in bed,' said Cardini.

'Damn it, Chris,' said McCloud, cheerily, 'you don't know everything. I'm telling you, the more you use your body during the first hours, the better it recovers.'

'A likely story,' grumbled Cardini.

McCloud came to a halt in front of Jim and Cardini. He took his right hand off the Zimmer frame. 'I was very rude to you earlier and I'm sorry,' he said. 'It can be hard to come back from the dead – when I start coming round it makes me as cranky as hell.' He shook Jim's hand.

'No problem, Mr McCloud,' said Jim.

'I appreciate that,' said McCloud. 'Please call me Howard – or Howie, even.'

'Thanks, Howard,' said Jim.

McCloud laughed. 'Why does no one ever want to call me Howie?'

'You're not a Howie,' said Cardini, dismissively.

'There you are,' said McCloud to Jim. 'Apparently I'm no Howie.'

The waiter appeared with the Coke, the gin and tonic and a whisky with ice.

McCloud was hardly leaning on the frame now. He took his

glass and raised it. 'To a sustainable future,' he said, clinking Jim's glass and then Cardini's. 'So what do you say, Jim, about the world population crisis?'

Jim sipped his Coke. 'I don't see one,' he said.

'You don't see any problems with seven billion people on this earth?'

'No,' said Jim. 'There they are, here I am.'

'And you think there is enough of everything to go around?'

'Sure,' said Jim. 'Energy prices are below food prices.'

Cardini looked at McCloud as if McCloud might understand what Jim was saying.

'What do you mean?' asked McCloud.

'Well, if you can economically turn energy into food – you know, use petrol to plough fields, make fertilisers, that kind of thing – you have more food and you have progress.' He shrugged. 'That means more people.'

'Is that it?' said McCloud.

Cardini was looking at Jim in the way that 'word people' always looked at him when he talked numbers.

'Yes,' Jim continued. 'The day you have to make food into fuel, corn into ethanol, for example, because it's more economical to do that than the other way around, that's when progress stops. That's when progress goes into reverse. Then people die of hunger. When the cost of energy means that food isn't going to the hungry, but into creating energy, that's what limits population. Obvious, right?'

Cardini was looking at him now as if he had said something utterly unintelligible.

'That's not going to happen, not soon anyway,' Jim went on. 'Technology keeps coming up with the goods, just like it always has. You should look at the ancient stuff I collect. In those days there were three hundred million people on the planet and most of them were diseased and starving but, boy, they had plenty of great natural environments to live in.'

McCloud was gazing at the flame-red sky. 'Hope you're right, son,' he said, 'but I fear you're just a young optimist. I was once, but there was less than half the world's current population then.' He took a sip of his whisky. 'You could catch thousand-pound marlins off Florida in those days, two, sometimes three fish in a day. Now they're all gone. Life was fat back then, wasn't it, Cardini?'

'Didn't you die of blood poisoning if you got a septic finger?' said Jim.

'I'm not talking about what we've gained, Jim,' said McCloud. 'I'm talking about what we've lost. Whole ecosystems simply wiped out, natural environments stripped bare, the deserts of the world slowly but surely creeping over the face of the earth. Dead earth, soils without life, a dying planet, Mother Nature on the edge of extinction.'

'Commodity prices aren't going anywhere in the next twenty years,' said Jim. 'Well, not inflation-adjusted. That suggests you might be wrong.'

'How can you know?' said Cardini.

'It's my speciality,' said Jim.

'Maybe you should check out cocoa,' said McCloud, laughing.

'Why cocoa?'

'Hell, it's been going through the roof!'

43

Kate and Stafford watched the ambulance turn in front of the house and trundle away.

Stafford was pleased with the result. 'That's that, then,' he said, and smiled.

'What happens next?' she asked.

'Nothing, I should hope.'

'What do you think I should do?' she said.

'Very little,' said Stafford. 'At least till Jim gets back.'

'Will that be all right?'

'Of course, my dear, of course. In any event, a house like this needs to be lived in. The more feet moving around the boards, the slower the place falls to pieces.' He cocked his head at her. 'Now, I'm afraid I have an appointment to attend. I will return in due course.'

He set off for the kitchen. In a crate of groceries there was a large white paper bag. He tore it open to reveal a hare, obtained from the butcher. It was a wild animal that some farmer had shot locally and would make fine eating. Holding it with one hand he placed it into his game bag and slung it around his neck. Then he went outside and walked down the garden to the ha-ha, his broken shotgun over his arm. His puttees made his tweed trousers flare out nicely at the calf.

Lady Arabella had signalled to him with a wave from the far side of the barley and was walking her mount round the edge of the field towards him. It wasn't her normal point-to-pointer but an enormous beast that looked more like a dray horse, which made her seem waif-like instead of rather robust. There would be no vaulting hedges on this steed, though crashing through one seemed an option.

She pulled up below the ha-ha and acknowledged Stafford. 'Hello again,' she said. 'Potted anything?'

'Funnily enough I have,' he said, and produced the hare.

'That's a jolly good-looking catch,' she said.

'I was wondering if you would like it,' he replied. 'I have a canvas bag if you want to take it.'

'That's very kind of you,' she said. 'I can't remember the last time we got sight of a hare.'

'One less to be seen now, I'm afraid,' said Stafford.

'Never mind,' she said. 'I'm sure it'll be marvellous.'

Stafford slid the hare into an off-white canvas bag. He pulled the strings to tighten the neck, walked to the edge of the lawn and handed it to her.

She slung the bag over her shoulder. 'I say,' she said, 'it's very heavy.'

He smiled at her and sighed unconsciously. 'Yes,' he said, 'quite some weight. Enough for a fine roast.'

'I won't let Mummy near it,' she said, bending forward. 'I shall cook it myself.'

'Good show.' He wondered whether she would ask after Jim, as she sometimes did. She must be waiting for an invitation up to the house and a chance to impress its wealthy owner. Most English aristocrats were genetically programmed to marry money. Their assets were often just giant money-draining liabilities masquerading as the family mansion and a traditional way of life. To them marriage was a ruthless business of survival. Without a sharp nose for a moneyed man or wealthy heiress, they would already be extinct, like so many of their class before them. One mistake or mishap, and the family tree crashed back into the proletariat from which, at some stage, it had risen. The trouble was, there weren't many men or heiresses with the right kind of money.

Stafford was admiring her glowing beauty.

'If there's enough left for a stew I shall bring you some,' she said, with a twinkle in her eye. 'I can be quite economical when the mood takes me.'

'Please don't waste any on me,' he said, bowing a little.

'Tsk,' she said, pushing the horse on. She looked back at him as she went, then sent him another little wave.

Tsk? thought Stafford. Was she speaking to the horse or to me?

44

McCloud put the Zimmer frame to one side. 'Let's go in and get something to eat. I have one helluvan appetite.'

Cardini smiled at Jim triumphantly. Behold and wonder.

Jim grinned back. TRT truly was amazing.

They followed McCloud, who was walking unsupported, if bowed and unsteady, back to the lounge.

'Where is my freakin' Segway when I need it?' McCloud said jokily. He looked back at Jim. 'Should have put a monorail in,' he said, then set off again shakily.

With a mix of horror and awe, Jim watched the determined old man forcing himself over the acres of carpet, hobbling to some distant location. Why was he hanging on to life so desperately? Jim was sure he'd shoot himself rather than be in such a terrible state. Yet he knew that the will to live was overwhelming. When he had lain in a hospital bed, drifting in and out of consciousness, he hadn't hoped to die. Then all he had wanted was to feel better, to be back in control of his mind and body. McCloud was the man he would one day become, if he lived long enough, a frail, brittle vehicle for a mind that wished to go on and on. It was a sobering and rather depressing realisation.

'Come on,' called McCloud, waving them forward. 'We've got a meal to eat.' He started to hobble faster, his arms swinging.

'Really, Howard,' complained Cardini. 'You are incorrigibly irresponsible.'

'Use it or lose it,' grunted McCloud, pressing on.

'Use it and lose it is also a potential outcome,' Cardini remarked. A twisted smile broke on his lips.

The dining room was a vast restaurant-cum-cafeteria. The door plaque said, 'Dining Room Four'. A waiter wearing a badge with 'Andy' engraved on it took their orders.

'This is an amazing house you've got here,' said Jim.

'Thank you,' said McCloud.

'Was it, like, a hotel before?' asked Jim, secretly wondering why it was so institutional and not homelike.

'No,' said McCloud. 'I designed it myself with Perry.' He paused. 'My late wife. We built it in 'ninety-two.'

Why would you build a house like a Las Vegas casino? thought Jim. Maybe it was meant to be a casino, but they'd built it first and planned to get permission later. He had heard that there were casinos outside Nevada on Native American land: perhaps this would turn into one when some legislation got passed. McCloud was clearly either very mad or very clever. Both seemed likely.

'You've got the most massive chunk of land,' he added.

'Has Cardini been telling you all my secrets?' asked McCloud, grinning.

'Only the important ones,' said Jim.

'OK, OK,' nodded McCloud, 'I'm down with that. Well, son, if you see the apocalypse coming and you've got the money, it makes sense to give yourself a buffer zone.' He took a mouthful of iced water. 'I wanted a piece of land so big that when the marauding hordes arrive they'll think hard about coming my way, purely on the basis of the energy they'd expend getting here.'

'Marauding hordes?' queried Jim. 'Do you get many on the east coast?'

'You know, Jim, I hear ya. No, we don't get many this way, but there have been a few around these here parts over the last few hundred years. One every fifty to a hundred years in fact.'

'Really?'

'Well, son, this used to be Indian land, until they got wiped out by us European marauders. Then there was the army of the north and then again the army of the south. Just because there's been no marauding for the last fifty or so years doesn't mean there won't be any tomorrow.'

'Howard worries that when the environment collapses so must civilisation,' said Cardini. 'War and ecological stress are closely linked.' He was drilling Jim's skull with his unblinking stare again. 'It was, for instance, a period of hard weather that set the Mongols on their course of destruction and conquest that in its turn brought the Black Death to Europe.'

McCloud gave Cardini a hard look. 'That's right, Chris. War, famine, disease and death. That's what happens when the environment breaks down.'

'We've been kind of getting on well without them,' said Jim. 'Well, a lot less of them than in the past.'

'It's down to a stroke of luck that's about to end,' said McCloud.

'You should mix an anti-depressant with your serum, Chris,' said Jim. 'What's the point of living for a million years if you're going to be as miserable as sin the whole time?'

'You're a live wire, Jimbo,' said McCloud. 'And you're right. It's time to lighten up. You know, I'm not really so unhappy about things because I do what I can to avoid the bad angles. I think of the bad things that may happen and I do what I can to fix them.'

Andy returned with a heavily laden tray, popped open the tray support and set it down. It was salads, steak and beer all round.

Jim's steak looked like it would keep him going for a week and he wondered if he was meant to eat all of it. He set to work immediately. It was the sort of steak that just didn't seem to exist in England, almost as if it came from a different kind of cow, which was quite possible, as far as he knew.

'So, Jim,' started McCloud, 'how come a young guy like you gets to have so much money?'

Jim looked up from sawing a large chunk of bloody flesh

from his personal beef joint. He swallowed the piece he was chewing. 'Well, I used to say I made my money from guns and drugs, but people always believed me, so I've stopped saying that.' Cardini was watching him rather as a teacher watches a child take a test. 'I'm a trader.' He half grinned and corrected himself. 'I was a trader.'

'And how come you came by such a big Japanese honour?'

Jim was eyeing a forkful of steak that he felt needed to be in his mouth. 'I sold some antiques to a museum there for a very reasonable price.'

'You get a medal for that in Japan?'

Jim had the piece of steak between his teeth, 'Umm,' he said.

'What was it? The freakin' Crown Jewels?'

'Umm.' Jim nodded.

McCloud laughed. 'You're a crazy guy.'

Jim began sawing off another piece of juicy red steak.

'Hedge funds,' said Cardini, as if it was a sentence with a subject, object and verb in it.

'That's right,' said McCloud, as if that meant anything.

'What about you?' asked Jim. 'How did you make your money?'

'Guns and drugs,' said McCloud. 'Legal ones ... They call it satellite TV, but it's a drug and you can be pretty sure that they show plenty of guns.'

McCloud was recovering his youth before Jim's eyes. From a doddery old man with a quivering voice, he was quickly becoming merely elderly. There was a sparkle in his eyes and the tremor was fast disappearing. His cheeks, which had been pale and almost translucent, were now rosy. 'I borrow a ton of money, build businesses and sell them on to someone else who can also borrow a ton of money. It's a shell game.' McCloud looked a little sour as Jim failed to react to his pithy revelation.

'I don't really understand businesses,' said Jim. 'So many balance sheets look bust to me – I don't understand how some of the companies even exist.'

'Money's an illusion, son,' said McCloud. 'A company is a poker hand you play. You just have to make sure you're not holding the bag when it has to fold.'

'What do you think about business, Chris?' asked Jim.

'I'm a biologist, not an anthropologist,' said Cardini. 'Such activities are a mystery to me.'

'Says the man with the ultimate product,' said McCloud, waving his steak knife at him. 'A man who sends me invoices that make me weep.'

Cardini ignored him.

'So, you gonna buy your way to immortality, Jim?'

'I doubt it.'

McCloud examined Jim as if he was scoring him against a pre-set check list. 'Why the hell not?'

'To be honest,' said Jim, 'I'm more interested in what it could do for medicine than in living for ever.'

'Really?' said McCloud. 'Why is that?'

'I'd've thought it was pretty obvious. The medical implications of wide-scale production would be miraculous.'

'Miraculous?' McCloud suddenly shrieked. 'Catastrophic, more like!' The atmosphere had chilled, as though Jim had uttered the most obscene blasphemy.

Cardini had reached over to McCloud and grasped the old man's shoulder. 'I don't think this is the right time to debate the hypothetical impact of the serum. There is no near-term likelihood of mass manufacture. Indeed, when this kind of technology is possible, chemistry will be on such a plane as to change much else besides simple human lifespan.'

'I'm interested in that, too,' said Jim.

McCloud was clearly fizzing inside.

'Good,' said Cardini.

Jim put another piece of steak into his mouth so he had no need to answer quickly if any more questions came his way.

McCloud relaxed a little. 'Let's hope we all have the luxury of time to see things turn out for the best.' He put down his knife and fork. 'What do you think about global warming?'

Jim looked up from his steak – it was a lot smaller now than it had been when it first arrived. 'I don't know,' he said. 'The world's been warming for ten thousand years, right, since the ice age ended. I'm pretty glad there's no glacier in north London any more.'

McCloud was fizzing again.

Jim went on, 'I mean, the sea has come up, like, three hundred feet since then, and that's pretty good. If it hadn't the UK would still be part of France.' His joke didn't seem to have gone down very well. 'What I don't understand is why islands like the Maldives are only a few feet above sea level. Were they poking up three hundred out of the water in 8000 BC?'

'The coral grows faster than the water rises,' said Cardini, quietly.

'Ah,' said Jim, 'that explains it. Someone needs to tell them that. They seem to be really worried over there about getting flooded.'

'But not if you concrete over your goddamn island,' said McCloud.

'Right,' said Jim.

McCloud was shaking his head. 'You're not a nature lover, are you, Jim?'

'I love nature,' said Jim. He held his fork up. 'This bit of it tastes just great.' He hoped that would get a laugh, but it didn't. He felt suddenly angry. 'Look, Howard. I don't think nature is better than people. That's kind of a fundamental for me.' He shook his head. 'You think the end of the world is coming because you're getting confused. The end of the world *is* coming – but for you, not the rest of us, not yet anyway. The world's not going to die, Howard, you are.' Jim regretted pointing his fork at McCloud but it was too late by the time he'd done it. 'It's the end of the line for you, Howard, not the planet.'

McCloud let out what might have been a laugh. 'We'll see,' he said, suddenly looking certain about something and pleased.

'Howard has a baseball team,' interjected Cardini. 'Do you follow baseball, Jim?'

Jim was bemused by the sudden change of subject. 'Hell, no,' he said, influenced by all the Americans he had ever spoken with.

'Pity,' said McCloud. 'It's the greatest game.'

Thank Heaven, thought Jim. Maybe they'd cheer up now.

45

Renton sat by the glass case and watched the bald rat shivering in the far corner. The mosquitoes were all over it and drinking. Others, having fed, had taken to their perches and hung there upside-down, red and bloated. He loved watching them feed. Eat, reproduce, die – that was all they did. Now that pointless cycle had a bigger purpose, to clear the world's tropical realms of a much larger parasite, which, like the mosquito, would mindlessly kill its host.

The mosquito's proboscis was an object of enchantment to him. He got an almost sexual buzz as it penetrated the white flesh of the rodent. It was like watching a thousand tiny deaths inflicted by innumerable miniature stilettos. The insect was so beautiful, so perfectly designed for its purpose of feeding on the mighty, draining and poisoning them.

He had been sitting there for two hours watching the tiny spectacle, the beginning of the end for five billion people. He was loading the insects with Ebola, something to kick off the initial plague, an accelerator for the process, a mathematical guarantor of epidemic. The true killer, however, was the breeding aggression of these engineered mosquitoes. They were male, irresistible to females, and carried all the genes necessary to reproduce their breeding proclivities as well as their flaw: the regurgitation of their last meal, the poisoned blood of their hosts.

Just like the dirty hypodermic syringes that had done for so many in the past, the mosquito would spread disease to all it bit. Its release would be the tiny spark on the dry haystack of mankind, a vast tinderbox. His action would turn the desert back into virgin jungle, savannah and plain.

He would soon be a god, a dark Ajax who would deliver the scourging message of pestilence. Where there was malaria, there would soon be plagues untold. Into all of the hideous places where man heaved in heat and filth, the first horseman would ride unchecked and scythe them down. Then the northern people would be left to a pristine world released from inevitable ecological collapse that would otherwise destroy civilisation.

His palms were sweaty as he watched, and he bobbed up and down on the raised stool.

46

They sat in a corner of a huge bar area by the window. Jim marvelled that, although it was staffed with a barman and a waitress, and they were clearly the only customers in a hundred square miles, the service was still slow even though the owner was sitting beside them.

When their drinks arrived, McCloud got up. 'Got to make a call,' he said.

As soon as he was out of earshot, Jim sat forward. 'Does your TRT make people paranoid and depressed?'

'No,' said Cardini. 'At least, not to my knowledge.'

'Is Howard always like that? You know, it's the end of the world.'

'Ever since I've known him,' said Cardini, quietly. 'He has two people collecting evidence of imminent collapse. Of course, if you search far and wide for evidence that fits your world view, you'll find enough to entrench yourself in your hypothesis. Then again, he may be correct. Humanity has ebbed and flowed many times in its short history but never before has it put such strain on the resources of its environment. As you know, I am not optimistic about the outcome if things are left unchecked. '

'Have you seen his evidence?' asked Jim 'You're a scientist so you'd know if it hung together.'

'Newspaper articles,' said Cardini, frowning. 'Popular science clippings, YouTube videos ...' He made YouTube sound like a six-syllable word. 'People always agree with data that is aligned with their own belief, whatever the source. However, bad science and even delusion is no guarantee that the outcome of a flawed hypothesis will not be as its adherents suggest.'

'So what do you believe?'

'I believe, Jim, in my work. Environmental collapse will come unless something is done, and I am confident that progress will be achieved through population control.'

'So you don't believe in a runaway climate event.'

'I think over the next few years mankind will come up with a solution to the world's population crisis.' He smiled. 'It may be unorthodox but I'm hopeful it will strike ...' he let the word hang in the air '... the right balance.'

McCloud was striding towards them. 'Got so much catching up to do,' he said. 'You lie on ya death bed for too long and all the work starts to build up.'

'I hope you are duly impressed by my results,' said Cardini.

'Yes,' said Jim.

'Impressed by what?' said McCloud.

'Your recovery.'

'You know something, Cardini,' said McCloud, 'now you've got Jimbo to fund you, I need to renegotiate what I'm laying out to you. I want to cut that by half.'

'I'm afraid that won't do,' said Cardini, 'unless you want to lower your consumption of the serum by half.'

'How about some economies of scale here?' protested McCloud.

'There are none,' said Cardini, flatly. 'The whole point is to use Jim's investment for yet further research. Without significant strides, the future remains uncertain. For instance, I know you wish to be thirty again. It may take me a century to achieve such results. With luck, Jim's investment will allow me to push back your core age by ten years, which in itself would be an important step, most of all for you.'

'You're smooth, Cardini, but I'm not falling for ya silver tongue.'

'Howard, why are you trying to negotiate?' asked Jim. 'Aren't you just happy to be alive?'

'No, son,' said McCloud, shaking his head. 'Never have been and never will be.'

'It's getting pretty late for me,' said Jim. 'I'm five hours ahead so it's like three in the morning in my head.' He got up. 'I'm going to crash.'

'You know where to go?' asked McCloud.

'I think I can find it,' said Jim. 'It's kind of back there, around the corner and down that way ...' He was waving his hand around as he spoke.

'That should get you there.'

Jim got up. 'Night,' he said.

47

A helicopter was droning over Jim's head. Was he asleep in the jungle? Was he heading towards a volcano?

He sat up in the huge bed in total darkness. Which way up was he? Where was the door? Where was he? He struggled for what seemed a long time and then remembered. He reached across the bed and switched on the light. A helicopter was doing something outside – landing, he thought.

Jim was suddenly very awake.

McCloud met Dario straight off the landing pad. The helicopter was lifting off before they were even inside the mansion. 'Thanks for coming out on such short notice, my friend,' he said, patting the man on the back.

'It's always a pleasure to see you,' said Dario. 'How you been?'

'Getting back into shape,' said McCloud.

'You're looking great.'

'Thank you.' He looked Dario up and down as they walked. 'I can see you've been packing it on.'

'Pure muscle,' said Dario, his New Jersey accent jarring to McCloud's Southern ear.

'How are the kids?'

'Good, you know, growing up. The youngest is getting so tall, she's looking down at me now.'

'Hey, that's cool, isn't it?'

'So, what problem can I solve for you tonight?'

'Let's get to my office so we can talk.'

'Sure thing.'

McCloud's office was small in comparison to the grotesque size of everything else in his palace. It was a compact and cosy room, with a shelf of show books, a window behind his desk with a view of the mountains and two walls of photos showing McCloud with just about every important American on the A-list of rich, famous and/or powerful over the preceding forty years. His favourite was of him towering over Martin Luther King, shaking his hand. It had been a pure fluke that it had happened but it had opened many doors. He could have collected stamps or racehorses; instead he collected Impressionist paintings and famous people. He hung both on his walls.

As far as he was concerned, those people were there to drive his passion for autographs, not on photos or in books but on contracts. He had built his fortune by getting ink at the end of important documents and for that he had to know everyone of power and talent in all walks of life, from the arts, sport, politics and science. He had made it his priority in business. That was how he had discovered Cardini and stayed alive long past his normal span. It was how he had become a friend of Dario and how he had found a way to make the really difficult people in his life simply disappear.

'You smoke, don't you, Dario?' he said, lifting a heavy ashtray from its place on the bookshelf.

'Sorry to say I do.'

'Don't let me stop you,' said McCloud. 'This is an old-fashioned establishment.' He put the ashtray on the coffee-table, and sat in the single armchair next to the other man.

Dario snapped open the gold lighter with a click and inhaled. 'Thanks,' he said. 'It was a long flight.' He shook his head. 'For a smoker like me, anyways.'

'I have a problem guest upstairs and I want him checked out.'

Dario took a long puff. 'Now I could take that either of three ways, Mr McCloud, and I always like to be clear. "Checked out" could mean "asked to leave", "looked into" or …' he took a quick puff '… "killed". I don't want to kill a guest of yours if all you want me to do is investigate him.'

McCloud nodded. 'I understand. By "checked out", I mean as in a ticket attached to his big toe in the morgue. Let's just say he's a competitor who's a threat to one of my monopolies. You know how I hate competition.'

'OK,' said Dario, stubbing out his half-smoked cigarette.

'And I'm coming with you. I want to see the look on his face when he knows he's finished. Then I want to see him beg. Then I want to see him die.'

'OK,' said Dario, getting up, not the slightest bit perturbed.

'Once we're done we can throw his body in the bio-gas generator. We're real eco-friendly here.'

'OK,' said Dario. 'I'll follow you.'

'First we need to pick up another friend.'

At a knock, Cardini opened the door to his suite a crack. It was McCloud. Cardini looked at him questioningly for a moment.

'Put your pants on, Chris. We've got a meeting to attend.' The door flew wide and a small, strong, thuggish man pushed into Cardini's room.

McCloud followed. 'While you're getting dressed, Chris, I got to tell you I need another shot of that medicine before we go any further.'

'No,' said Cardini. 'I have told you many times before, overdose will later set your core age forwards. You burn the candle at both ends and you will suffer accordingly.'

'I need more.'

Cardini fastened his trousers and reached for his shirt, which was neatly folded on a table by the window.

'I'll ask Dario here to help me,' added McCloud.

Dario pulled out a small revolver from under his arm.

'You're not going to shoot me,' boomed Cardini. 'I keep you alive. Not even you are that mad.'

'I don't have to shoot you,' said Dario, slightly put off by the authority in Cardini's statement. 'Do you know how many bones there are in a human body?'

'Yes,' snapped Cardini. 'I am fully aware of how many bones there are in the human body.'

'Well, unless you give Mr McCloud what he wants I'll start cracking some.'

Cardini looked down his nose at the short Italian. The TRT regenerated the body's tissues but not the bones to the same extent. Underneath the vigorous organs, the muscle and nerves, they remained weak and vulnerable. 'Very well,' he said, putting on his shirt. 'But you have been warned, Howard, and the consequences when they occur will be on your head and on yours alone.' He rummaged in his bag and took out an ampoule. 'This is all I have.'

McCloud took the glass capsule and flicked the end off it. He put the open end in his mouth and sucked in the juice. 'Argh.' He sat on the end of the bed and stared at the floor.

Cardini was putting on his jacket. 'What now?' he said.

'Just give me a minute,' said McCloud.

'Is he OK?' asked Dario.

Cardini didn't reply.

McCloud jumped up. 'OK, let's do this. Let's go down the hall and pay the punk a visit.' He took a swipe card from his pocket with a grin on his lined face. 'Trick or treat!'

'What do you plan to do?'

'Just shut up and watch.'

McCloud strode off, the others following. When they came to the door of Jim's room, he stuck the card into the lock mechanism. There was a twitter and a green LED flashed. Dario opened the door with his left hand, the pistol in his right. He hit the light and charged in. He veered off to the bathroom and barged in. 'Damn,' he said, coming out.

McCloud was looking around. 'Check the wardrobes and the balcony.'

There was a pause. Then: 'Nothing. Wherever he is, he isn't here.'

'Well, I know how we can find him.'

48

Jim looked at the double doors that separated the front office from the back stage of the huge building. Like a hotel, casino or restaurant, portals separated the consumer from the service areas. Doors segregated the plush from the Spartan, the idle from the functional, the spotless from the grubby, the loved from the loathed. He wanted to know what made this place tick.

He walked through the doors and saw three parked Segways. He fired one up and began to ride down the hallways setting off the lighting units one by one. The building was cavernous, its corridors monotonous and empty.

He came across a great lift, stopped and summoned it. When its doors opened, it was big enough to take a small truck. The floor rattled metallically as he rolled inside. He looked at the control panel. 'This place goes down nine levels,' he muttered. 'Wow. Well, let's start at the bottom and work our way up.'

The lift began to descend. What would you keep nine storeys below ground? Perhaps he'd find a giant swimming-pool or even a bowling alley. Why not a shooting range? With so many gun nuts in the US, what could be a more natural feature for a man like McCloud? He was rich enough to have his own personal baseball pitch down there. For a moment Jim imagined a skating rink. Or the world's biggest train set, a scale reproduction of all the railways in America laid out like some Disney attraction on steroids.

The lift halted and the doors opened. He drove out.

'Fuck me.' He rolled out into what looked like a giant warehouse. Rows and rows of racking towered up to a ceiling a hundred feet above. He drove forwards, lights flashing on in waves as he sped into the giant space. He reached the end of the aisle and set off down a parallel row. About halfway along he stopped the Segway, got off and went to a rack. He looked at the white sacks. 'Sugar?' he muttered.

49

McCloud opened the control-room door with his pass card and strode in. It was in darkness, save for the bank of screens taking their video feeds. Twelve panels were playing the drama-less events outside and within the building. The screens were empty.

Jimenez, the security operator, was fast asleep in his chair, snoring loudly.

McCloud put on the lights and looked unhappily at Cardini, who did not respond. He went to Jimenez, jammed his foot under one of the chair's castors, heaved, and Jimenez fell to the floor, waking with a yelp. He looked around, dazed. 'Oh, Mr McCloud,' he said, half crouching, 'you surprised me.' His eyes focused on Cardini and the hulking outline of Dario behind him. 'Is anything the matter?' He picked up his chair awkwardly.

McCloud seemed ready to hit him. Instead he said, 'Jim Evans, where is he?'

Jimenez scrambled back into his chair. 'I'll check the logs. It won't take me long to find him.' He hit some keys on his console. 'In warehouse five,' he said. He glanced at McCloud's furious expression, looked back at his screen and tapped. He pointed up to the top array of three monitors. A light was on off-screen but Evans was not in view. Jimenez clicked with his mouse and the central screen pulled up a picture of him Segwaying down an aisle.

McCloud looked at the screen, then grabbed Jimenez by the arm. 'Now close the whole system down and delete the last twenty-four hours of files and directories, in addition to the bedroom-floor streams I asked you to shut down earlier. Once I've seen you do it, I'm going to give you ten minutes to get your hide out of here or you'll be sorry you hung around.'

Jimenez typed fast. The screens blinked out. 'Done,' he said.

'Show me.'

'Here, look, the directory's empty.'

'I said kill the directories too.'

Jimenez typed with incredible speed. 'See? Gone,' he panted.

McCloud peered over his shoulder. He knew the system: he had trawled the videos on many occasions in the past. 'OK,' he confirmed.

McCloud took the pass from around Jimenez's neck and threw it to Dario. 'Now git,' he said, stepping back to give Jimenez a route to the door.

Jimenez jumped to his feet. 'Yes, sir,' he said, watching Dario from the corner of his eye. He stumbled towards the door, flinching as he passed Dario. He pressed the button that operated the door release and yanked it open, went out and pulled it smartly closed behind him.

'Should I go deal with him?' said Dario.

'No,' said McCloud. 'He won't cause any trouble. Let's get on down to that warehouse.'

50

Jim jumped back on the Segway and drove. There seemed to be acre upon acre of food, but a grey shadow drew him to the far side of the space. 'Holy cow,' he muttered. 'Guns.' He stopped. Each rack had an example gun on display and behind it dozens of boxes or crates. There were rifles, pistols, RPGs, five-millimetre sniper cannons, machine guns, mortars and mines. There were also tons of ammunition. He looked towards the far wall. 'Hummers,' he murmured. 'Military Humvees.'

He ran back to the Segway and jumped on, riding further down the canyon of armaments. He stopped and stared at the line of hardened vehicles. He was standing in an arsenal, looking at the provisioning for the army that would use it. McCloud really was prepared for the apocalypse, ready to hold off the marauding hordes with more than just a gate and a long driveway.

He turned around and set off back the way he had come. The sooner he was out of McCloud's asylum the better.

There was a distant flash as lighting came on far away at the entrance. He slowed. Someone was there.

51

Jim was preparing what he would say to whoever was waiting for him by the lift. If it was a staff member, he would try to bluff. A friendly 'hello' would be a good opener, and it would soon become apparent whether or not he was in hot water. Or if, after all, no one was there to meet him, perhaps he should stay on the Segway and ride on out of the complex.

The Segway was fully charged and he thought it would take him twenty miles. That was enough to get him to the highway. He accelerated to the machine's top speed. He wondered about zigzagging across the huge warehouse, snaking his way towards the lift to appear alongside it, but with the lights switching on and off above him he'd hardly surprise whoever was waiting there for him. If he popped up beside them, rather than riding the last couple of hundred yards in full view, it was unlikely to make any difference to their reaction.

He rounded the final corner and looked down the concourse. There were three figures. Two he recognised as McCloud and Cardini but the third was unfamiliar. He waved at them and, when he was near enough, called, 'Evening.'

The third character was a thug. Jim could see that at a hundred paces. Not all thugs were bad people but in general they had only one purpose in life: to hurt someone. It had already occurred to Jim that McCloud might react badly to him traipsing all over his secret militia cache. After all, a man planning for the final battle was not going to have the most balanced reaction to someone uncovering his bizarre schemes.

The thug in black sparked a cascade of what-ifs in Jim's mind. At least Cardini was there. McCloud couldn't have planned anything too drastic with the English professor as audience and witness; that would be a shade too crazy even for McCloud.

It wasn't long before he found out how the cards would fall.

52

'Pretty amazing place you've got down here,' called Jim, jumping off the Segway and trotting up to them.

McCloud was furious and agitated. 'Had a good look, have you?' he said aggressively.

'Yes, thanks,' said Jim, and saw McCloud give the thug a nod. It was one of those nods that meant trouble.

The thug moved his hand, like a cowboy bringing his hand up to the pistol handle on his holster. There was no hip holster but the initial movement was the same, even though the hand was travelling inside his jacket for the pistol under his arm. He was watching for McCloud's signal, and McCloud was clearly enjoying commanding his executioner to step into action. Only Cardini was watching Jim, his eyes cold and his face impassive.

Jim had learnt never to hesitate at such an instant. You had to strike first and without warning. You did not entertain doubt; you did not take a second thought. If there was a chance that a fight would start, you had to finish it before it began.

The thug saw the first blow coming and just got a block in, instinctively reeling back to avoid the next. This was already on its way and landed a split second later, as did the third and fourth. Jim shot five punches into his stomach in the next second, four more to his head in a blur of fists that made even Cardini step back.

The thug collapsed as if he'd been shot. Jim straightened up, suddenly surprised at himself and the savagery of his attack. The man was shaking on the ground, a sickening croak rasping from his mouth.

'Swallowed his tongue, no doubt,' observed Cardini, stiffly, as

Jim gazed down at the convulsing body.

Jim bent to help the stricken figure – and a blow to his temple sent him skidding to one side. He spun round bent double, his vision blurred, his head pulsing. He took a guard and squinted at McCloud coming forwards at him. 'For fuck's sake,' he said, 'help that guy, he's choking to death.'

'I'm going to beat the crap out of you,' hissed McCloud.

Cardini was bending down to the quivering figure, whose croaks were dying away.

'Then I'm going to kill you.'

Cardini wasn't helping the thug: he was feeling inside his jacket.

'Then I'm going to burn your body and piss on your ashes.'

Jim was backing away, buying time for his head to clear. His eyes were getting their focus again. A primitive desire to say something bubbled inside him, but he bottled it up and focused yet more tightly on McCloud.

'Stop this,' called Cardini, suddenly, flourishing a revolver he had extracted from the prostrate man.

'Put it down, Chris,' spat McCloud, moving towards Jim. 'You ain't going to shoot either of us.'

McCloud was no longer the infirm old man Jim had met just a few hours ago. Now he was all puffed up and red, like a weight-lifter posing for a competition. His angry face seemed swollen and distorted, veins standing out on his skull.

'This is madness,' shouted Cardini. 'Stop it immediately.'

Jim stood still.

McCloud eyed him with a wicked smile. He stepped forward and swung a right. Jim blocked it with his left and drove his right fist onto the point of McCloud's chin. The old man's head snapped back and before Jim's next blow had arrived his body was already falling backwards, his head twisted to one side at an unnatural angle. It hit the concrete with an ugly crack.

Jim looked down at the lifeless McCloud, then at Cardini, who trained the pistol on him. 'You've killed him,' Cardini said.

He looked at the thug. 'You've killed them both.' Fear flickered in his eyes.

'You could have saved that guy.'

'Yes, I could,' said Cardini. 'But to what purpose?' He pointed at McCloud. 'That fool, on the other hand, had his uses.' He strode to McCloud's body, still training the pistol on Jim, and rolled the head from side to side. 'Yes,' he said, 'as I guessed. The body of a forty-year-old held up by the skeleton of a ninety-year-old. You snapped his neck.'

Jim didn't seem shocked, and a shiver of panic shot through Cardini. He tightened his aim.

Jim took a step towards him. 'Give me the gun, Professor.'

Cardini drew himself to his full height.

'Don't make me have to take it.'

'Stop,' commanded Cardini.

'It's on safety, you idiot,' said Jim, darting forward and wrenching it from Cardini's grasp.

Cardini gasped in pain and hugged his arm to his chest. 'I wouldn't have shot you,' he said, noticing how familiarly Jim handled the firearm.

'I know,' said Jim, 'but guns are dangerous, especially in the hands of someone who doesn't know what he's doing.' And it wasn't on safety. He flicked a switch on the pistol, then looked down at the thug. He imagined the agony of choking to death on his own tongue. It must be a most horrible way to die.

'You could have saved that guy,' he said again.

Cardini didn't reply.

'You're on your own,' said Jim. He trotted back to the Segway and jumped on, heading for the lift. His DNA would be all over the scene but so would a lot of other people's. The bottom line was, he had several friends where it counted and if anyone put him on the spot he would simply tell the truth. The set-up would speak for itself.

The lift closed, and as it rose, he thought about the Humvees. They must be able to drive out of the underground complex.

The chances were that one of the floors near ground level would lead out of the building. He looked at the lift panel again. 'G' appeared just below '1'. He hit the button. Was that G for 'Ground' or 'Garage'?

The space beyond was dark. As he stepped out, the lights tripped on. It was indeed a garage, empty but for a dozen black Town Cars. He hopped on to the Segway and drove over to the vehicles. There was a metal box on the wall with a clipboard below, the paper attached to it half filled with logs. Inside the box, the keys were neatly lined up and identified. No need for petty security inside a castle, he thought.

He matched a bunch of keys with a black limo and walked quickly over to it. He got in and turned the key without starting the engine. The petrol gauge flicked up and floated to 'full'. He took the pistol from his pocket and dropped it onto the front passenger seat, fired up the big engine and pulled out of the parking space, checking the armrest for a gate key. There was a black box in the visor – the key? He drove round the garage, following the tyre marks left by others on the smooth concrete, to the up ramp and a barrier. He edged forward.

It didn't open.

He stopped. There was a post with a grey device on it. He took the black box from the visor and waved it frantically at the device, then flipped it over and waved it some more. A green light went on and the barrier rose. He sighed with relief, the prospect of Segwaying miles into the dark banished. He accelerated up the ramp and out of a portal in the side of the massive building.

He wondered how far he would have to go before he had a mobile signal he could use. As soon as he was connected to the world he would be so much safer. He drove along the winding road that led to the highway. It seemed interminably long. At the end of it, he remembered, there was a gatehouse. Somehow he had to get past it. He could stick the gun into the guard's face, of course, but he'd save that for a last resort. Perhaps the transmitter in the car that he had used in the garage would open the gatehouse barrier. After all, the gatehouse was to stop people entering, not leaving. Anyone inside was already trusted. He shook his head. He had to be ready for more problems.

He wondered if he was heading in the right direction. He had been driving for what seemed like a very long time. Perhaps he was on his way further into McCloud's wilderness rather than back to the highway. He kept going. As long as the road stayed perfect he would carry on down it.

He came round a hilly bend and let out a little cry of relief. There was the gatehouse.

The transmitter didn't seem to work and the guard was opening his window. Jim buzzed down his. 'Going out for cigarettes,' he said. 'Your boss doesn't keep my brand.'

'Sure,' said the guard. 'Let me call the house.'

'At this fucking time?' snapped Jim. 'You want to piss me and everyone else off?' He gave the guard the hairy eyeball. 'I'm in a hurry to get my fix, so press the fucking button.' He was thinking about the exact position of the pistol. His hand flew out of the window and he was pointing something at the guard. The guard recoiled, then saw what Jim was holding: a hundred-dollar bill. 'Take it and do us all a favour.'

The guard said, 'No problem, Mr Evans, that's not necessary.' The barrier went up.

'That's OK,' said Jim. 'Have it anyway.'

The guard took it from him. 'That's mighty generous of you, sir. The freakin' control centre ain't answering, as usual. Bozos!'

Jim acknowledged him with a grin then, buzzing up his window, drove under the raised barrier.

53

Will hadn't spent many months in his own bed: his work with the US military took him from one place to another. Sometimes it was a hotspot, sometimes it was a backwater but wherever it was he would know he'd be on his way somewhere else in a few months.

Since his posting back to Virginia he had got used to the pleasures of home and family. He absolutely did not miss the action or excitement. On Sundays when the family went to church, he actually prayed he would never again be called away from home. It was a possible outcome and he did all he could to make it happen.

At home he let very little disturb him and his mobile took few calls after midnight. Only a dozen people jumped past silent mode and Jim Evans was one of them. In certain circles the Brit had become a legend and he was just the kind of close connection to make Will's presence in Langley that little bit more sustainable. As he answered his mobile he hoped Jim wasn't going to ask him about Jane.

'Will, I'm in a bit of deep shit,' came Jim's voice. 'I need your help. I take it I've still got plenty of good karma with you.'

'A shedload.'

'Good, because Howard McCloud, the satellite guy, is dead in his compound in South Carolina. He's lying in about a million square feet of his own personal military arsenal – mortars, small artillery, machine-guns, Humvees, the lot. There's more hardware under his mansion than it'd take to invade Cuba.'

Jim was talking fast and Will had to concentrate hard to understand his thick London accent.

'OK,' Jim went on, 'so I'm exaggerating a little bit but not too much. His whole estate is some kind of survivalist wet dream.'

'OK,' said Will. 'And?'

'Well, you guys should get down there fast because McCloud's got all sorts of connections and his set-up is going to make a lot of important people extremely embarrassed. No way is his shit legal. You might want to tidy it all up very fast.'

'What's your story?'

'Let's just say I'm alive while McCloud and one of his goons are brown bread.'

'Brown bread?'

'Brown bread, dead.'

Will was sat upright in bed, his wife turning restlessly next to him. 'So what's the narrative on this?'

'Will,' said Jim, suddenly sounding exhausted. 'Get your people down there. If or when you need more from me, just call.'

'You OK, Jim?'

'In the circumstances I'd say very well indeed. Got to drive.'

Jim hung up. His next call was to Stafford. 'Got to get out of here,' he said. 'I need to get back to the UK quick.'

54

Renton sat hunched forward, looking intently into the glass case. Catching a mosquito was no easy matter, even if it was feeding on a rat that he was holding down with his other hand. The blue rubber gloves, the gateway into the cage, were very thick and made the job yet more difficult, but the thick latex layer was what stood between him and the little flying syringes that, given the opportunity, would land on him and stick their feeding hoses through his skin.

Not that he would mind being fed on by a mosquito. It didn't hurt and he had watched it many times on himself with a kind of fascination. Under magnification it was exciting to see his own blood being drawn up into the tiny mindless creature. These mosquitoes, though, were feeding on a reservoir of rat blood infected with disease. Each insect was a little bio-weapon, primed with a terrible payload. In this case the disease was Ebola, a haemorrhagic fever that killed at least half of all those infected.

He was looking forward now to when they were freed, to swarm and breed, infect and multiply, then pick up other blood-borne diseases that they would spread onwards wherever they flew. The range was important: there was no point in him and Cardini killing everyone, including themselves, with their creation. These mosquitoes would be unable to travel beyond the current malaria belt, leaving the northern world untouched. It would be the hot primitive lands of the developing world that were struck. They would again become the fallow lands of Earth, the lungs of the planet. These once pristine continents so nearly destroyed by man would return to nature, leaving the north the benefit of a cleansed environment, with three-quarters of humanity gone from the disfigured face of the globe.

The mosquito was crushed by the tweezers. Renton groaned in annoyance. He shifted his grip on the almost lifeless rat and lined up the tweezers to pluck another insect from its hairless pink skin. His hand trembled slightly as he grasped the specimen.

They were all males, engineered to be ferocious in their reproduction. They were bigger and stronger, selected from hundreds of generations for their reproductive proclivities, then engineered yet further to dominate their species. But on top of this, he and Cardini had laid a flaw, the weakness that made them the first horseman: a broken digestion. Cardini had copied the vector that had slain half the world in the Middle Ages, the mechanism of the Black Death.

The vomit of insects was pestilential.

The Mongol hordes had brought the Black Death from Mongolia. The marmots there had carried the disease from the beginning of time and fleas had jumped from animal to man, killing him with the sickness they carried. Unprepared for the Mongol or the Black Death, medieval Europe had reeled. The flea, sick itself with bubonic bacteria, regurgitated its last meal as it tried to feed and hence infected its host. In a world that was covered with a layer of filth, the fleas became tiny angels of death.

Cardini had applied that lesson to the mosquito, an animal with a defined range, yet unstoppable where it still lived. In a few short years it would leave the world a place worth living in, a planet with a future.

Renton slipped the insect into the square container with the other specimens. When he had thirteen in the box, he would stow it and move on to the other cases: glass tanks that contained rats infected with newly prepared West Nile virus and equine encephalitis, commonly known as sleeping sickness.

He smiled to himself. In a way, loading the mosquitoes was unnecessary: without the prepared diseases, they would pick up and spread all those that they and their offspring drank. Yet the more sparks there were on the haystack of humanity, the faster the blaze would take hold and the higher the inferno would flame.

55

If Jim could have seen himself pacing around the gate area of the small landing strip in North Carolina he would have advised himself to sit down and look less suspicious. His jet was heading towards the airstrip. No matter how agitated he got, it was not going to arrive a minute earlier.

On the one hand he wanted to stay behind and sort the situation out, but on the other, the prospect of sitting for months in a US jail while facts were untangled was unthinkable. He had enough friends in high places, but it was clear that he would be better off explaining what had to be explained from the UK side of the Atlantic.

Will hadn't called him back and he wasn't sure whether that was good or bad. His phone was on, so if Will wanted him picked up, his guys would know exactly where Jim was. That was enough for him not to feel too bad about getting directly out of Dodge: they could grab him if they wanted to.

Whenever he heard a vehicle, he expected a posse of police cars to sweep into sight and someone like Will to get out and arrest him. But they didn't appear. Occasional light aircraft came and went, maintenance trucks mooched around on their day-to-day business, and that was all.

The sight of his G5 coming in to land was a huge relief, but he wouldn't be happy until he was aboard. Even then he'd still be dreading the thought of what was to follow. At the very least there would be months or even years of trouble, a cycle of legal worries churning on without a conclusion in sight.

The choking rasp of the guy he had felled echoed in his head. He could feel McCloud shattering at the end of his fist. Those sounds and sensations would take a long time to fade.

He watched the jet taxi on the apron. What the hell had the fiasco been about? What was Cardini doing now? What had McCloud planned to do to him? Kill him? Why? Because Jim was a threat to his supply of TRT?

He walked smartly towards the plane as the stairs dropped down. He heard footsteps behind him, trotting quickly towards him. He turned sharply, but it was only airport staff getting up to speed on the arrival. 'Get her refuelled as fast as possible,' he said to the captain, who met him at the top of the steps. 'We've got to be on our way, pronto.'

'Roger,' said the captain, flashing his oversized smile. 'We can refuel in the British Virgin Islands if you like.'

'Do it,' said Jim.

He slumped into a chair by a porthole overlooking the private terminal. Any minute now he would see a squadron of police careering in. He was praying his shedload of karma was going to be enough.

56

Stafford's right knee was giving him a bit of trouble so he'd brought his shooting stick to the ha-ha and now sat on it heavily.

Right on time, there was Lady Arabella on her hunter, cantering around the field. Something in the far right-hand corner of his vision piqued his attention. He looked towards it without moving his head. A giant wood pigeon was gliding towards the tree to his right. How unfortunate for it, he thought, snapping the breech of his shotgun. The stupid bird had flown at the wrong time and in the wrong direction.

Stafford had no desire to kill it, but he could hardly keep up his pretence of hunting if he let another pest float by him in full view of Lady Arabella. He raised the gun and fired, the pigeon falling a few feet from him. Suddenly another was on its way towards him. 'Good grief,' he muttered. He fired again and the second bird fell obligingly close to the first. He broke the shotgun gently so the cartridge did not fly and took the cases out carefully, putting them in his pocket. He reloaded but left the gun broken.

'Top shot,' said Arabella, still some yards away, her high, clear voice carrying to him through the still air.

Stafford gave a little bow. 'I think perhaps pigeon pie is now on the menu,' he said.

'Does your Mr Evans have you shoot his dinner for him?' she asked. 'How very economical.' She smiled.

'On occasion.'

'Perhaps I should invite him to sample some of our estate's produce.' The horse stood perfectly still under her.

'I'm sure he would be delighted.'

She studied him for what felt like a long time. 'You're interesting, Stafford,' she said. 'Yes. In your way you're almost as mysterious as Mr Evans.'

'I can't see how,' said Stafford, more than a little flustered.

'Good day,' she said, giving him a sideways look as she lightly pushed the horse onwards.

He watched her go, then collected the two birds. He would clean them and send them over to her.

57

Jim was on his way back and Stafford could tell from the message he had left that all was not well. He was therefore somewhat distracted when a car came up the drive and the familiar figure of Superintendent Smith got out. 'What's he doing here?' Stafford said aloud, and headed for the front door.

He opened it as Smith reached the steps.

'Well, well, well,' said Stafford. 'What brings you here?'

'You, as a matter of fact,' said Smith, his voice spiced with a hint of sarcasm. 'Saving your skin as always.' He skipped athletically up the worn stone staircase. 'Can I come in?'

'Of course. I take it it's about the package I despatched.'

'Yes.'

'I'm glad they've sent you, old chap.'

Smith strode into the grand hall and had a quick look around. 'We need to know right away where those samples you sent to Porton Down came from,' he said, after his quick survey. 'Is Jim about?'

'No,' said Stafford. 'He's flying back from America as we speak.'

Smith nodded. 'OK.'

'Right,' said Stafford. 'Wait here while I fetch the gal.' He turned on his heel and headed off.

So this was Jim's new pad, he thought. Very nice. Jim had once tried to give him ten million pounds as a present. He had just laughed and handed it back. 'Go on,' Jim had said. 'I'd be dead twice over if it wasn't for you.'

Smith had smiled rather grimly. 'It might not be a fortune to you, Jim, but it would kill my reason to be alive. I've got to have something pushing me to get out of bed in the morning. With ten mil I'd buy myself a big armchair and a tanker of whisky and drink till I rotted away.'

Jim had hopped up and down in frustration – it had made Smith's day. 'Well, consider it banked,' he'd said. 'So long as I've got it, it's yours.'

The hall walls were covered with fine old paintings and other ancient decorations. He found it hard even to contemplate what it all cost to keep up. You needed to be extremely rich to maintain premises like these, but Jim was a lot wealthier than that. 'It's another world,' he nearly said, as Stafford arrived with a pretty young woman in tow.

'Superintendent Smith, this is Kate,' he said, standing to attention. 'Kate, this is Superintendent Smith from Counter-terrorism Command.'

'Hello,' she said.

'It was Kate who came by the samples,' continued Stafford.

'Good to meet you,' said Smith. 'And where, may I ask, did you come by them?'

Kate's face was burning and she could tell she had gone bright red. 'Professor Cardini's lab in Cambridge.'

'It's far more complicated than that,' said Stafford. 'Kate was attacked there by some kind of mad lab technician. He followed her here.'

Kate was nodding and trying to watch them both closely at the same time.

Smith's head was bowed forward, his arms behind his back. 'Can you take me straight to where you got them?' he asked, lifting his face and peering at her intently.

'Yes,' she said.

'We'd better get going then, right away. I have half of Porton Down waiting on the road outside.' He turned to Stafford. 'Some of them will want to come in here and check everything. The rest will follow us.'

Smith put one hand on Stafford's left shoulder, the other on Kate's right. 'There's a medic in my car and he will inoculate you both immediately,' he told them.

'Against what?' asked Kate.

'Everything,' said Smith.

Kate went pale.

'Are you OK?' asked Smith, gently.

'Yes,' she said.

'We should get going then.' Smith threw a glance at Stafford, then led the way to the door. 'Is Jim involved in this?' he asked over his shoulder.

'To no great extent,' replied Stafford.

'I'll take that as a yes, then.'

58

From the car window, Kate watched the countryside rushing by. She turned to Smith. 'I'm scared,' she said.

'I don't blame you,' he replied. 'Helping us like this is incredibly brave.'

'I don't feel brave,' she said.

'But you are,' said Smith.

'I'm kind of excited too,' she said, laughing nervously.

'So am I,' said Smith, 'excited and scared. You can't beat the feeling.'

Kate shifted in her seat. 'What happens when we find Renton?'

'Hopefully your nasty lab assistant will be under arrest before we get there. They'll be tracking him down right now.'

'And if they don't find him?'

'Well, we'll go into the lab and you'll take us to his bit of it and see if he's there. I'll go ahead with my officers and you'll be at the back directing us.' He smiled. 'It sounds dramatic but it isn't in practice. We won't be breaking any doors down.'

'Superintendent,' called Stafford, from the front seat. 'I take it local officers can't investigate the labs before we get there because of the nature of the potential biohazard.'

'That's right,' replied Smith, watching for panic in Kate's face. 'How do you feel about that risk, Kate?'

'I've already been in his lab,' she said. 'It wasn't germs that were dangerous, it was Renton.' She sat up stiffly, suddenly resolved. 'But I'm relying on you to deal with him, OK?'

'Absolutely,' said Smith. 'If he's at the lab we need to swoop and grab him before he gets any ideas.'

Kate was scared but at the same time she seemed to be riding a wave of adrenalin. The conflicting emotions wrestled within her as the convoy charged along the country lanes, sirens shrieking all around.

Stafford seemed to know the police guy very well indeed. That was an odd relationship, a butler and a senior officer.

She had poured out her story to the superintendent. She didn't know why but she'd kept saying she was sorry, as if somehow it was her fault. He had reassured her that she was a brave and resourceful woman but that hadn't really helped. She felt weak and isolated, like someone who had set off an avalanche and was watching it sweep down the mountain towards them. None of this was her doing, but if she had done something differently, even something small, perhaps the whole mess might never have come about. She tugged at her hair. She was going to see it through with Smith and Stafford; she was going to do everything she could to make sure that Renton was caught. She was going to overcome her terror and do what had to be done to make sure she and everyone else was safe from this maniac.

59

Renton looked up at the tiny video feed window on his giant computer monitor. A line of vehicles had stopped outside the university grounds. He studied it in mild panic, then clicked on an icon, opening a series of video windows. He zoomed in on one of the vans. It had a 'hazmat' symbol on the side. He told himself not to jump to conclusions. It was almost certainly a coincidence. In a moment the convoy would set off and nothing would come of it.

As he watched, a sudden sweat broke out on his furrowed brow. He shot back in his chair as men appeared from the vehicles, some in biohazard suits. They appeared to be assembling and, as they did so, three cars passed them at speed and turned into the university. They were on to him.

He pulled out the bottom drawer of his desk and took out a small package covered with layers of clear Sellotape. He opened the top drawer, took out a scalpel, sawed it open and took out two ampoules. This was his treasure, the result of five years' devoted servitude to Cardini. Each ampoule would perhaps add a decade to his life or represent a month of heavenly bliss armed with supernormal intelligence. It was now his only escape. He opened the top drawer and took out a syringe, filling it as fast as his shaking hands allowed. They were in the building as he stabbed the needle into his neck. He pressed the serum into his blood, feeling it burning through him like acid.

He fell from his chair as the last of the liquid entered him and lay on the floor, panting. His mind raced. Perhaps so much of the elixir would kill him, just as an overdose of heroin or cocaine might. He grunted – his body felt as if it had been tipped into freezing cold water. He flipped on to his back. Every bone ached, and now a hot wave spread into his torso, as if his blood had turned to boiling metal.

His mind suddenly cleared.

They would try to take him but they were stupid and clumsy. He would overcome them as easily as any adult can outwit a child.

He jumped up and took a deep breath. 'Let's have some fun,' he said, grinning widely.

Stafford wasn't answering, so Jim gave up calling. The cab that picked him up at the airport was no substitute for a Maybach and appeared to have been modified to take people in wheel-chairs to hospital. It was less than comfortable, but Jim didn't mind that Stafford had not shown up as planned and had instead booked him a ropy old minicab. He didn't mind Stafford not answering his phone either: he was not in the mood for interaction.

He had recently killed two men with his bare hands, and a lingering self-loathing had settled on him. The world would be a better place if he sat quietly in his comfortable home and shut everything out. Maybe he should do as the previous owner of his house had done: go to bed and stay there for the rest of his life. Maybe he could become the world's next Howard Hughes, or turn into a crackpot like McCloud, addled by all the money he had almost accidentally accumulated for himself.

He looked out of the small passenger window to his left. Was it an ugly-looking day or was his mood colouring the horizon?

60

There were three policemen ahead of Smith and Kate. They looked as though they spent a large part of the day either practising controlled violence or wielding it. They rolled down the concrete stairwell in the way doormen or rugby players do.

The silence unnerved her.

Then the lights went out. There were curses.

'Hold on,' she heard Smith say, among the commotion. 'Let's get those torches on.'

She took a step back up and looked around, attempting to see something, anything, in the pitch black. She held out her arms and grasped the banister in her left hand, stepping up.

Seconds later, Smith took her right hand and led her up the stairs. She wanted to run, but he was already leading her faster than she would dare to go in the dark. She knew they had to get out of there fast.

Was it Smith's hand?

Smith turned on his flashlight and turned to Kate. She was gone.

61

'This is not the way out,' said Kate.

A door slammed behind them.

'No,' said a voice she didn't immediately recognise.

A beam of light lit Renton's face and his hand was on her mouth.

'I will slit your throat if you disobey me even once. I may slit it at any time anyway, so do exactly as I tell you.' He let go of her mouth.

She could see a scalpel illuminated in his hand, which he held in front of his face, just below his wicked grin.

'Come.' He grabbed her hand and drew her along the dark corridor.

'Where are you taking me?'

'Don't talk,' he said. Suddenly his head shuddered with a violent tic. He grasped her arm and yanked her forward. They ran, Kate lurching behind him, down dark passages illuminated only sparsely by dim skylights or flickering emergency lamps. He opened a door and pulled up a hatch. 'In,' he said.

She reared back but checked herself.

'Tunnels,' he said. 'Miles of them. They run under the university. Get in,' he said softly, pointing at the hole with the scalpel. 'Now.'

She shuffled forward, sat on the lip of the hatch and lowered herself down to a ladder, banging her left leg as she went. She stifled a cry and tried not to lose her grip as the pain went through her.

He came down directly after her, pulling the hatch closed behind them. 'Keep going. It's not deep,' he said.

Every step down in the dark was agonising, each rung a vast gap in time and space. It was pitch black in the tunnel, not the slightest flicker of light. As she lowered herself, she felt she might slip and fall to her death. Her hands were wet with perspiration, thin strands of cobweb catching her face. Her left shin was throbbing painfully and she banged it again as she climbed down. She cried out.

'Faster,' he said. 'Not much further now.'

The smell of stale dust filled her nostrils as she went down another rung.

'Hurry,' said Renton, 'or I will punish you.'

Her right foot hit the ground, with a gritty echoing crunch. She had the sudden impulse to run. It was so dark that there might be a place to hide. If she ran, she might come across an alcove to squat in. If Renton missed her, he would never find her again in the dark.

Yes, no. Yes, no. Go, stop. Her mind froze. She heard Renton's feet on the concrete. There was a shuffling sound, followed by a rattle, then a metallic click and ping.

She was dazzled by the light of a torch. When her eyes adjusted she could see Renton in outline as he lit her and the path ahead. Where was he taking her?

62

Smith was pacing up and down outside the lab, speaking rapidly into his phone. 'I want the whole college cordoned off,' he barked. He swung round. 'If necessary, the whole university.' He pivoted again. 'The entire city.' He walked past Stafford. 'That's correct … Yes … Yes.' Pain and fury were etched on his face. 'I feel such an idiot,' he said, in Stafford's direction.

Stafford's expression conveyed 'Quite,' but he said, 'One cannot simply vanish into thin air.'

Smith's face screwed into a caricature of disgust.

A sergeant in plain clothes ran up to them. 'Power's back on, Chief.'

'Right,' said Smith. 'Let's get to it.' He added, to Stafford, 'You stay back.' He turned and began to jog for the lab entrance.

Stafford sighed. Smith was doing both the right and the wrong thing. He should have remained behind to direct matters and would be criticised for not doing so, yet to wait was to condemn Kate. She had to be found fast or she would not be found at all.

His phone rang. It was Jim again. If he told him what was going on he was sure to have yet more insanity and chaos on his hands. A thought struck him: perhaps Jim wasn't all right. He answered the phone.

'Is everything OK?' he asked.

'What's going on?'

'Having terrible trouble with my phone, what was that?'

'What is going on? Are you OK?' asked Jim.

'Sorry, can't hear a thing. Running out of batteries to boot.

Will try to get back this evening.' He hung up. No need to worry about Jim.

More police were showing up, some in uniform, some not. Soon an incident centre would form, but unless Smith managed a rescue in minutes it would likely be to no avail. Instead Renton would be wanted for murder and Kate would be dead.

He was imagining the dog's mouth around Renton's throat. If only he had issued the command. He had added another regret to the mountain.

63

Jim walked through the house, the smell of beeswax polish pervading the air. Something was wrong. He knew it. He had the ache in his gut that he got when he was caught in a losing trade. It told him something was draining away, like clean air turning lifeless in a stuffy room.

Stafford would be here unless something was badly screwed. Whatever was happening, Jim couldn't let it lie.

He went into Stafford's office, which was effectively the control room of their lives. Here, Stafford ran Jim's empire, puny as it might be. Twenty billion dollars was a lot of money, but a trivial amount when placed in US treasuries at next to zero per cent interest, alongside another twenty trillion of American debt. He had tried to do some good but his money, like blood dripping into an ocean, had seemed only to attract predators.

Stafford's office was small and Jim felt as if he was breaching trust by being there to discover where his butler was. The Mac was asleep but it awoke at a click. Stafford had put a Post-it note on the screen with the password. Jim logged on. He went to the Apple cloud and asked it where Stafford's iPhone was, then converted the location to a Google map. His mouth fell open. 'What are you doing at Cardini's lab?' he shouted. 'For fuck's sake!'

He called Stafford but got no reply. He leapt to his feet, ran for the door and flung it open.

64

Jim gazed at the long line of sleek sports cars Stafford had bought for him. Every one had cost at least half a million dollars. He was sure Stafford was reliving his youth vicariously by trying to make him buy the most perfect version of everything in the vain hope that it would attract happiness to him. Instead Jim felt like some spoilt Arab princeling showered with jewels he didn't deserve.

He looked at the first car, a Noble, by the man who had designed the vehicle that had broken the sound barrier on the salt flats of Nevada. It looked amazing and it was the closest. He walked over to it and got in. The keys were in the ignition and he fired it up. All his toy cars made a loud noise: the stupid rich demanded such.

He wondered if it would get him to Cambridge faster than a Ford, but he'd find out soon enough. He felt dread in his gut in the same way he felt deep uncertainty when the market was going to crash. Something horrifying was happening and, once again, he was about to enter the eye of the storm.

He lost a little control as he pulled out, the back wheels slipping, and took his foot off the accelerator. No point being a man of destiny if that meant smashing side-on into a wall. The garage door was opening. He pulled out of the stable block and swept around the gravel courtyard. He accelerated as he used a remote to open the gate he would soon reach. He might not break the speed of sound but he was going to try; he'd have to get himself a Polish driving licence – he was about to throw the British one away.

He drove touching 160 m.p.h., headlights on, and the rest of the traffic seemed to melt away, leaving his route clear. His mind was focused on the road ahead, which seemed to pass no faster than normal now that his senses had adjusted to the speed.

(There was a maniac on the road, other drivers observed, and as they saw him pass, they cursed and marvelled. Whoever was at the wheel was taking a short-cut to the crematorium; it was just sad they were bound to take some innocent with them.)

The world had turned to liquid. It flowed around Jim as he hit 200 m.p.h. The Cambridge police were alerted but no one could respond to a vehicle travelling so fast, and today was not the day to stop some drugged-out footballer in his Ferrari: today was the day the whole of Cambridge might be cordoned off.

They watched the unidentifiable car streak up the M11 and wondered who was driving. The number plate wasn't recognisable by the computers at such speed and was just partially readable by eye as it flashed past the camera. But there was more to worry about than that: something very bad was happening elsewhere.

65

There was the growl of an engine behind Smith and Stafford, and a bright red sports car shot through the lab's gateway.

'Oh dear,' said Stafford.

'Oh dear?' said Smith.

'Jim,' said Stafford.

'Jim?' said Smith, immediately breaking away from him and heading for the lab.

The car had pulled up and was suddenly the focus of half a dozen policemen.

Jim jumped out, immediately catching sight of Smith. He acknowledged the string of officers as if the prime minister had sent him.

'What the hell?' said Smith, bounding over to him.

'What the fuck?' replied Jim.

'Do you know what's going on here?'

'Elixir of life,' said Jim.

'Bio-warfare toxins.'

'Oh, shit,' said Jim.

'Elixir of life?' queried Smith, raising his eyebrow as far as it could go.

Stafford was waddling as fast as he could towards them.

'Cardini has developed a medicine that can extend life almost indefinitely,' said Jim.

'Renton has turned disease into bio-weapons capable of wiping out everyone.'

'Christ,' said Jim, putting his hands on his head.

'And Renton's got a girl kidnapped somewhere in this college and we can't find her.'

Jim looked at Stafford. 'Don't tell me.'

'Kate,' said Stafford.

Jim spun around. 'Argh.' He pulled himself together. 'Where?'

'Come with me,' said Smith.

66

Renton held the bag. It was perfectly warm. He undid his shirt and laid it on his belly. It felt good, comforting. It was a gorgeous ruby colour, fresh from the woman who was strapped to the chair. He had built the room years ago and upgraded it as technology had changed. It was the garden of his inner life, a dark cinema to the movies he would play in his head. It was a sanctuary protected by silence, profound blackness, isolation and a shield of security. He watched the ground above from his chair, the bag of hot blood soothing him, the elixir taking his mind to planes of intellect he had only guessed existed.

He might be in a squalid concrete bunker but his mind flew far above it. There was no good or evil, no right or wrong, just equations that cycled through our reality and brought pain and pleasure to the ignorant as day and night brought flowers to bloom and wilt.

He was above that now, looking down on existence from a distance at which he could gain true perspective. Draining the woman's blood was no more wrong than eating a black pudding for breakfast. Humans were animals as pathetic and exploitable as any cow or pig.

He was elevated, he had seen the truth and even when he returned to his former faculties he would remember that all life was worthless, nothing but a collection of sterile information elevated by the few basic principles of physics. There was no god, only agony and ecstasy. There was no personal divinity, only the positive and the negative that balanced the universe.

Smarter, stronger, faster, more agile than the others, he was true to the purpose of existence. The weak were but raw materials for the existence of the strong; the feeble were bags of resources to be exploited for his higher form of life.

The woman was just a plaything to be pulled here and there, to be broken and thrown away. He held up the bag of cooling blood. In a few minutes he would draw another.

67

Jim looked through the hatch. 'Down there?'

'Most likely.'

'Give me a torch,' said Jim, staring at Smith.

'Can't let you do it,' said Smith.

Jim sat down and swung his legs into the hole.

'We don't have any idea what's down there, Jim,' said Smith. 'I'd go down myself but I might as well tender my resignation right now.'

Stafford handed Jim a silver flashlight and held up one for himself.

Smith looked at them both.

'I'm going alone,' said Jim.

'I won't slow you down,' said Stafford.

Jim smiled. 'My arse you won't.' He looked at Smith. 'You mean to tell me you don't have a gun or a night-sight for me?'

Smith's head drooped. 'I'm a policeman, these days. We don't use that kind of thing.'

Stafford handed him his pistol. Jim stared at what looked like a relic from a museum. 'Thanks,' he said. 'Does it work?'

'It's cocked. Just take it off safety. Don't yank the trigger. Squeeze.'

Jim tried not to grimace. 'Thanks,' he said, smiling as best he could.

'Don't lose it,' said Stafford, as if that was the biggest thing to worry about.

Jim grabbed Smith's calf. 'Got to go.' He shook Stafford's hand. 'See you later.' He began to descend.

*

Something caught Renton's eye: a little window on the computer screen was flashing. He looked at her arm muscle, red and gently pulsing beneath the opened skin. It was a fine cut, only a little blood extruding; it revealed the marvellous structure below. He had parted the skin without severing a significant vein, so that his view of the underlying tissue wasn't obscured by a flow of blood.

Someone had entered his labyrinth. He looked down at the oval opening, glittering with silvery liquids. He could deal with the visitor, run, or continue his exploration of his subject. He took the adhesive suture and pulled the top of the incision shut. He took another and closed it completely.

The woman looked at him, eyes wide and full of tears. The tape over her mouth stopped her saying anything and more tape fixed her head to the table. The local anaesthetic in her arm meant she felt nothing but the terror of his examination.

It seemed to Renton that pain was as nothing to the rack of fear. He could feel, as he cut into her, that there was great power to be had from bathing in the hopeless terror of a victim. Was it possible that, as ancient cultures believed, he had been drinking in the soul of his conquest? He had felt as though he was drawing in an essence, like the scent of a crushed flower.

He looked down at the female. She had no more right to life than the billions of animals herded to their death in the abattoirs of man. A few generations ago the slaughter of tribes and nations had been cause for celebration. It was only since people had swarmed into every corner of the planet that humans had somehow gained sanctity.

Now that the elixir allowed him to soar over the stupidity of mankind he could see it for what it was: just another life form preying on others in the primordial soup. Power, experience and longevity were the only purpose; all other dreams were just flames flickering against the wall of superstition.

There was a pleasure in domination, and dismantling this subject creature would give him such a joy. The primitive emotions delivered a wonderful payoff that even his elevated intellect could revel in. Now that they had sent someone into his maze, he might use his superhuman mind and accelerated body to crush the visitor for sport. He would enjoy the killing. He would watch the progress of the intruder and consider what action to take.

How long the serum would keep him on this high plain, he did not know, but long enough, he was sure, to execute his plans.

Kate looked up at Renton. His face was red and grotesquely swollen, as if inflated by an allergy. His skin seemed to glow and his brow hung forward over his eyes. His hair seemed to bristle, like that of an animal shocked into aggression.

She was floating in and out of her body. She knew it wasn't a nightmare: she was praying for salvation, for a quick death ... for a miracle.

She felt as if she had been lying there, taped to the table, for ever.

She had looked away when he had injected her arm; she had looked away when he had begun cutting her. She had tried to reach out for comfort, a place to hide her mind, a way to hide from the horror, but all she could do was try vainly to imagine it wasn't happening.

Now she was looking up at Renton, his face lit in the gloom by overhead lights that shadowed his face. The whites of his eyes glinted as he seemed to look past her at something far away. What was he about to do now? He had done something to her arm, cut it open, she guessed. She closed her eyes.

68

Renton's face, which had been clear in his mind as he had climbed down the ladder, had faded to that of a demonic goblin, a sneering, leering, bearded troll. Jim gritted his teeth as he walked slowly along the tunnel. Everything that had been somersaulting through his mind as he climbed down had fallen away. There was only the dark tunnel and himself. His eyes had become accustomed to the light of the torch and now the tunnel was as bright as any room.

What kind of D&D fantasy world had been built down here? The tunnels cried out for flakes and nerds to explore and hide in. It was just the sort of place he would have loved if he'd ended up at Cambridge doing some silly arts course. While those kids had been drinking, shagging and smoking weed, he had been fetching coffee on the trading floor of a big bank, happy to kiss the arse of any trader who demanded it.

Those thoughts, too, were falling away.

There was just him, the tunnel and the freak who had taken Kate. He was going to find Renton and wring his neck. To do that, he had to focus. He had to be in the moment. He had to keep his whole consciousness in the immediate now. He mustn't get distracted.

By the faint light of the torch he could see as far ahead as he needed. This was Britain: anyone wanting to take him would have to do it hand to hand. His thinking fell away again. Now there was just him and the tunnel ahead, the smell of dust, silence, a veil of darkness beyond the reach of his torch's beam.

*

Renton sat by the monitoring equipment and watched the screen. He could see a figure coming down the primary tunnel. To have any chance of finding his lair, the man would need to go left at the second spur. If he went down the first, he would travel the best part of half a mile before a dead end forced him back. Then several branches would overwhelm him and hopelessness would force whoever it was to surface, lost and disorientated.

If the intruder took the wrong route, Renton would return to work on his subject.

He looked at the body on the table. It was stiff and alive, not malleable and inert. He had dreamt of this moment for so long. He had fantasised about this scene a thousand times. He had planned and imagined every detail, himself a terrifying god, bending the puppet to his will, twisting, cutting and dismembering it.

69

A little something flashed white in front of Jim; he flicked his light down. It was a small piece of tissue, a crumb on the dusty floor. Next to it he saw footprints, two sets, in the grime. The tissue looked fresh, unlike the rest of the tunnel. Was it a sign from Kate? Were they Renton's footsteps alongside hers? It felt right, it felt real, and all he needed was a trend to follow.

Renton's hairs prickled inside his nose as they stood on end. The figure had passed the first fork and was continuing down the primary tunnel. It was a long artery with seven spurs; the man would travel the full length and then, seeing the exit, go through it into the basement of the main college building a quarter of a mile ahead. When the intruder passed the second turning he would get up, turn the monitor so he could keep a better eye on it, then start the vivisection of his subject.

He smiled comfortably to himself as he watched. He was the master of the labyrinth: he knew all its forks and tributaries. No one would find him in his private sanctuary. It would take days to track it down on a branch of a branch of a branch of a branch of the maze.

Jim followed the footsteps as they seemed to turn a corner into another alley. At the fork lay another piece of white tissue a little way in. Jim's face tensed. He had found the trail. She was leading him on.

Somewhere down these dark, dusty tunnels the creepy Renton was with a girl Jim barely knew, a beautiful, sensitive woman who had put a smile on his face and, for a few fleeting hours, made him happy.

He looked up the tunnel. There was only him and the silent, shadowy forms lit by the flashes from his torch.

Renton stood up, pushing his chair backwards. He was bobbing up and down with anxiety. The intruder had made the correct turn.

There were two turns to the right, then more to the left. The first turn to the right was the correct route. If he came down it, he would be getting warm.

Renton stared at the screen, his brow furrowed. What were the chances of that? The first might be a logical route to take, but after that, one turn was as good as another.

Kate was trying to look at Renton, but her eyes could not swivel that low. All she saw were her cheeks and a blurred image of him staring at something. The muscles in her eye sockets ached and she strained the few millimetres the tape would allow.

She dropped her head as her neck muscles cramped.

Renton squealed. The figure had turned right. The man was coming for him as if he knew the exact route. How could that be? He stared at the screen, his head jutted forwards.

'Footprints,' he cried. Then he reprimanded himself: 'You're getting complacent, you idiot.'

Jim stopped in his tracks. Had he heard a distant cry? He strained to listen, but there was only the sound of his breathing and the thud of his heart.

Renton stood tall on the balls of his feet. 'Ha!' He laughed. 'Let's meet.' He would be able to see better by the light of the man's torch than the intruder could. His senses were supercharged: he could hear more, feel more and see more. Not only was he smarter, he was stronger, quicker and more alert than any ordinary mortal.

While the elixir rebuilt his body, repairing all the faulty and broken DNA, his metabolism raced. As Renton's life clock reversed, so the biomechanical process was unencumbered by his biology. He flipped the scalpel into the air and caught it by the handle. He would cut the trespasser into chunks.

There was another piece of tissue, torn and balled up at the junction of the next tunnel. Now that he had grown accustomed to the footprints, it was reinforcement rather than his only clue.

He turned into the tunnel.

There was a kind of humming. Someone was there. He stopped and listened. He could hear nothing but he could feel the faint vibration.

He took out the pistol. He couldn't remember if Stafford had said the safety was on or off, whether it was cocked, half cocked or otherwise. He put it back into his pocket.

His heartbeat quickened. He paused and inhaled deeply. Calm was strength.

He had long since played out his natural luck. He had lived beyond the point of no return for so long that he was not going to let fear overwhelm him. Thoughts of the future faded as he refocused; there was only the now. He moved forward deliberately, putting one foot in front of the other, watching the path ahead.

There was a left turn and, with a flick of his torch, he saw that the footprints went in that direction, one trail making a long, just discernible arc into the dark gap, like an elongated arrow.

He moved slowly towards the gap. He shone the torch back and forth into the gloom.

He turned to enter, and as he did so, a white shape shot towards him. He jumped back and to one side, dodging it.

A figure emerged from the darkness, arms raised, the metal of a blade glinting in one hand.

Renton struck down at Jim.

Jim swept the torch up, dodging so that Renton's blow would miss him. His forearm smacked into Renton's face. His adversary fell forward on to the floor as Jim swung round to face him. He prepared to step forward and attack, but Renton was scuttling away, twisting and jumping up faster than Jim imagined possible. Renton was running at him empty-handed. As he reached him, Jim grabbed Renton by the scruff of his shirt and, with a judo throw, catapulted him down the tunnel.

Renton was up again in a second and lunged forward. Jim punched his temple, sending him into the tunnel wall. Renton bounced back at him and rammed him into the other wall. He punched Jim in the side, at the site of his old injury.

Jim's strength drained away and his knees buckled as pain shot through him. He fell to his knees. Renton aimed a blow at the top of his head as Jim punched upwards between Renton's legs.

Renton doubled up and staggered backwards. Then he hobbled away.

Jim raised the torch and staggered to his feet. He stumbled after Renton, who was lurching ahead at a terrific speed, his feet barely touching the ground.

Jim's pain was dissipating now, his vitality oozing back into him as he forced himself after Renton, who took a left into another tunnel. Jim didn't hesitate to follow him. There was a kind of cold hatred in his spirit that he hadn't felt before.

His torch picked up a figure in the near distance, disappearing into another entrance. He had to keep up or Renton would get away. He ran up to the turning. It was a door.

He hesitated. Renton would be on the other side. He flung the door open. Renton was standing in the middle of the room. As the door swung closed again Jim pushed it open. He stepped inside.

Renton was smiling at him. 'Hurt, that did,' he said.

'Fuck,' said Jim, seeing Kate prostrate on the table behind the technician.

Renton registered his reaction. 'She's OK,' he said, 'but once I've killed you I'll do to her alive what I'll do to you dead.'

Jim didn't say anything, his focus returning solely to Renton. Renton's face was bleeding on both sides, but that didn't seem to bother him.

Renton held out his right hand. He was holding a long boning knife.

Jim heard the voice of his personal trainer: 'When you see a knife, the best tactic is to run. Any other response is speculative.' He stepped forward.

'Aren't you afraid?' said Renton, waving the knife at him.

'Aren't you?' Jim said involuntarily.

Renton didn't reply.

Renton held back. Doubt swept through him. He didn't know how to fight. He was faster and stronger than he could ever have imagined being but now he was facing someone who clearly knew fighting, someone who was his match, even while he was accelerated by TRT. The inner confidence that had welled up in him had drained.

Were the elixir's powers failing him already? Were his moments of basking in a godlike consciousness leaving him? He swayed.

It was a signal to which Jim knew how to react. He grabbed Renton's knife hand and threw the man to the floor. Renton rolled away, the knife spinning from his grasp. He was up amazingly fast again, too quick for Jim to get his punch in.

Renton darted to Kate; there was something in his hand, another blade grabbed in a flash from his workspace. He slashed at her and there was a jet of blood. 'I've cut her vein wide open,' he screamed, backing away from the table. 'Deal with it and she may live. Come after me and she dies.' He turned and darted for the door. His screaming cackle filled the room and the tunnel outside as he ran down it.

Jim dashed for Kate. Blood was pouring from her left wrist. She was twisting against her bonds. Jim tore away the tape holding her head down with his right hand, his left stuck into her armpit to try to slow the bleeding. He forced his knuckles deep into her, the pressure on the artery stemming the flow of blood from her wrist. He pulled the clear plastic bag from her mouth.

'Behind you,' she screamed.

Jim spun around. Renton was standing in the corner of the room, the boning knife in his hand. Jim snatched the pistol from his pocket and took aim. Renton froze, already halfway to him. The trigger wouldn't pull. Renton registered the failure and lunged forwards. Jim pulled the trigger again and a shot sounded. Renton toppled forward.

Kate moaned and Jim looked back. Blood was everywhere. He stuck his right hand into her armpit again and pushed, looking around wildly for Renton and a chance to shoot.

He saw Renton's crouched figure making for the door. He tried to fire again but the trigger didn't snap back, and when it did, Renton had flung the door closed behind him. The bullet ricocheted off the metal frame.

Jim slammed the gun on to the table.

'Tourniquet,' gasped Kate. 'In the dish there. Tourniquet ...'

He located the leather strap curled in a kidney-shaped metal tray.

'Tie it on my forearm,' she said, her body struggling as she spoke.

He slipped the strap around her arm, his hands now slippery with her blood, and threaded it through the buckle. He pulled it tight, then took a scalpel from the table and, keeping the strap tight, cut away the rest of the tape.

She was naked, her skin white and cold.

She half sat up as he sliced the tape that bound her feet to low metal stirrups. She was hugging him limply, with barely enough strength to hold herself up. Her feet fell on to the table top and she sagged back. He dropped the blade and cradled her. 'Lie back,' he said. 'I'm going to call for help.' He took out his phone. There was no signal.

He looked at her. 'Are you strong enough to walk out of here?'

'No choice,' she said. 'True?'

'Probably.'

'My clothes are over there,' she said vaguely. 'What's left of them.'

Jim glanced at her wrist. The blood had stopped gushing.

'Get them,' she said. 'I'm so cold.'

Jim went to pick them up. They had been cut to pieces, apart from her jeans. He carried them and her shoes back to her.

'Better than nothing,' she said.

He helped her into the jeans and slipped her shoes on to her feet. 'Put your good arm around me,' he said.

She looked at the smashed torch and then at him. 'God is on our side,' said Jim, putting Stafford's gun in his left hand.

'I can walk,' she said, as she stood, wobbling.

Jim steadied her, ready to grab her if she began to collapse.

Her head drooped a little. 'Please let's get away from here. I'm not sure how long I can hold on.'

'I know the way.' Jim looked at Renton's screens. They were all empty, nothing moving in front of the camera's infrared gaze. Renton had watched him every step of the way. He took a deep breath. 'We're going to be OK, Kate. It's not far. It'll be like a slow walk on a warm summer's night.'

70

They were moving forward by the dim light of his mobile phone, which flickered off every few seconds and barely illuminated their feet. Every step appeared to take a minute, every few yards felt like an interminable mile. In the near-absolute dark the passages seemed never-ending. He listened for any sound other than their hesitant footfall, sensing Kate's grip on his belt that left both his hands free in case Renton attacked them.

'Are you OK?' he would whisper every minute or so.

'Uuuumm,' she would reply.

Every bend felt like a trap that a demented Renton might spring, every heartbeat a roll of thunder that might drown the sound of him moving in the darkness ahead.

Jim could feel the hum of life in the tunnels but was that Kate or Renton? The pitch black of the way ahead was almost unbearable, a paralysing blanket that dragged at their progress like sticky mud underfoot.

Was he retracing his steps or sending them further into the maze?

Kate pulled at him and he stopped. 'Ssh,' she whispered.

He listened but heard nothing. They were at another corner: was Renton waiting for them on the other side?

Jim took a deep breath and listened. A faint scratchy sound came from beyond. A moment later he realised quick footsteps were coming their way. He pulled her hand from his belt and touched her face. It was cold. He stroked her cheek as the steps drew nearer. There was no light, no torch beam. Someone was almost upon them.

He was going to jump out, wrestle Renton to the floor and beat him with his fists until he stopped moving. He had to do it blind and without hesitation.

The steps were seconds away. He counted them down as they approached.

He dived out into the space he estimated Renton to have reached.

'Christ!' someone yelled, as Jim launched a series of blows into the darkness. 'Jim! Stop, for fuck's sake.'

'Smith?' said Jim, startled.

'Yes.'

A torch came on and he could see part of Smith's face: the rest was covered with night-sight goggles, which were now askew.

'Get us out of here fast,' said Jim.

'You've got the girl?' said Smith, apparently in some pain.

'Yes. Follow me.' Jim turned and headed into the other tunnel. 'Kate?'

Smith's torch illuminated the passage.

Kate was slumped on the floor.

Jim threw himself down beside her. 'Kate – are you OK?'

'Just about,' she said.

'We're getting out now – we've got help. Can you stand?'

'Almost,' she said.

Jim jumped up and took her good hand.

'I'm OK really,' she said, Jim's arm around her waist now, hauling her up. 'I'm just shaky.'

Jim looked at Smith. 'I hope you know a fast way out.'

'Yes,' said Smith. 'I've a map.' He tapped his goggles. 'All in here.'

'Can we go, then?' said Kate, sagging in Jim's embrace. 'I've almost had it.'

71

Renton pushed the manhole cover up and slipped it to one side. For now, his immense frustration was overwhelmed by the tension of emerging into the light, like an insect breaking out of a pupa. It was not normal to appear from the earth like a phantom – it might expose him to those hunting him above.

He glanced about. Across the road there was a line of white vans and policemen looking towards fields and the far building of the campus. Their focus was exactly wrong. To them, their challenge lay within the bounds of the university so they were blind to him. He stepped off the grass verge on to the pavement and turned right, walking away from them, now a mere ninety degrees from their gaze. He smiled: that was all it took to foil these simple people.

Smith and Jim knelt by Kate as the paramedics strapped her into a stretcher, then got to their feet as she was hoisted up from the tunnel to the hatchway above.

Jim's hands were over his mouth.

'She'll be OK,' said Smith. 'Now we've got her she'll be fine.'

Jim saw the tail end of the stretcher disappear. 'Let's get the hell out of this place,' he said. 'And when we're above ground again I'll leave you to catch that creep Renton.'

Smith shook his head. 'This is a right old Pandora's box. Let's just say this Frankenstein shit we've uncovered is funded by people in a lot of important places. You can break the rules for the people who make them. You know how it is.'

'So what are you going to do?' said Jim.

'Get Renton for a start. It might be the only action I'll be allowed before I have to start covering my arse.'

Jim's fingers were sticking together where Kate's blood had dried. He looked up at the light coming through the hatch. 'I'm off,' he said, and made for the ladder.

72

Jim lifted himself carefully out of the hatch into the cramped space. Stafford was offering him his hand but he didn't take it. His butler and a policeman were clearly shocked by his appearance. He looked down at himself. He was covered with blood and grey dust. He stepped out to let Smith up.

'Well done,' said Stafford, grabbing him by both arms and almost shaking him.

'Thanks,' said Jim, as Smith stepped out of the hole, stooped as if he was in danger of banging his head.

'Christ you're a mess,' Smith said to Jim.

'Thanks,' said Jim. 'You don't mind if we scram?'

'Go on,' said Smith. 'I'll keep you up to date on any developments.'

Jim clapped him on the back. 'Thanks again,' he said.

'For what?'

'Coming down there.'

'Shouldn't have let you go alone,' he said. 'That was rubbish of me.'

Jim shook his arm. 'Thanks anyway.' He grinned.

'I'm going to have to ask you later why you showed up here,' said Smith.

'Sure,' said Jim, as Stafford stepped past them. 'There isn't much of a story, apart from a mad genius, bunkers full of military equipment, the fountain of youth, you know the kind of thing.'

Smith nodded. 'Just the usual, then.'

'Come on, Jim,' said Stafford, throwing him a beady look. 'Mustn't linger.'

'Yes,' said Jim, casting an eye at the open hatch. 'Let's get home.'

73

Cardini was seated at McCloud's desk, in the huge leather chair that McCloud had used as a throne.

Marius had taken the rather strange investigators away. They had seemed to Cardini remarkably relaxed. Was the locale so violent that dead bodies were treated in the same way as minor road accidents?

He had expected rounds of heavy questioning but instead had received little more than a request for his personal details. He had had almost no opportunity to tell them he knew nothing of what had gone on.

They had immediately accepted that he had been asleep in his bedroom. It was almost as if they had decided already that everything was in order. The whole situation was bizarre. Perhaps it was just the beginning. Perhaps he'd be trapped there for weeks as the investigators tried to snare him with a game of cat and mouse.

He rocked in the chair as he tried to think through all the things that could possibly happen next and how he should react.

It was impossible to predict what the outcome might be. He had no idea how these things developed. It was fortunate that McCloud had disabled the surveillance systems, or Cardini's goose would have been well and truly cooked. What a recording that would have made.

Cardini began to dwell on Jim. Who, or perhaps what, exactly was he? Cardini had met many rich men, many titans of industry and politics, but never someone so apparently plain on first impression yet so clearly dangerous. The man was a killer.

What freak of probability had thrown his DNA together to produce such a remarkable chimera?

The door opened and Joe Marius came in. He closed it behind him carefully and approached the desk. 'Professor, I'm so sorry – what can I say? I'm horrified by what's happened. I just want to say I'm so deeply shocked and upset by everything I can hardly contain myself.' His face didn't match his words.

'What now?' said Cardini.

'I shall arrange for you to go back to England,' replied Marius.

'Go back?' boomed Cardini, surprised. 'How soon?'

'As soon as you wish,' said Marius, pressing his hands together. 'I can organise the jet whenever you want.'

Cardini studied him for several seconds. Could it be that he was free to leave? 'That is very good of you.' He fixed Marius with a stare. 'Do they know what happened?'

'Yes,' said Marius. 'Apparently Mr McCloud disturbed a guest who was out of bounds in the mansion. They got into a terrible fight and both died in the struggle.'

'Incredible,' said Cardini.

'It's almost too much to take in.' Marius was fixing Cardini with his own stare. 'Professor …'

'Yes?' replied Cardini, slowly.

'Now that Mr McCloud is no longer with us …'

'Yes?'

'… I need to ask you something in all confidentiality.'

'Yes?'

Marius wrung his hands and began to quiver. 'The treatment.'

Cardini nodded.

'It's always seemed to me a miracle.'

Cardini nodded again.

'And I wondered … What exactly is it?'

'Indeed.'

'And what would its effects be on someone young, like …' he smiled nervously '… myself?'

'The effects are remarkable,' said Cardini.

Marius looked at him, agog. 'Could I ... might I ... ?'

'Experience it?' Cardini leant forward, looking deep into Marius's eyes.

'Yes.'

Cardini sat back. 'Certainly. Now?'

'Now.' Marius twisted from right to left, like a puppet yanked on its strings. 'Of course, yes, of course.'

'You realise the consequences?'

'The consequences?'

'Of looking into infinity ...'

Marius stared at him, clearly riveted at the prospect.

'... and of infinity looking back into you?'

Marius gasped. 'Please, Professor, give it to me.'

'Very well,' rumbled Cardini, and picked up his doctor's bag. He rounded the desk and loomed above Marius. He placed the bag on the table and opened it. There was a rattle of contents. He took out a small vial and removed the top. His hand dipped into the bag and returned effortlessly with a thin strip of paper. He dipped it into the liquid, the perfume of pears filling the space around them.

'Open your mouth and put out your tongue,' commanded Cardini.

Marius stuck it out as far as it would go.

Cardini dabbed the paper on it. 'Hold your tongue still in your mouth and try not to wash the extract from it.'

Marius felt something like chilli burning on his tongue, a searing sensation simmering and hissing inside his mouth. Suddenly the burning was spreading, like a flame across a crumpled piece of paper. He threw back his head and grabbed his mouth. The feeling was something between pain and pleasure. Suddenly the heat was travelling up his tongue and then down his throat and thence along the nerves of his neck, up the side of his face and into his brain. His eyes opened wide in shock as his mind came alive and his whole being seemed to leap from some shadowy internment into a bright landscape of revelation.

'My God, it's beautiful,' he moaned. 'I can see – I can feel everything. Everything makes sense. How could I have been so stupid?' He looked at Cardini, awestruck.

'Be still,' said Cardini. 'Let these feelings pass through you. They will not last long.'

Marius gazed around the room as though he was seeing it for the first time. 'So, ' he said, and laughed, 'now I get it.'

'I'm glad.'

Marius stiffened. 'How long have I got?'

'Another five minutes, perhaps ten.'

Marius sighed. 'OK, I get that too.'

'Good.'

'I know what I need to do,' said Marius.

'And what is that?'

'Have more.'

'How can that be, Joe? That one taste was more costly than a year of your salary.'

'There must be a way.'

Cardini said nothing.

A moment later Marius slapped his forehead. 'Of course. The foundation.'

'The foundation?'

'McCloud's foundation. It has hundreds of millions of dollars. If I controlled it, I could fund you.'

'You could indeed,' agreed Cardini. 'And how could you gain control?'

'With enough of the treatment I could outwit anyone – I could do whatever I wanted.' He smiled at Cardini. 'The trustees think they're clever but I can see now how easily they could be manipulated. Stein, for example, would get behind me if the foundation was to fund his favourite museum. Gomes is easily scared – the slightest fear of litigation and he will go along with anything I ask him to agree to. Kelly is a fool. He'll back any proposal I make so long as he gets his money. Can you believe that?' He laughed contemptuously. 'A billionaire caring so much about a few thousand bucks and expenses. What a Scrooge McDuck.' He smirked. 'That just leaves Walton, and I know how to deal with him. He has a mistress in Charlotte, some old gal he's been tight with for thirty years. A little nudge and he'll fall into line.'

'Simple,' said Cardini.

Marius's eyes widened. 'I can actually feel myself losing it. I can totally feel my mind shrinking. You said five minutes. Has it been that long?'

'No, Joe, but perhaps you are not blessed with a mind that can hold such thoughts for long.'

Marius held out his hands beseechingly. 'Please tell me you'll help me. Please let me come back to this heavenly state.'

'I will help you, but only once. The elixir is so precious that I can risk only one full treatment on you. You must succeed in your quest or I must let you wash up, like everyone else, an empty carapace on the beach of life.'

'Oh, God,' groaned Marius. 'I can feel myself slipping away. It's like my brain is going blind.' He let out a half-laugh. 'Wow, the lights are going out in my head.' He looked at Cardini hopefully. 'Give me more and I'll hand you the McCloud foundation and all its money on a plate.'

'You beg now,' said Cardini, 'but it will not be easy. Fail once and you will never have another chance. Are you prepared?'

'Yes.'

'Sit down,' ordered Cardini. He delved into his bag and produced an ampoule. 'You must understand that the cost of saving a life in the developing world is just two dollars. This treatment costs one hundred million dollars.' He looked once more into Marius's soul. 'By accepting it you are extinguishing by proxy fifty million lives. Are you prepared to cross that line?'

'Yes.'

'Sacrifice the population of a whole country for your personal desires?'

'Yes.'

'And you understand that only I can manufacture this and that you will be for ever in my thrall?'

'Yes.'

Cardini extracted a syringe from the bag without taking his unblinking eye off Marius. 'Very well.' He loaded the syringe. 'You will have one day, perhaps two, three at the outside to effect your plan. Open your mouth.'

Marius did so.

'Write down your plan as you will neither understand it nor believe it when you return to your normal existence.' He aimed the needle. 'Raise your tongue!'

Marius rolled it back.

Cardini pushed the needle home and pressed the barrel. 'You must move fast or you will not succeed. The elixir will not keep you accelerated for long. This is your single chance, your only hope, your one throw of the die.' He withdrew the needle.

Marius was gripping the seat of his chair. He was staring at Cardini in silence, his mouth open, trying to say something. 'Professor,' he said finally, ' I will not fail you.'

'First get me back to London.'

Marius jumped up from his chair. 'Right away.' He turned to Cardini. 'I love you.'

Cardini held up his right hand. 'For now at least.'

74

Arabella walked the horse up to the ha-ha. There was no sign of Stafford. It wasn't odd, of course, almost the opposite. It was odd that he should always be standing there and that she should ride by at roughly the same time each day. Yet she had a purpose, and she was sure it amused the butler-cum-estate-manager to be there. At some point the invitation would come and then she would see what the mysterious Mr Evans was all about.

Stafford was a good fellow. His old-fashioned manner brightened up her day. He seemed exactly the sort of retainer that every aristocrat dreamt of having. Her meagre retinue hated the family, as it seemed most servants did. Their heartfelt resentment manifested itself in little acts of sabotage passed off as fawning incompetence. She wondered whether, if the family could afford to pay more, they would get better results, but her friends, many in a significantly better financial position than her family, seemed beset by the same problems with their staff.

If only her family could improve its finances, but there was no prospect of that. They had tried everything they could think of to boost their income but were reduced to scraping by.

The Chase, on the other hand, had seen a complete reversal in fortunes. The grade-one listed Jacobean pile had been stripped down and repaired by an army of restorers from all over Europe. The sums expended on the red-brick monstrosity were rumoured to be colossal. The locals said millions had been poured into the structure and yet more millions into the contents, which included an unbelievable collection of paintings by Reynolds, Gainsborough and Hogarth, to name but three of the more famous artists.

The mysterious Mr Evans had even had the grounds excavated by his team of archaeologists, who, it was said, were forbidden to remove any finds from the earth until he was there to help. That seemed a trifle eccentric, yet at the same time rather fascinating.

She pulled up and looked into the grounds. Definitely no sign of Stafford. She spurred the horse and it jumped on to the ha-ha, halting immediately. She looked over the rhododendrons to the red house, set back a quarter of a mile. Her aristocratic nose twitched: a whiff of atmosphere emanated from the old pile, thrilling her. I can put up with a certain amount of waiting, she thought, but if it continues much longer I'll have to take matters into my own hands.

She had made up her mind.

She turned the horse. It was a pity Stafford hadn't appeared, she thought.

The chestnut hopped off the ha-ha on to the margin of the field. They cantered towards home.

75

Jim was watching the US stock market close. It was the best way he knew to clear his head. He could certainly go to sleep, but he wanted to get through to midnight and avoid falling into a jetlagged sleep pattern. Watching the market calmed him. He forgot the questions that flew around his head, crazy and unanswerable, as the market traded, jittering from one price to another.

He threw a few million at the moves and made a few thousand in the process. It was like watching ducks on a lake: you had to throw some bread into the water or the spectacle was boring.

No one from America had called him. That was a small relief, but he knew the authorities were never in a hurry. The call for him to explain the goings-on in McCloud's palace might come at any time, within hours or not for months. It would be years before he forgot the unpleasant episode.

With five minutes to go, the market was plunging down, just as it had at the start of trading hours before. It was a regular pattern these days: a tradable event that would vanish as soon as too many people cottoned on to it. He didn't have to trade that kind of thing. He could look at a chart and trace out its progress as if he had next year's market records in front of him. Market moves were so obvious to Jim. Armies of market analysts claimed they had such talents, but when it came to it no one but Jim appeared to possess them. While their claims seemed plausible, the fact of the matter was that if you could predict the markets just a few seconds into the future, let alone days, you could make all the money in the world.

Jim had stopped trading seriously and resorted to playing at it instead. Money was a great thing to have a lot of, if you could keep it simple. The trouble was, money was like honey: it oozed and dripped and flowed so that pretty soon you were surrounded by an uncomfortably sticky mess. He closed out all his Dow shorts and wondered about trading some forex to keep himself occupied. He was feeling pretty tired.

The phone buzzed. It was Stafford. 'We have a visitor.'

'Who?'

'It's a taxi-cab and I think it might be Kate.'

'Oh,' said Jim, getting up from his desk. He hung up.

Kate was paying the driver when he trotted down the stairs. She seemed to be hunting in a purse. He waved at the man, who wound his window down. 'I'll get this,' he said. 'How much is it?'

'Ninety-five pounds, boss,' said the driver, with an element of satisfaction.

Stafford held out two fifty-pound notes past Jim. 'Keep the change, driver,' he said.

Jim walked swiftly around the car and opened the door for Kate, who was putting something into the tote bag Stafford had had delivered to the hospital a few hours earlier. She got out. 'I didn't know where else to go,' she said apologetically.

'That's OK,' said Jim. 'How come they let you out?'

'Nothing wrong with me,' she said, shrugging. Her arm was bandaged. 'Just stitches.'

'Outrageous,' remarked Stafford, behind them.

The minicab pulled away slowly and circled back.

'You don't mind, do you?' she said. 'I'll—'

'Of course not,' said Jim. 'I've got forty bedrooms here.' He laughed.

'It's just—'

'It's fine.' He took her bag from her.

'I didn't feel safe going home,' she said, hunched up. 'It's right by the lab.'

'Don't worry,' said Jim. 'It's fine, really, come in.'

'I'm sorry.'

'Sorry?' said Jim. 'I should be sorry for not coming to visit you in the hospital. I was going to in the morning. I mean, what was I thinking?'

Stafford took the bag from Jim.

'No,' she said. 'I would have been embarrassed.'

Jim thought about that for a second. It didn't make much sense to him. A few hours ago he had been freeing her, stark naked, from a makeshift operating table. Why would she be embarrassed by him visiting her in hospital? His brain struggled to compute. The markets were so much simpler than people. The markets went your way and you made money; if they went against you, you lost. There were no ifs and buts, no non-computes, no illogical results. People said things that were infinitely more inscrutable than any stock price ticking up or falling down on a trading screen. They said things that made no sense on so many levels that his brain would spin. How could anyone begin to understand people? How could an army of traders be so predictable when each individual was so obviously random?

'Let's get inside,' he said, nearly putting his arm around her. He checked himself. 'Hungry?'

'A little,' she replied.

'How's your arm?'

'Sore, but fine,' she said, as Stafford went through the front door.

She was looking at Jim with an expression he didn't understand. He was unsure how to reply. 'What?' he said finally, for want of anything clever.

She blinked at him and smiled, then looked away from him to the front door. He followed her gaze and she looked back at him. He thought she was very beautiful in the soft light coming from the house. He raised his hand, acutely sensitive to her reaction, and stroked her cheek, as he had before. After a fraction of a moment she smiled.

It felt wrong but he was going to kiss her and she was probably going to shriek and run off down the drive. He leant forwards slowly and their lips met. Her eyes were closed. Her lips were warm and responded to his. His right arm was around her waist and he felt her embrace him.

Inside he could feel himself sighing. His loneliness was dissolving, like snow falling into water.

'I'm sorry,' she said, after an indeterminate period had elapsed.

He looked down at her. 'No, I'm sorry,' he said. 'I shouldn't have.'

'It was nice.'

Nice, he thought. Fantastic, more like. 'Yes,' he said. 'It was.' She was looking at the door again.

'Let's go in,' he said, taking her hand and leading the way.

76

Renton sat on the chair, his head in his hands. The effects of the serum had almost worn off. He had ruined everything. In the space of a few short hours he had destroyed his life, exposed the lab and become a fugitive. There was no way back for him now. He was a non-person, completely dependent on Cardini for haven and sustenance.

What would Cardini do when he returned and found out? Would he forgive him? Would he shelter him? Would he do him to death? He wouldn't mind so much if Cardini killed him. His life was over. What kind of sentence would they give him for what he had done to the girl – and what if they found out about the others? He'd be banged up for life. He was crying silently, occasionally snivelling into a large tissue.

They would be searching his home now, rifling through his drawers, tearing up his carpet, collecting all his implements. They would have seized his computer and soon be trying to unencrypt all his hard drives. They must have ways of breaking into them, he thought, sobbing. Would they be able to piece together his life from them? Would they be able to find his servers and their contents, get access to them? Would they bother?

Someone was entering the building. He wiped his eyes and blew his congested nose.

He shook. It was Cardini.

Renton jumped up and ran for the door. He dashed up the hallway. Cardini was at the end of the corridor.

'Master,' screamed Renton, running, arms held aloft. He threw himself at Cardini's feet. 'Master,' he wept.

'You wretch, what have you done?' boomed Cardini.

'Forgive me,' wailed Renton. 'Forgive me.'

'Why are you still here?' Cardini delivered a kick that sent Renton backwards. 'Go to my office immediately. I will hear your account there.'

77

Renton was slumped in front of Cardini, distraught and defeated.

The report had sounded plausible. Renton had gone to deal with the girl and she had escaped. That was extremely unfortunate and an unforgivable lapse on Renton's part. Then he had followed her to Evans's house. This had sent the police to the lab, a very unfortunate train of events but not necessarily one that would drag Cardini into it. Renton had then overdosed himself with the serum and become delirious, rather as Evans had, with his wild tales, on the plane. The revelation about the tunnels under the university was a new development. Cardini had been unaware that they existed and Renton had elucidated to him what had been in store down there for the girl.

All fiendishly clever but unhelpful.

How Evans had ended up down in the tunnels was beyond his ken, but it was the most worrying factor of all. Evans knew the location of his second secret facility, the THT lab, and it wasn't a giant leap of deductive genius to place Renton there now. Renton risked exposing everything not only through his actions but his presence.

Renton was staring at him, the low light covering his long face in deep shadow. It had been many minutes since he had finished his tale and Cardini had said nothing.

Cardini picked up his mobile phone from his desktop. 'Marius, I need a private flight from Cambridge to Cairo as soon as possible.'

'Professor, our plane is at Gatwick right now. Can you meet it there?'

'Certainly.'

'I'll email details.'

'How is your project progressing?'

'Well, sir, it's all just a matter of paperwork, past and present.' There was a smile in his voice. 'I'm recovering all the necessary pieces of documentation from the files. I was very careful to make sure it was all kept close at hand.'

'Very efficient,' said Cardini. 'Please remember to write down your project plans before you revert to the norm.'

Cardini saw Renton's head jerk up. He'd know what that meant. Cardini had inducted someone else. He hung up. 'Tomorrow you must go to Cairo and unleash the first horseman. Then you will travel to Rome. There you will stay till I call for you.'

'Yes, Master.' He clasped his hands together. 'Thank you, thank you.'

'Do not fail me again, Renton.'

'No, no,' he said, jumping off his chair. 'I swear I would rather die,' he said, bobbing up and down on the balls of his feet.

Cardini stared at him, filled with pent-up fury.

'Master?'

'Yes, Renton?'

'My serum is all used up.' He hung his head. 'Will you replace it?'

'No, I will not,' growled Cardini. 'It is too rare, too precious.'

'But, Master, I had to use it to escape.'

Cardini rose from his chair, looming above Renton, who cowered even though a desk stood between them. 'I will give you more on your return, but not until then. You have squandered the precious little you had and by rights you should have no more.'

'But you will give it to me,' he said, grovelling.

'Get out of my sight, Renton. Prepare the horseman so that you can travel first thing tomorrow.'

'Yes, Professor.' Renton straightened. 'I'll do it now.'

78

Renton made the final fiddly selection of fragile mosquitoes from the lethargic bald rat: a swarm of Ebola-infected bloodsuckers. He placed the last one in the Perspex box with its mates and put it into the airlock. He opened the airlock and held the box up to the light, dimly viewing the insects inside. The night's job was complete. He was ready.

He put the last container into its protective box, then slipped it into his shoulder bag and checked it for balance. It was three a.m.

He slung the bag over his shoulder. A small wheeled suitcase stood by the door, waiting for him to add the bag. It would pass through the X-ray machine at the airport as a jumble of soft lines. The four small boxes would be undetectable. 'No,' he would say, when they asked him about liquids and toiletries. Of course, carrying creatures over borders, infectious or otherwise, was highly illegal, so if he was caught his plan would be foiled. This gave him a moment of concern, but he was sure that, beyond another stroke of sheer bad luck, no one would have any idea that he was carrying the most devastating weapon ever created to its destination in Egypt.

He thought it was ironic that, as the Angel of Death, he would be flying by private jet, but genocide didn't have to stick to an economy budget. He scratched an itch on the back of his neck and glanced round the lab, with its array of humming, flickering equipment. This was where he and Cardini had fashioned the future of mankind in a test tube, he mused. Then he shook himself, picked up the case, walked out and closed the door with a click. He would soon be a god in a world renewed, responsible for the long overdue pruning of *Homo sapiens* before its ultimate regeneration. He was on his way to remake the destiny of man.

79

Jim registered a cry. He sat up in bed. Kate had jumped out. He looked at the side he normally slept on. The drawer was open. He was suddenly very awake.

'What's going on?'

Kate was on her way to the door. She stopped and turned. 'There's a gun in that drawer,' she said, pointing.

'So what?'

'So what? *So what?*'

'Yes. So what?'

'It's not normal,' she said.

'Normal?' he said. 'What's normal?'

'I don't know,' she said.

She made a dash for the door but he intercepted her. He took her in his arms. 'Come on,' he said, 'it's OK.' He kissed her.

'And what about that?' She pointed at his mangled side.

'Bitten by a shark,' he said. 'I was surfing.' He kissed her forehead. 'But I punched it on the nose with my free hand and it let me go.'

She looked up at him, her eyes glinting in the moonlight. 'Am I just meant to believe you whatever?' she said quietly.

'No. Trust me. That's all.'

'And the gun?'

'I've got a licence for it,' he said. 'Do you want to see?'

She shook her head.

'Let's go back to bed,' he said.

'I can't sleep.'

'That won't be a problem,' he said, smiling at her.

She pushed him away gently. 'I was trying to find something

to read but instead I found a gun.'
  'Welcome to my world.'

80

Renton's alarm was buzzing and he sat up with a jolt. He had barely slept. The little bedrooms above the lab were Spartan but serviceable. Many a time he had slept in one of them, too tired to go home. Now home wasn't an option. He felt hot and he needed an urgent pee. He got up and went into the bathroom cubicle.

He caught sight of himself in the mirror and did a double-take. He looked like a student again, a good ten years younger than the man he had last seen in the mirror. His face was red, glowing with sweat, and hot. His skin had a youthful softness. His cheeks were thinner and he thought his ears had shrunk. The lines and wrinkles that had collected around his eyes were gone, along with the black rings, the bags and creases.

He relieved himself – an immense quantity flooding out of him – then looked into the mirror again. He seemed at least five kilos lighter than he remembered.

He smiled. He noticed that his gums were red and swollen and his teeth ached, as if he had been chewing long and hard on something tough, like beef jerky. The dramatic change wrought by the elixir was bound to take its toll on his body, he thought. But bleeding gums and sore teeth seemed like a fine price to pay for becoming ten years younger overnight. He hopped into the shower and switched on the water.

When he came out, his pay-as-you-go phone, his emergency line of communication, flashed with an incoming message. 'Mr Renton. The car has set off and is on its way.' He read it, then looked at himself in the mirror again. It might take a year for someone of his age to revert to his rightful position on the clock face of ageing. For the next month or two he would be twenty-one again. He could feel the difference in his whole body: the new younger Renton was just that bit more flexible and, in a strange way, moist and smooth. He had never spotted his deterioration, but the difference between twenty-one and thirty-one was giant when you could jaunt back a decade during a few hours' sleep.

He dried himself, peed again – another vast amount – then rubbed his hot face with a damp flannel. The serum was still burning through him, although the mental acceleration had all but left him. His mind felt numb and stultified.

He went into the bedroom, dressed, collected his suitcase and went outside, bouncing determinedly along the corridor past Cardini's suite and down the stairs. He would wait outside in the fresh early-morning air for the cab. The heat racing through his body was making him feel uncomfortable.

Cardini sat up a little straighter in bed when he heard Renton's footsteps coming down the hall. He dropped his iPad on to his lap and listened as they passed his door and faded. He picked up the tablet and sent the email to the lab technicians not to come to work today. They were all on twenty-four-hour call so the chance of them missing the message was remote. Of course, he mused, if it had been an instruction to do some work it would not have been universally received, but as it was an invitation to indolence it would be acted upon by all.

He got out of bed and adjusted his cotton pyjamas, his great hands trembling. The clumsiness was rising quickly in him, his fingers heavy and fumbling. He sat down on the bed and dipped his head in thought.

Tonight would bring the optimal moment at which to administer his treatment. A second too early, and his overall life span would be shortened; too late, and he would live as though he were much older. He had begun the treatment far later than would be truly effective for him, but far earlier than McCloud, who had started after his human span was already past.

Yet, like McCloud and Renton, Cardini too was now gambling with the elixir to buy himself more than just time. He had formulated a simple plan that revolved around Evans. The strange young man was the simple solution to all of his concerns, if only Cardini could convince him.

Yet there was a serious risk. Evans was dangerous, unpredictable and strangely hard to read. Cardini had dealt with many rich men but none as young or as mysterious. The super-rich were normally either born into it, lucky or a decadent mix of smart, brazen criminality. Jim Evans didn't fit into any of these categories.

Cardini would treat himself and use the temporary acceleration of the TRT to bend Evans to his will. It would be but a tiny sacrifice to his optimum lifespan but it had to be done. He took the vial from his bag. Was it truly worth swapping a whole day of his life just to feel strong enough to deal with a young man of the same age as his worshipping students?

He broke the end off the glass ampoule.

81

Jim woke up. The sun was shining through the mullioned windows, throwing a glowing dusty light across the bedroom. Kate was dressed, putting her shoes on. 'What's up?' he said sleepily.

'I've got to go,' she said.

'Oh,' he said. 'Go where?'

'My folks,' she said. 'I haven't seen them in ages.'

'Do you have to go now?'

'Yes,' she said, not looking at him.

'OK.' He watched her put on her second shoe with an almost balletic grace. 'Did I do something wrong?'

She turned and gave him a shy smile. 'No,' she said.

'Are you sure?'

'Yes,' she said.

'Then why not stay a bit longer?'

'I need to get myself together,' she said. 'I've got to get back to something real.' She smiled at him again, as if she was about to say sorry for the umpteenth time.

'I was hoping I was real enough.'

'Nothing feels real to me right now, not this, not yesterday, not anything.'

He didn't reply, just watched her looking at him.

'You know?' she said.

'Not really.'

'Give me some time. I'll work everything out.'

'OK,' said Jim, wanting to ask what exactly she had to work out.

'Can Stafford help me?' she said, glancing at the door.

'Sure,' said Jim. 'You go down. I'll be along in a couple of minutes.'

'Thanks,' she said, heading to the door. It clunked shut behind her.

He dropped back on to the pillow and stared up at the moulded ceiling, its plaster flowers in the grasp of happy cherubs. Wasn't he meant to be the most eligible billionaire bachelor in Europe? Hadn't he just saved her from a fate worse than death by fighting a knife-wielding fiend in an underground cavern? What exactly did he have to do to win a girl's heart?

He threw off the sheets and climbed out of bed, went to the window and gazed out over the grounds. Maybe she did just need time to decompress. She must be in shock. He grimaced. There was no point in trying to understand women. They weren't from Venus: they were from another galaxy altogether.

82

Stafford seemed even more crestfallen than Jim. 'I shall accompany Kate and her car to her flat. When she has her things and is on her way again, I will drive with her until she is on the motorway.' Stafford had a reproving look on his face as if he was scolding Jim silently.

'What?' said Jim, in slight irritation.

'I'm sorry, what do you mean?'

'Why are you looking at me like that?'

'I'm not sure I understand you.'

'You're giving me a funny look,' said Jim, pulling a face back at Stafford.

'You're mistaken, I'm sure,' said Stafford, his eyebrows busier than usual. 'You perhaps take my sadness at Kate leaving for some other emotion.'

'I'm gutted too,' said Jim, the fan on his computer rig kicking in as it booted.

'I'll be on my way, then,' said Stafford.

'I'm going to nail that ridiculous fucking Italian retail chain,' he said, watching his trading screens open. 'It's been riding high in Fantasy Land long enough. Today it's going to go off the cliff with my boot up its backside.'

Stafford looked back. 'There is terrible unemployment in Italy,' he said.

Jim threw himself back in his chair and gave Stafford a gimlet stare. 'I know, I know.' He stood up and threw his wireless mouse towards Stafford in a gentle arc. 'You'd better take this with you.'

Stafford brought it back to the desk. 'I'm almost certain I

won't need it for the journey,' he said. 'I'll see you later.'

Jim took the mouse and sat down again. Emporio-mundo wasn't in a business that the man in the street would recognise. It had long since stopped making profits from selling people stuff they needed at a commercial price. It was like so many modern businesses, a derivative enterprise of a derivative of the business it had once been. It didn't make much money on selling things off the shelf. Instead it made a bomb from selling the store-card debt it created to banks, and from property, which always seemed to go up whatever the economic environment. It wasn't a collection of stores buying cheap and selling dear: it was a huge sack of debt, finely encrusted with a layer of respectable commerce, a thin gloss of brand and the smoky dry-ice effects of frantic PR.

On the apparently highly regulated stage of a European stock market, the investment audience couldn't care less about how the chain made its money, as long as it was part of a major European index. As an index constituent, it became just another of the many financial instruments that made up the multi-correlated world of global market trading.

If a Bloomberg terminal said it correlated with the yen, then people would buy and sell the shares of this Italian store chain to hedge their yen. If the yen was correlated to oil's rise against the dollar, then millions of euros a day of Emporio-mundo would trade because, down the line of causality, something was happening to the dollar. As a result, Emporio-mundo was a way of insuring some Arab sovereign wealth fund against a change in price of a tanker of Liquid Petroleum Gas heading from the US west coast to Japan. Yet go through the door into the Emporio-mundo store in Rome's main shopping drag, Via Condotti, and the fact it could sell Chanel shoes at roughly the price of manufacture would not be linked to the volatility of dollar, yen and oil. Emporio-mundo was financed by a world in which finance had become so complex that only a very few knew how all the linkages fitted together or cared that, although the correlations might be real, the business of the company was not.

The 'new lira' would swing violently from day to day and the media would ascribe it to one piece of news or another, but the truth was, no one knew why the market moved as it did, any more than ancient astrologers understood why empires fell or floods rose. Even Jim didn't know why things moved as they did. All he could see was that they would move, by how much and when.

Jim looked at the Emporio-mundo stock chart: the company's price hung in mid-air, like a ball at the apex of its flight. It couldn't stay airborne for much longer, and when it fell, it would plummet, perhaps, all the way into bankruptcy. He could easily make $200 million shorting it. He could ring up his prime broker and borrow five to ten per cent of the company's stock, then sell it in the market over a number of days. In the process of selling the borrowed shares, the price would tumble. The rumour mill would begin to turn, and if any skeletons were hidden – and they most certainly were – they would pirouette out of the closet to land on the front pages of the financial media. The whole world would start to sell, which would highlight the hollow balance sheet of a company held up purely by the sort of fiction that had recently brought the developed world to the brink of financial extinction.

All he had to do was click his mouse and the end of one of Italy's best-known companies would begin. He would chop down a rotten old tree and make space for a healthy new one. The human misery would be short-lived. Within a few years Emporio-mundo would be just another almost-forgotten historical brand, its retail locations long since repopulated by other stores. It was how the market worked. It had no fear, it had no remorse and it never slept.

His hand hovered over the mouse.

His mobile rang. 'Argh.' He pushed the mouse aside. 'Let some other fucker have the trade.'

He picked up the phone.

'Jim,' said the deep voice he immediately recognised as Cardini's. 'I would like to talk with you.'

'What about?' snapped Jim.

'Matters.'

'Matters?'

'We never came to a final conclusion.'

'We didn't?'

'No, we didn't.'

'Let me think about it,' he said, although it must have been clear to Cardini that he would not.

'Please come and see me this morning.'

'No, thanks,' said Jim.

'If you do not come this morning I will no longer be reachable, ever.'

Good job, thought Jim. He nearly said it too. 'Where's your psycho assistant?'

'Renton?'

'How many do you have?'

'He has disappeared. Apparently he has created a panic on the campus. I have not been back there, so I have no further information.'

'Where do you think we should meet?'

'At my lab outside Cambridge.'

'Will Renton be there?' said Jim.

'No,' said Cardini. 'As I said, he has disappeared.'

'Pity,' said Jim. 'I could have wrung his neck.'

'If I see him I shall immediately inform the authorities.'

'Did you inform the American authorities about McCloud?'

'That is one of the things I need to discuss with you.'

'Right,' said Jim. 'What else?'

'The project.'

'The TRT drug?'

'Yes.'

'The drug that turns old men and lab assistants into

psychopathic nut jobs?'

'It does no such thing.'

'It seems pretty obvious to me that it does. A bit of a coincidence, don't you think, that both McCloud and Renton are psychotic?' said Jim.

'Nevertheless, will you come?'

Jim's eyes turned to the samurai sword on display above the fireplace. He got up and walked over to it.

'Jim?'

'I'm thinking,' said Jim, running his hand along the length of the scabbard. His eyes narrowed. 'OK, I'll come straight away.' He hung up and took the sword down. He drew it, the blade flashing blue and red. It was a savage blade, a killer, its iridescent steel surface forged in ancient times and tempered in blood. He fancied taking it with him but that would make him as crackers as Renton. He slid the blade into the scabbard and put it back on its ebony stand on the marble mantel. He turned and headed upstairs to get the Glock pistol from his bedside table.

Jim looked down the long line of supercars. Their number plates might as well have been replaced by a sign that said, 'Arrest me.' He peered hard at the Veyron, then took the Glock out of his pocket and examined it. If the police pulled him over and came across it that would be the end of his day for sure. Stafford had undoubtedly filed all the licences in their proper place but he had no idea where or how he was meant to carry the firearm. And if he was stopped with it, bulging in his pocket, he might never get to confront Cardini or Renton.

He looked at the gun. He didn't need it against either of them. He laid it on the wall beside the nose of the Bugatti, then got into the Veyron. It was his favourite car, even if it did attract trouble.

83

Renton was sweating heavily. He lowered the window and let the air flood him. He wondered whether this was like a drug come-down. Perhaps his body was going into some kind of withdrawal after such a huge dose of the serum. The symptoms were very uncomfortable. His nose was blocked and the back of his mouth was sore. He was starting to grumble out a dry cough, struggling to clear something from the top of his windpipe. He wondered how long the effect would last.

He was feeling depressed and tired. He shifted in the back seat and rested his head on his fist, which he supported on the arm rest. A sleep would be the best thing all round, he thought, trying to get comfortable. In a couple of hours he would be taking off for Egypt, and soon after he landed he would let the horseman fly into the night skies of Cairo.

The motion of the car was making him nauseous, which was unusual. The TRT had clearly taken its toll, which was hardly surprising: it had jammed his cellular time clock back a decade. It was lucky that he'd stopped pissing like a horse – the trip would have been a nightmare if they'd had to stop every fifteen minutes. In fact, he was thirsty. The bottles of water in the back were tempting but he thought the liquid might go straight through him. He'd go without till at least they were in sight of the airport.

He closed his eyes and his vision lit up like a red firework display as he saw into the capillaries of his eyelids. It would have been a fun lightshow if he had been feeling better, but instead it was just a blazing red inferno of sparks, which stopped him dozing off. He let out a groan and coughed. Sleep would come:

he could feel it welling up in him.

How had so much gone so horribly wrong? Not long ago everything had been running like clockwork.

He was so hot – he might have been wrapped in a blanket. As he fell into a doze, strange distorted images flitted through emerging dreams. Flaming devils were running and jumping across blazing fields— he woke, his vision blurred. He rubbed his eyes. They were on a motorway he didn't recognise and a freezing wind was blowing on his face. He closed the window and rubbed his eyes again.

A big blue road sign said 'Gatwick'. A few moments later another told him that the distance to his destination was five miles.

He was burning up. He wiped the perspiration from his brow. This isn't right, he thought. He took a piece of kitchen roll from his pocket and blew his nose, which relieved the pressure in his sinuses. As he folded the paper, he saw in it a large red blob. Then he felt warm liquid rush his nose. He put the kitchen roll to it quickly and tasted his own blood.

This was terribly wrong. His eyes were filled with tears that burnt. He rubbed his eyes with the back of his hands and squinted at them. The tears appeared pink, not clear.

'Cabby,' he cried.

The driver glanced at him in the rear-view window and gasped. 'Are you OK, mate?'

'Take me back to where you picked me up.'

'I can take you to A&E,' offered the driver, whose face was lit with concern at the prospect of blood on his seats.

'No, just take me back.'

'OK,' said the driver, 'but if you change your mind, tell me.' He picked up a box of Kleenex from the passenger seat and held it out to Renton, who snatched it.

Renton glimpsed himself in the driver's mirror. His face was red, the whites of his eyes bloodshot. He was ill. It looked to him like Ebola. He thought back to the lab and the loading of the specimens: had one escaped and bitten him? It must have – how else would he have the disease? His high temperature was not an after-effect of the serum: it was the accelerated onset of the disease. Ebola took a week to incubate, perhaps as little as three days in the aggressive strain they had grown and enhanced. The serum had accelerated his metabolism and the virus with it. He had to get back to the lab. Cardini would know what to do. He might survive.

He could go to the Hospital for Tropical Diseases but he was known there by the medical specialists as the famous Cardini's assistant and would be quickly recognised. Then if he pulled through he would only be arrested and spend the rest of his life in prison. He had to get back to Cardini. It was his only hope.

'Please hurry,' he said, his throat hurting with the effort.

'I'll go as fast as I can, mate,' said the driver, coming off the motorway to go back in the opposite direction. 'If you pass out I'm taking you to a hospital,' he said.

'OK.'

84

He had driven up the same roads like a lunatic only a few hours before but now he was cruising like an old guy in a clapped-out twenty-year-old banger. He didn't want to attract any more attention to himself and risk getting waylaid by the police. There had been something very final in Cardini's voice when he'd said it was Jim's last chance to speak with him. Did he know something that Jim didn't? He needed to get to the bottom of whatever the hell Cardini was up to.

Jim was used to things being linear in his world. One thing followed from another. This situation was fragmented into a mosaic and the picture it portrayed was a garbled mystery.

He had seen the TRT at work; he had felt it work on him. He had seen an ancient dying man made a generation younger. He had met a wonderful girl. He had killed two men and fought a maniac. The only common factor was Cardini, the daunting professor with a cure for death.

Everything revolved around Cardini, but he had no idea how it all fitted together. He knew something awful was going on so he had to find out what Cardini was planning.

At legal speeds the journey was excruciatingly slow. He wanted to travel much faster and so did the car, but he didn't want his number plate flashing up on a traffic police computer somewhere, which might link him up with the road events of the day before.

Vehicle after vehicle passed him, passengers glancing at him as they went by. Some people smiled. One white-van passenger gave him the finger. Jim decided he was going to get a really boring car to add to the collection, a shabby old Volvo, perhaps, or a generic people-carrier. A million pounds' worth of wheeled rocket wasn't a sensible means of transport and he owned no vehicle that wasn't flashy or extravagant.

He found himself wondering about Kate. Somewhere ahead, Stafford would be chaperoning her to her door in the bullet-riddled armour-plated Maybach, driving behind her at exactly the right distance and speed.

The miles ticked down slowly.

Cardini held out his once-quivering hand. It was as steady as it had been when he was a surgeon. The steady hand was the proof of cold blood and an incredible concentration, both vital to him as he tacked and spliced nerves, bound sinews and mated capillaries. He was proud of that work, but he had always been proud of himself, even as a child. All men were not born equal and they never would be. There was talent, there was breeding, there was the alpha human of Huxley's Brave New World and there were the epsilons. Yet now there was no room for them all and the epsilons had to be purged, just as the weak shoots of a planting had to be thinned.

The cull would change everything. Death would make life more precious. In initiating a plague against man he would be its saviour. In the following decades, he would be the master of longevity and, as his knowledge, power and wisdom grew, of human biology. There would be no cutting down of his mighty oak, no felling of his majesty by aged decline. As other minds wilted, he would become an ever greater mental colossus. Within one or two generations he would be unassailable, the grey emperor of a new world, a latter-day Methuselah.

But things were not going to plan.

The hot-headed youth had torn his plans to tatters. Jim Evans, however, could be the perfect remedy to the very problems he had created. Under Evans's patronage, Cardini would be unimpeded for decades, enough time for the world to be cleansed and for him to have transcended the intellect of other mortals.

Evans would provide the bridge to the fruition of his master plan and a simple solution to what had become a set of complex problems. All Cardini had to do was bend him to his will using the ultimate promise of eternal life. It had never failed before. In the end it would surely overcome Evans.

85

Jim drove slowly up the drive through the scrubby woods that surrounded Cardini's hidden lab. He was starting to have second thoughts.

He should have called Smith – he still could. If he involved the authorities, though, he would never find out what Cardini was really up to and, knowing Cardini, the professor would simply use the serum to seduce someone very senior and get from him whatever it was he desired. As such, something worse might come out of an intervention from Smith: another patron to fund Cardini's sinister plans.

Would Renton be there?

Renton hadn't been an easy opponent, obviously high on the serum, but Jim had been able to take him on, even though he was wielding a knife – but what if it had been a machete or a fire axe?

He'd been an idiot to leave the gun at home and drive straight into Cardini's trap. Sometimes he thought he was the stupidest guy in the world and right now was just one such time.

He could turn back even now. What could Cardini tell him that he didn't already know? He wasn't going to sell his soul for a promise of eternal youth. He wasn't going to be a pawn in Cardini's game for anything. The drug clearly turned a frequent user into a barking psycho. He had experienced the effect on his mind, which, even after a small dose, had been remarkable, but he didn't long to take it again. It was like when he had driven along the motorway at 200 m.p.h. It had been thrilling but it had also been scary.

His nan had liked to say, 'What you see is what you get,' and as he had grown up, the phrase had morphed in his mind from a meaningless adage into something profound. There was little or no truth below the surface. If you wanted to know what the truth was, all you had to do was look at it with innocent eyes. When the market was going up, it was going up; when it was falling, it was going to carry on falling. Not much looked ugly that wasn't; little looked beautiful that wasn't.

This was an ugly situation, populated with terrible people up to something horrible. That's enough evidence for me to turn around and head away from the whole set-up, Jim thought.

But instead it drove him on.

86

Renton had lost track of time. His world was a blur of strange images and the sickness that racked his body. He had to get back to the lab.

He wanted to ask how much further it was, but he didn't dare utter a sound. He could taste blood in his mouth as it leaked from his gums and mixed with pooling saliva, which he forced himself to swallow. His heavy breathing filled his head with white noise as he shielded his face with his hands. If the seatbelt hadn't held him so securely, he would have slumped forward.

He pulled his consciousness into a ball inside his crumbling body, desperate to hold out against his disintegration. He concentrated on making it to the next moment, surviving by willing himself into the future. The TRT would be healing him just as the accelerated virus was tearing his viscera apart. Streaks of pain, like thin needles skewering his trunk, came in showers, and he winced as they passed.

If he could get more TRT, it would boost his body's fight against the infection. It had accelerated the effect of the virus but it could accelerate his recovery too. With enough serum, he dreamt in his delirium, his body would fight back and overwhelm the disease. He had to stay upright in his seat. He had to get back to Cardini.

The driver looked at his passenger in the mirror. The man was cradling his face like he was having some kind of migraine. He was worrying about getting paid, but at the building where he had made the pickup, there'd be plenty of people to bail out the guy if he wasn't up to it. At a hospital he might be left holding the bag. As long as his passenger looked awake, he'd keep going to Cambridge.

87

The front door of the lab was locked. There were venetian blinds down across the main reception windows so Jim couldn't see in. The door had no give at all, suggesting it was a lot sturdier than it looked. He peered at the entry system. You needed a swipe and possibly a pass code to get in. The door clicked. Jim stood back a pace to give himself room and turned side on. If Renton was on the other side he would be able to attack or flee.

The door opened slowly as if the person on the other side was also showing caution. There stood Cardini, looming large. 'I'm so grateful that you came.'

'Grateful?' queried Jim, stepping forwards.

'Yes,' said Cardini.

Jim shrugged and walked in. The door clicked shut behind him.

'Please come through.'

Jim followed.

'We have had a torrid time in our short acquaintance,' said Cardini.

'Yep,' said Jim, carefully registering everything around him. He might have to come back down the corridor in a hurry and wanted to know every little detail along the way just in case.

'I must, of course, apologise for everything,' said Cardini. 'But I was eager to prove the value of my work to you as quickly as possible.' He opened his office door. 'McCloud was simply out of control.'

'After you,' said Jim, not wanting to go into the room ahead of Cardini.

As Cardini walked ahead of him into the lab, he said, over his shoulder, 'McCloud was never satisfied and was constantly trying to force me to increase my dosages so he could be younger than I believed desirable.'

Jim sat down in front of the desk, Cardini opposite.

'You see, Jim, some people are a law unto themselves.'

'You mean people like you?'

Cardini appeared to think for a moment. 'I suppose so.'

'So what happened after I left?'

'I was about to ask you that.'

'I asked first.'

An expression of delight came over Cardini's face. 'Practically nothing happened.' He threw his hands up. 'A pair of serious men appeared unannounced and asked to see McCloud, and when he couldn't be raised the staff set about looking for him. In the end, they discovered him and the other man in the lower complex.'

'Then what?'

'It was all very odd.' His eyes narrowed. 'Clearly they knew something because someone must have tipped them off. Then more people appeared and there was a hive of activity. They took my details and basically told me to go.'

'Didn't they interview you?'

'No. They asked me who I was, what I was doing there and what I had done the previous evening. I said I had seen McCloud in the evening, gone to bed and woken up in the morning for breakfast.'

'Is that all?'

'Yes. I am gambling that all the video of the day was erased. If not, we are all in the soup.'

'Possibly.'

'What about you, Jim? What's your story?'

'I drove to Raleigh and flew back here.'

'And then what?'

'Well, you know or you wouldn't be asking.'

'You came up to my lab and fought Renton in the tunnels below the university.'

'Yes,' said Jim.' Your assistant was off his face on your drug and about to chop Kate – one of your old students – into little pieces, like one of those poor monkeys you keep.'

Cardini didn't flinch. 'I'm very shocked,' he said. 'I haven't gone back to the main lab, as you can imagine. Not in the circumstances.' He looked a trifle unsure. 'None of this was meant to happen.'

'Well, it has and it's all your fault.'

'Mine?' boomed Cardini, in outrage. 'How can it have been my doing?'

'You're the common factor, aren't you?'

Cardini looked at him gravely. 'Are you not also a common factor?'

It was Jim's turn to think. 'If the maniacs were my friends then you might have a leg to stand on, but as they're yours I think I'm safe in reckoning you're the guy in the frame here.'

'We could continue this debate, Jim, but that would serve little purpose.' Cardini smiled. 'I can see so much in you that was in me when I was your age. You are full of drive and energy. You have the courage to challenge the situations you find yourself in and overcome the barriers that others find insurmountable. You have a brilliant mind and you have the character and foresight to use it to rise above the rest. You and I shouldn't be at odds. We should work together. Together we can overcome the petty considerations of our finite lifespan and be the first to transcend this shoddy existence.'

Cardini's face suddenly seemed fatherly and benign – he was beaming at Jim. 'Now that, to all intents and purposes, I have overcome mortality, at least for someone as young as you, I can expand my work on the human mind.' He leant forward on the desk. 'The mind may appear a wondrous thing, but it is as simple as any muscle. It just takes a little more intellect than we are naturally blessed with to understand it.'

There was a twinkle in his eye. 'I have, of course, been able to leap above that limiting intellect and see the mind for what it is and how one may interface with it. Our predecessors knew that a little electricity would make the leg of a dead frog kick. It has long been a scientific dream to be able to fuse the mind with electricity and somehow expand it. Of course, with a gross understanding of electricity and the mind, treatments like electric-shock therapy were the initial brutal steps towards developments that now, in our still-primitive era of medicine, mean some mental processes, which cause Alzheimer's, Tourette's and epilepsy, are at last being ameliorated by electrical charges discharged deep within the brain.

'I have gone much further than that. I am on the edge of another breakthrough that is as revolutionary as my elixir: the ability to connect the mind with the machine.' He sat back. 'We can think and move a muscle and we can read that muscle, but I know how to connect a mind directly to a machine, a computer. That computer in turn offers mental processes far in excess of human capacity. A computer can calculate in a second what a mind might calculate in a lifetime. It can remember everything. Every piece of knowledge ever discovered, every song sung, book written, formula proved or postulated, it can simulate in its silicon mind environments beyond our ability to conceptualise. A human mind is the soul and spirit of a human, but it is a weak calculating device and a poor, slow thinker. Soon I will be able to expand our consciousness by orders of magnitude, increase our intelligence by a thousand-fold, then a million-fold.'

He smiled at Jim.

'Imagine what would happen if you could be even a little bit smarter than everyone else. The world of limitations as we know them just falls away, doesn't it?' He was nodding, clearly fishing for Jim's agreement. 'Then imagine again if you were ten times smarter.'

'You'd be very lonely,' said Jim.

'Pah!' exclaimed Cardini. 'Lonely! Why would you care when you would be the ruler of the world?'

'I'd care,' said Jim. 'It's bad enough being richer than everybody else, but if you were that much cleverer, it'd be like living on your own at the top of Mount Everest. You'd freeze to death.'

Cardini let out a sigh. 'Why can't you see the grandeur? How can you not want to embrace an expanded potential?'

They looked at each other, like two totally different species wondering which was the more dangerous and which was about to be the other's lunch.

'Where's Renton?' asked Jim.

'How should I know? He is, or rather was, just one of my many lab technicians. I don't run their lives.'

'Just one of your technicians?'

'Well, an important one, but still just another.'

'He needs to be taken off the streets,' said Jim.

'Jim,' said Cardini, 'there are more important things right now than Renton. I'm sure the police will find him soon enough. It's not for me to turn into a sleuth. My concerns are just as pressing. Now that McCloud is dead I need to replace him with a new source of funds and, as you know, the cost of my project is significant.'

'Not my problem.'

'Jim, you simply cannot pass up this opportunity! You cannot turn away the one and only chance you will have to live for ever. I am not prepared to believe you are mad enough to turn that down.'

'I'm mad enough,' said Jim. 'I don't want to live for five hundred years as a paranoid lunatic like McCloud.'

'I did not do that to him. That was always his personality.'

'Or as a psychotic sadistic sicko like Renton.'

'That was not my doing either. Look at me – do you see madness in my demeanour? Do I demonstrate behaviour like that of either McCloud or Renton?'

'Maybe, your experiments are pretty sick.'

Cardini moaned in frustration. 'The experiments you saw are the norm for medical research,' he said, waving his hands in the air as his voice rose. 'They are science, plain science. I appreciate they are not pretty for the non-scientific observer but they are normal, quite normal.'

'Whatever,' said Jim. 'I'm not interested.'

'What if I can show you the serum is safe? After all, you can go without it for many years, perhaps as long as decades, and still have the prospect of hundreds of years ahead of you.' Cardini slumped back in his chair. 'I must say, the request is not totally unselfish. The project will fund my longevity too. Funding the project funds my research. Without money, you will see the end of me and my knowledge.' He looked dolefully at Jim. 'Why not think of my project as the ultimate life insurance for yourself, and a way of helping me to extend my research?' He fixed Jim with a penetrating stare. 'What I have in store will truly change the world for the better, for ever.' A powerful, confident smile lit Cardini's face, but there was something knowing in it too – and something evil.

'If you publish the formula of TRT in the public domain I'll fund you.'

Cardini sat bolt upright. 'Publish the formula?' His forehead creased and his nostrils flared. 'Are you mad? Do you realise what that would mean?'

'Yes. Everyone would live a lot longer.'

'Yes, yes,' replied Cardini, almost laughing with contempt. 'The population would explode – eight billion, twelve billion, thirty billion, fifty, a hundred ... Where would it stop?'

'But you said it would make people smart enough to overcome our barriers.'

'We can't all be gods,' said Cardini. 'When everyone is a giant we are all dwarfs again. If I released the formula and knowledge behind TRT, and it could be manufactured like aspirin or penicillin, the world would be set on a course of destruction. Its population is already too large to support itself. With TRT, the whole of humanity would be pitched into a vicious circle of conflict and resource depredation that would throw the whole of civilisation into the abyss within a generation.'

'So instead you want the two of us to rule the world as immortals, like two Greek gods sitting on Vesuvius?'

Cardini looked pained. 'Olympus.'

'Wherever,' said Jim.

'Doesn't the idea appeal to you? Haven't you earned it?' said Cardini.

'You're mad as well,' said Jim. 'You might not be as off your trolley as McCloud or Renton, but you're still in Cloud Cuckoo Land.'

Cardini put his hands on the desk and lifted himself up a little. 'Do you mean to tell me you cannot see the amazing opportunities I am offering, that you cannot comprehend the vast potential for you and your line? Can you not appreciate that, in the history of the world and of mankind, this is the first time that anyone has had the chance of escaping their mortal fate? This is not a fable or a myth. This is the destiny of humanity. If it is not you, or it is not me, it will be another at some time in the future. If not you, if not me, then who?'

They heard a crash in the hallway and jumped to their feet. They stared at each other, shocked.

'I have no idea what that was,' said Cardini.

Jim suddenly regretted being unarmed. Someone or something was coming down the hallway. Now they could hear a whining, screeching, crying noise that sent a shiver down Jim's spine.

The door was flung open. A figure, bent double, tottered into the room supported on the door handle.

'Master,' cried Renton, red drool spiralling from his mouth on to the floor.

Jim jumped forward and vaulted over the desk to Cardini and stood beside him, aghast.

Renton fell to his knees. 'Master,' he squeaked. His eyes were red orbs, and blood streamed in tears down his cheeks. 'Help me,' he begged. 'Save me. I couldn't release the horseman because one has infected me.' He held up the box, then thumped it to the floor. 'Forgive me. Forgive me.' He shuddered, belching, and blood poured from his lips. 'But save me, save me, so I can try again.'

'Be still,' shouted Cardini.

'Save me.' His head fell forward, the blood trickling from his face in long red streams.

'Be still and I will save you.'

Cardini pulled open a drawer and took out a syringe. He shuffled among a collection of small bottles.

'What are you going to give him?' barked Jim.

'Be quiet,' snapped Cardini.

Renton looked up, his face a mass of sticky blood. 'Master?' He turned to Jim, staring blindly at the space he occupied. 'Master?'

'Be still, child,' boomed Cardini.

Renton coughed blood, which showered across his chest.

Cardini filled the syringe and stepped around the desk. 'Be still,' he commanded again.

'Master,' croaked Renton.

Cardini's long arm stretched out at an angle to avoid contact with Renton and his blood and he pressed the needle into the man's neck. He pushed the barrel in and stepped away quickly.

Renton looked up at him and then at Jim. His eyes widened, his head tilted and then he fell backwards.

Jim looked down at the lifeless body. 'You've killed him.'

When he glanced up, the needle, still in Cardini's hand, was swinging towards him. He caught the professor's wrist and his left fist was on its way. It connected. The old man fell back and landed on the floor.

'The tip of this syringe is laced with the Ebola virus. If you come towards me I will make sure it pierces your skin.' Cardini struggled to his feet, holding it out like a knife. 'The tiniest drop will finish you, just as it killed Renton.'

Jim regarded him with a gimlet stare.

'Contact with even a drop of Renton's blood will be enough so leaving this room uninfected will be difficult. A struggle with me will doom us both to a terrible death. I did Renton a service in ending his misery and now I am letting you go.'

'What's in the box?'

'Go, before it's too late.'

'If I die, you die,' said Jim, 'so tell me.'

'What?'

'What's in the box?'

'Don't you want to live, you fool?'

'Less than you do, so tell me what's in the box.'

Cardini straightened. 'You really want to know?'

'Too right I do.'

'You would stay in a room that is dripping with death to know?'

'Get on with it.'

'Very well.' He paused, then sighed. 'Bio-weapons.'

'What for?'

'Ridding the world of its excess population.'

Jim's mouth fell open. He closed it hurriedly. 'Is that what you and McCloud were up to, ridding the world of its excess population?'

'It was McCloud's idea but I warmed to it. It is just accelerating the inevitable, managing the process, separating the winners from the losers.'

Jim vaulted back over the desk. Cardini turned to him, too far away to lunge but gripping the syringe with evident intent.

Jim glanced at Renton's body and the bloody mess around it. 'Stay back, Cardini, I'm out of this room first.' He inched along the wall, one eye on Cardini and one on the pool of bloody filth around Renton's prostrate body. The technician's face looked much younger than he remembered it: it was like his own, still holding the trace of the teenager he had been. Jim was shuddering with revulsion as he stepped around the body slowly, watching Cardini in case the old man decided to come at him with the syringe.

The door handle looked clean. He took it and swung the door open. One touch of the wrong thing and his life was over. He leapt awkwardly out of the room and sighed with relief. He was clear.

Then he looked at the wall just in front of his nose. 'Oh, fuck,' he cried.

A bloody handprint was still dripping just a few millimetres away. He balanced back without moving his feet and peered down the hallway. Renton's blood was splashed everywhere, on the floor, the walls – it was even sprayed on the ceiling.

He looked back at Cardini, who was eyeing him. The professor was backing away now, pressing something behind him. He smiled. 'Good luck, Jim,' he said, in a deep voice. 'You'd better get yourself to a hospital as soon as you can.' A panel in the wall behind him slid to one side and he stepped backwards. The panel closed over him. There was the click of a latch and a locking sound.

Jim was going to have to play hopscotch for his life.

88

Cardini walked quickly down the spiral stairs and into the main production area. McCloud had made him build a failsafe device and had actually come to check it had been installed. He had wanted Cardini to be able to destroy the lab so that no one could ever work out what had gone on there.

It was child's play for Cardini to turn the place into an inferno. He had actually enjoyed building a system that would create a fire so hot that it would turn anything inside into a charred wreck or a pool of molten metal. Iron had been the solution, an everyday material, cheap and innocuous: it burnt under the right chemical conditions with a heat that was unstoppable. When the trigger fired, the lab would become one giant thermite reaction and a ball of fire as iron turned to rust in hours rather than years.

McCloud had been right: the world was more complex than even Cardini could have calculated. McCloud had thought that for every action there was an equal and opposite reaction. Of course, that was childish physics, but he had believed it applied to human action as much as it did to a rock floating in space. He had felt Cardini's plan would magically conjure an opposing force and that only by extremely careful planning could this human cosmic mumbo-jumbo be overcome.

Cardini had thought it superstitious nonsense yet now the paranoid McCloud's preparations were proving necessary. It was ridiculous, of course: McCloud had been right for the wrong reason. Such were the outcomes of luck.

He headed for the store room, entered his code and pulled the door open. In racks before him lay container after container of

TRT, ten tonnes in total, two million treatments. He held the key to a million cures for a thousand terrible diseases in his hands, like a butterfly he would pin to a card. Everyone who died – and they died at every moment – had had a life that he had taken because it was in his power to save them. He smiled at the rows of white containers. Now he would remove enough for his purposes, destroy what remained and be gone.

He walked to the rear of the store and typed a code into a panel. It asked for another, then a third, followed by the number five. He had five minutes to be clear of the building, which was more than enough.

He grabbed a heavy bottle from the shelf, his other hand still holding the infected needle: life in one hand, death in the other.

89

Jim was scrubbing his hands and face in the washbasin. He had hopped, skipped and jumped down the corridor and thought he had avoided Renton's bloody trail. Then he had spotted the toilets in Reception. If there was a trace on him it was best that he tried to wash it away. He washed, rinsed and dried himself again and again. Then he grabbed some towels and headed for the front door. He would open it with the towels and get clear of the building. He wouldn't relax until he had reached the car.

He'd call his butler. Stafford would know what to do next.

First, though, he had to get clear.

Cardini was walking swiftly towards the back entrance. He wondered if Jim would be there waiting for him. But why would he? He would surely head away as far and as fast as he could. He might have got out without infecting himself but, even if he had, any sensible person would head for a hospital and wait out the incubation period there.

If Jim was still out front Cardini would simply get into his car and drive off. The needle would keep Jim away: it was the ultimate weapon.

He swung open the rear door, the fresh air hitting him. It was an invigorating blast. The canister of TRT was enough to buy off the world, a blank cheque from a hundred megalomaniacs, dictators, oligarchs and other men of destiny. This time he would sacrifice a few years of comfort for the smooth execution of his plans. A few carefully chosen people had an inkling of what he could do for their health; they had been given a hint that he could add a few years of life expectancy to an ageing person. They had seen how robust he was for his age and would contact him with offers of fabulously well-paid work. It was yet another ploy, another safety net for his master plan.

If Marius did not succeed in his takeover of the McCloud Foundation he would turn to the others and quickly release a new set of the first horseman. This time he would have no interference from someone like McCloud, distracting him with constant demands. This time he would be unleashed.

Cardini rounded the building and balked. Jim was sitting on the bonnet of a sports car, holding something. Cardini stepped forward, putting the canister down. He fumbled in his pocket and pulled out a container. He held the top between his teeth and bit it off, then spat it out and sucked at the open end as he broke off the other. The TRT shot into his mouth. Jim approached him, the tyre iron in his hand.

'Drop the needle, Cardini, or I'm going to brain you with this.' He waved the metal bar at him.

In a moment the TRT would kick in and he would take on the younger man.

'Jim, you do realise you are also as mad as I?' He laughed. 'What exactly are you going to do?'

'I'm going to take you to the police. You've made bio-weapons, for fuck's sake. You have to be stopped.'

Cardini laughed long and loud. 'Stopped? By you? I've offered you the world and in return you want to destroy me. Don't you think that's mad?'

'Drop the needle, Cardini.'

Cardini was feeling the TRT flood his body with power. This was the sensation McCloud had craved, of going back to a time when the energy and vigour of the body were more than they had ever been. He felt as if he was growing, his muscles blowing up like balloons.

Jim watched Cardini. He seemed to grow: his posture straightened, first his back and then his neck. He looked a good two inches taller than he had a few seconds earlier.

'Jim, don't make me infect you. Don't make me take your life. This is all so unnecessary.'

'Drop the syringe. It's all over for you. There's nowhere for you to go.'

Cardini took a step forward. 'Get into your car, Jim, and drive home to your beautiful life. Go now if you want to live.'

A calm had come over Cardini that gave Jim a horrible sinking feeling in the pit of his stomach. The syringe in the man's hand would be lethal with just the slightest prick. A knife could cut, scrape, gouge and still not be lethal, but one touch of that needle and he would be infected, his death just a matter of time.

Jim moved between Cardini and his black Mercedes.

'It seems that you really are going to make me fight you. You are beyond foolish.' Cardini squared up to him, out of the range of the tyre iron.

'Drop it, Cardini. This is your last chance.'

'No, Jim, this is your last chance. Stop this insanity and join me instead; together—'

'Forget it, Cardini. Let's get this over with.'

Cardini was a big target, but the needle was out in front. A miss would leave Jim open for a fatal counterattack.

Jim had no idea how fast Cardini was, pumped up with the serum. He was younger than McCloud, who had been pretty fast, but much older than Renton, who had been almost too quick to handle.

He would go for the obvious shot: to knock the syringe out of Cardini's hand.

They were sizing each other up, swaying slightly from side to side. Cardini certainly wasn't moving like an old man: he was as limber as anyone Jim had fought.

Jim chose his moment and swung for Cardini's right hand. Cardini drew it back, and as Jim pulled the bar away, Cardini caught it with his left hand. He swung the needle towards Jim's exposed forearm.

Jim let go of the bar instantly and jumped back. 'You can go now,' said Cardini. 'I set you free.'

'I'm not going anywhere, and neither are you.'

'So, you are going to force me to kill you,' said Cardini. 'Very well. You have received all the mercy in me. I will show you no more.'

Cardini stepped forward and slashed the tyre iron at Jim's head. Jim ducked under it and danced to one side. Cardini changed hands with the weapons, giving Jim no time to rush him. Cardini nodded to himself. 'It looks as if it is I who will brain *you*, Jim,' he said, with relish in his voice. He swung again, this time with his best arm, and Jim jumped back just far enough for it to miss the side of his skull.

It was going to be very difficult to get inside the arc of the iron bar to strike Cardini, yet be out of the way of a blow from the syringe. He turned away so that as Cardini advanced he wouldn't get pinned with his back to the Veyron.

There was a sudden roar and Cardini started. His eyes darted to the building and he shielded himself from the sudden heat of the blast.

The rupture did not break Jim's concentration: it had been like a soft, unexpected punch, not distraction enough for him to take his eyes off his opponent. He saw Cardini flinch. He pushed off from his back foot, the left heading straight for Cardini's right kneecap. It made contact and Cardini's leg, which was braced, providing the push-off he needed to spring away from the arc of the professor's reach.

Cardini's kneecap spun under the force of the kick and fractured, the joint shattering. Cardini fell to one side and Jim sprang away from him. He ran to the plastic container Cardini had been carrying and swept it up. He unscrewed the top and began to pour the contents on to the ground.

'No!' cried Cardini, trying and failing to get up. 'No!' He dropped the syringe. 'No! Don't do that! Don't waste it.'

The heat of the blaze was baking Jim's back as he poured the pear-smelling liquid along the road and on to the grass verge.

Cardini was weeping helplessly. 'Please.'

Jim walked around him, picked up the tyre iron, and threw the container into the shattered front door of the lab, flames billowing towards him. He smashed the driver's side window of the Mercedes and climbed inside to riffle the glove compartment. He popped the boot and took out Cardini's bag, which he opened.

'Don't!' screamed Cardini, as Jim lobbed the bag through the fiery doorway. He rolled over and snatched up the syringe.

'Drop it!'

Cardini held it, defiant.

Jim gritted his teeth. Then, with a brutal blow, he smashed it out of the professor's hand.

Cardini screamed as the syringe flew across the forecourt. Jim bent down and rummaged through his pockets. He stood up with a vial of TRT, threw it on to the ground and crunched it under his foot.

Cardini was sobbing, a desolate wail.

'You don't have any more, do you?'

Cardini stared up at him with hatred.

Jim smiled. That had told him all he wanted to know. There was no more TRT. He turned and walked to the Veyron. It was hot inside the car. He reversed, looking across at the black Mercedes, which was now smouldering. He turned the car and drove around Cardini, who was crawling towards the puddle of TRT that remained. Make the most of it, thought Jim, looking up as a raindrop struck his ash-covered windscreen.

It began to pour, and as he headed towards the road he put on his wipers; they smeared the black detritus across the glass.

He rang Smith.

90

Stafford came into the study. 'You called.'

'Yes, Stafford,' said Jim, who was scanning the gardens.

Stafford waited. 'How may I help?' he asked finally.

Jim turned away from the window. 'I've found something I want you to have.' He pulled it out of his pocket.

Stafford raised his eyebrows. 'Is that what I think it is?'

'Yes.'

'The serum.'

'Yes. It's the only one left. I don't think a single dose turns you into a maniac.'

'Can you be sure?'

'No,' said Jim, 'but I've had some and it didn't turn me into a loony.'

'You should keep it.'

'It needs to be destroyed and you may as well take advantage of it instead.'

Stafford let out a little cough and opened his mouth as if to say something. He checked himself. 'As you will,' he said. 'How can I refuse?' He smiled.

Jim held out the vial to him. After a moment's hesitation Stafford took it. He unscrewed the top and gave another little cough. 'Just drink it?' he asked.

'Yes,' said Jim.

Stafford sipped, then braced himself and poured the rest into his mouth.

He stood stiffly, concentrating on the effect, if any. 'I can't say I'm noticing much,' he said, with a hint of disappointment. 'No, nothing.'

'Really?' said Jim. 'Nothing at all?'

'Nothing.'

Jim shrugged. 'Sorry. It must have gone off.'

'Gorn off?' said Stafford, suddenly laughing. 'Gorn off? You must be joking, old chap. My whole body's on fire. Why, it's amazing.' He ran his hands down his sides. 'Are you sure this is safe? My insides feel quite peculiar – as if I'm filling up with hot chocolate fondue.' His face had gone red and he was beaming. 'I think, if you don't mind,' said Stafford, 'I'll go to my quarters and have a lie-down – no, perhaps a walk in the grounds. This is quite extraordinary.' He took off his glasses and squinted at Jim. 'By George, I can actually see you,' he said. He put his glasses back on, then took them off again. 'This is remarkable, quite remarkable. If I suddenly turn into a power-crazed maniac, promise you'll shoot me.'

'I promise.'

'I think I need to experience this in private,' Stafford said, 'or I might die of shame later.' He put the empty bottle on Jim's desk and walked out of the room.

Jim dropped it into the wastepaper bin.

91

There was a man on the ha-ha but she couldn't make out who it was. Perhaps it was the mysterious Mr Evans. She was glad she was on the shire. It was a giant and made her look small and frail, rather than slightly too strapping, which her mother had told her was her fatal flaw. 'Men don't like tall women,' she had been informed, as if that would somehow curtail her growth.

Arabella saw that he was getting up as she approached. He was going to do more than wave as she walked past: he was going to engage her in conversation. She wondered whether Stafford would appear. That would be nicer than chatting with this stranger, even if it was the mystery man. She had got used to the daily acknowledgement, the smile, the few passing words, the relaxed but long gazes.

The man looked like Stafford, like a younger brother, a son, even. He was particularly handsome, in a way Stafford must have been twenty years earlier when she had been running through head-high wheat in that same field.

'Good day,' called the man.

She raised her hand to him, riding his way. 'Good day,' she said, when they were close enough.

A tartan rug lay on the grass with a hamper on it, a bucket of ice and a bottle of champagne. Next to it there was an extraordinarily large dish of caviar.

'I've been told that the most beautiful gal in the whole of the Home Counties rides this way each day,' the man said, smiling up at her. He was undoubtedly Stafford's son. 'And, by George, it's true.'

'Surely he didn't mean me,' she said, smiling down at him,

taken completely off guard by such extravagant flattery.

'I'm certain he must have.' He waved at the picnic. 'So I have laid a trap for you.'

'It is a rather obvious snare,' she said. 'What is the champagne?'

'S,' said Stafford.

'Oh, really? S for "super", ' she said. 'And the caviar?'

'Russian Imperial Beluga, in strict contravention of the CITES accords.'

'That is so illegal,' she said, looking down at him, 'but rather tempting nonetheless. Will your father be along?'

'No,' said Stafford, 'he's gone away for a few weeks.' He held his hand up to her. 'Can I help you down?'

'That's very gallant of you but I prefer to dismount in my own way.'

He stepped back and she swung down to the ground, bouncing a little. She took off her helmet and her hair fell on to her shoulders.

'You've caught the sun,' he said, looking so closely at her cheek that she thought he might kiss her.

She smiled. 'You are perhaps the most forward man I have met all year.'

'I must apologise for being enchanted,' he said, looking down bashfully.

'Don't,' she said.

92

Stafford marched into the study.

Jim looked up. 'Bloody hell,' he said.

'Quite,' barked Stafford. 'Bloody hell indeed,' he said, with a military clip to his delivery.

'You're wearing my clothes.'

'Yes, I am. Force of circumstance, I'm afraid. Mine no longer fit and, what's more, they are no longer in fashion.'

'Right,' said Jim. He grinned.

'I have a favour to ask,' continued Stafford. 'In fact, several.'

'Anything,' said Jim.

'I wish to take some time off, perhaps as much as a month.'

'Of course,' said Jim.

'I would like to make the most of this Indian summer, if I may.'

'Of course.'

'I wondered if I might borrow one of the cars.' He turned away as if to give Jim the space to say no.

'You're covered in straw,' said Jim.

Stafford spun round. 'Am I?'

'All over your back.'

'Oh dear.'

'Oh dear?' queried Jim.

'Would it be all right …?'

Jim was pulling straw off Stafford's back. 'You want to borrow a car?' he asked. 'Of course, however many you like.'

'And perhaps the jet?' said Stafford, a trifle sheepishly.

'Sure,' said Jim. He looked out of the window. His jaw dropped. 'There's some bird riding over the lawn on a warhorse.'

Stafford followed his gaze. 'Good grief, it's Arabella.'

'Arabella?' said Jim. He burst out laughing. 'Charter a yacht too.'

'That's too much,' said Stafford, panic in his tone.

'Go for it,' said Jim. 'Show her the bright lights – you're only young twice.'

'I'd better get out there,' said Stafford.

'See you later.'

Stafford dashed for the door, appearing a few moments later on the drive, the gravel crunching under his stride. He walked smartly towards her, about to break into a skip and a jump.

Jim shook his head.

93

'Why have you come here?' Cardini said, his voice trembling.

'Just checking up on you.'

Cardini was sitting in a cheap armchair, wrapped in a blanket. He looked much older than he had two months before when Jim had left him lying on the ground, his leg smashed. 'Come to see me crumble away?'

'Yes, I have. If I could drive a stake through your heart I would.'

Cardini was nodding as he thought of his reply. He raised his mottled, gnarled hands. 'Take a good look, child. This is your sorry future. One day you will be sitting here. You will be dying and then, as you look into the void of death, you will –' he gasped '– you will know that you gave up your only chance to survive. You will have died through your own stupidity.'

'Well, I promise you one thing. Unlike you I won't give a monkey's cuss.'

His mobile bleeped, it was an SMS. No one sent him SMS. Maybe it was Kate. He took it out.

It was a slap in the face for Cardini. 'You'll be like me one day,' his trembling voice spat, 'a worthless broken vessel.'

Jim looked up at him, distracted. 'Right,' he said. He looked back at the message. It was from some crazy foreign number and it was Jane. 'Am I worth $100 million? J.'

He turned away from Cardini and walked out, desperately trying to call the number back. The line didn't answer. He looked at the message again. What the hell had happened?

There was another bleep. This time it was from Kate. What?

thought Jim. 'Jim, I'm sorry for running off like that. Can we perhaps have a coffee?'

He slapped the screen to his forehead and groaned. More insanity and chaos, he thought.

94

Cardini raised his head slowly and peered at the nurse, his misty eye barely able to make out her features. 'Is there a package for me?'

'No, Professor,' she sang. 'Are you comfortable there?'

'There must be a package for me.'

'No package for you today, Professor.'

'Can you check?'

'Of course, Professor. I check for you every day.'

'Please check again.'

'Tea time first, Professor. It's your favourite.'

'I'm expecting an important package,' he said slowly.

'Yes, Professor, I know.'

'I must have it as soon as it arrives.'

'Yes, Professor.'

'It's very important,' he said, his head nodding from side to side with anxiety.

'Of course, Professor.'

'Has it arrived yet?'

'Nothing for you today, Professor.'